HOPE NEVER DIES

This Large Print Book carries the
Seal of Approval of N.A.V.H.

AN OBAMA BIDEN MYSTERY

HOPE NEVER DIES

ANDREW SHAFFER

THORNDIKE PRESS
A part of Gale, a Cengage Company

Farmington Hills, Mich • San Francisco • New York • Waterville, Maine
Meriden, Conn • Mason, Ohio • Chicago

LIBRARY OF CONGRESS CIP DATA ON FILE.
CATALOGUING IN PUBLICATION FOR THIS BOOK
IS AVAILABLE FROM THE LIBRARY OF CONGRESS

ISBN-13: 978-1-4328-5841-4 (hardcover)

Published in 2018 by arrangement with Quirk Books

Printed in Mexico
1 2 3 4 5 6 7 22 21 20 19 18

FOR UNCLE JOE

IT IS BETTER TO
LIGHT A CANDLE
THAN TO CURSE
THE DARKNESS.
— W. L. Watkinson

ACKNOWLEDGMENTS

THANKS, OBAMA.

1

The night this all started, I was in a black Irish mood.

And that was *before* I learned my friend was dead.

I was sitting at my computer, and I'd stumbled across one of those so-called paparazzi videos. It opened with a wide shot of Cape Town's fabled Table Mountain. The camera panned down to the white-capped waves in the harbor. An impossibly long speedboat entered the frame, cutting through the surf like a buttered bullet. A parasailor trailed behind the boat, high in the sky, tethered to the stern by a thin rope. The camera zoomed in on the daredevil's face, and I saw that my old friend Barack Obama was having the time of his life.

Unencumbered by his dead-weight loser vice president, 44 was on the vacation to end all vacations. Windsurfing on Richard Branson's private island. Kayaking with

Justin Trudeau. BASE jumping in Hong Kong with Bradley Cooper. Barack wasn't simply tempting the fates — he was *daring* them. And why not? If he could survive eight long years as the first black U.S. president, he could survive anything.

Not that I was worried about him.

I was done getting all worked up over Barack Obama.

I forced myself to look away from the computer. I turned to face the dartboard on the back wall of my office. It was an old Christmas gift from my daughter. I'd kept it in storage for many years, but now I finally had some free time on my hands.

Maybe too much free time.

"One call," I said to my faithful companion, Champ. "Is that too much to ask?"

The dog glanced up with indifference. He'd heard it all before.

"Just one phone call," I said.

With a snap of the wrist, I sent the dart sailing across the room. It hit its mark, right between Bradley Cooper's piercing blue eyes.

"Eight years." I plucked the darts from the shredded magazine cover taped to the board. "And not even a gosh-darned post-card."

Barack even had the gall to tell *People*

12

magazine that we still went golfing together on occasion. To save face, I repeated the lie. The truth was, there hadn't been any golf outings. No late-night texting. Not even a friendly poke on Facebook.

I watched the skies for smoke signals; I read the *New York Times,* dissecting headlines, looking for clues he might have left me. Nothing. Sometimes late at night, after Jill was sound asleep, I scrolled through the old text messages Barack and I had exchanged a lifetime ago. It was an exercise in futility. If I kept picking at the wound, it was never going to heal.

In the darkness outside my office window, I glimpsed a tiny flickering light.

I turned off my desk lamp to get a better look, and there it was again: a pinprick of orange light, like a firefly . . . or a cigarette.

A prowler? Maybe.

Only one way to find out.

"Let's go, Champ."

The dog's ears perked up. I spun the dial on the small closet safe. There were two things inside: my Medal of Freedom . . . and my SIG Sauer pistol. The bean shooter was a gift I'd bought for myself, in spite of Jill's objections. "Aren't your shotguns enough?" she'd asked. "What on earth could you need a handgun for?"

For times like this, Jill.

I slipped the pistol into the waistband at the small of my back, then tucked my polo shirt over it.

I called to my wife, "I'm letting Champ out." She didn't answer back. I could hear the TV playing in our bedroom. *Law and Order.* I should have been watching with her. Instead I opened the back door.

As soon as I did, Champ raced across the lawn and tore off into the woods. The motion light over the back porch should have kicked on, but the bulb was burnt out.

It was an old one, I guess.

Old bulbs were meant to burn out.

The moon was full enough to light up the backyard. Our 7,000-square-foot lake house sat on four acres of property. Late at night, it was possible to imagine you were all alone in the world.

Tonight, however, I wasn't alone.

Ahead in the woods was that pinprick of light.

And now I smelled tobacco, a familiar brand.

Marlboro Reds.

Don't get your hopes up, I told myself. *"Hope" is just a four-letter word.*

I crossed the yard, walking to the spot where Champ had disappeared into the trees. At the edge of the clearing, I spied a vertically challenged man in a dark gray suit and matching tie. He had short, spiky hair, like he'd recently been discharged from the Marines and was letting it grow out. An earpiece wire disappeared into his collar. Secret Service.

My heart was beating faster than a dog licking a dish.

My own security detail had been dismissed several weeks earlier. Vice presidents were granted six months of protection following their time in office and not a day more unless there were extenuating circumstances.

"Nice night for a walk," I said.

Secret Service nodded toward the woods, showing me the way. I ducked under a low-hanging branch and kept walking. The heavy foliage overhead diffused the moonlight. I had to tread carefully to avoid the underbrush. The smell of burning tobacco grew stronger. I called for Champ.

In response, I heard flint striking metal. A lighter, close by.

I swiveled around. There. To my left, by the big oak. Ten paces away. A man crouched low, scratching Champ behind the ears. German shepherds don't take to strangers, but this man was no stranger.

He rose to his feet, a slim figure in his

15

black hand-tailored suit. His white dress shirt was unbuttoned at the neck. He took a long drag off his cigarette and exhaled smoke with leisure.

Barack Obama was never in a hurry.

2

I offered a handshake. Barack turned it into a fist bump. It was a greeting I'd never been able to master, but I gave it my best shot.

Barack smirked. Just like old times.

"Thought you quit smoking," I said.

He took another long drag off his cigarette. "I did."

I wiped my brow. It had been an unusually hot and humid summer. In the past couple of years, I'd become more sensitive to temperature extremes. I was either too hot or too cold. Never comfortable.

"It's been a while," he said.

"Has it?" I asked, tracing a circle in the dirt with my foot.

"You keeping busy?"

"I've been laying tile in the master bath."

Barack laughed. "If I'd known Jill was putting you to work, I'd have dropped by sooner. Michelle wants granite countertops, and I don't even know where to start."

"I'm sure Bradley Cooper could help."

"You saw those pictures, huh?"

"Everybody saw them."

"Well, you know me. Laying low was never my style."

I grunted a response.

He put out his cigarette on a tree. "I'm sure Jill's waiting, so I'll get right to the point." He returned the extinguished butt to his pack of Marlboros. Even when he was smoking, he was still a Boy Scout. "There's been an incident I think you should know about."

Of course. Now it all made sense. Barack wasn't here to rekindle our friendship. He was here on business.

"An incident," I repeated.

"Does the name Finn Donnelly ring any bells?"

Of course it did. Anybody who rode the Wilmington to DC line knew Finn Donnelly. "He's an Amtrak conductor," I said. "The finest one I know."

"He was hit by a train this morning. I'm sorry, Joe."

The news struck me in the chest like an open-field tackle. I tried to speak, but the words caught in my throat. Barack said something else, but I'd stopped hearing him.

There was a time I'd seen Finn every day.

Back when I was commuting to and from the Senate. We'd traveled thousands of miles together. After I became vice president, riding Amtrak was too challenging — too many Secret Service agents and security protocols. I'd only seen Finn once since the election, in passing. I'd spent the last few weeks thinking I ought to reach out to him, maybe try to catch up, but now . . .

Barack put a hand on my shoulder, steadying me. "I had a hunch you knew him. I wanted to tell you myself, before you heard from somewhere else."

He told me everything the Wilmington PD had learned about the accident. Finn hadn't reported for work in the morning, and by the time a replacement conductor was found, the 7:46 a.m. Acela was a half hour behind schedule. While rounding a corner on the way out of town, the engineer spotted somebody lying on the tracks. At the speed the train was going, there was no safe way to avoid a collision.

"Why didn't he move?" I asked.

"Could be he suffered a heart attack, or some other medical emergency. The state medical examiner couldn't tell, based on the condition of the body. They're running some blood samples. It's going to take time before we know more."

It was unbelievable. Preposterous. I'd known Finn better than most of my fellow committee members on Capitol Hill. I knew his favorite singer was Michael Jackson — even after all the hoopla, Finn stuck by his man. I knew he was a Patriots fan — through all the hoopla with them as well. I also knew Finn had a wife, and a little girl, Grace. Finn had been a decade younger than me, and close to retirement age (or what used to pass for retirement age). His girl wasn't so little now. She was probably just starting college.

And now her father was dead.

"The police found something," Barack said, holding out a piece of paper.

It was a full-page black-and-white printout of an online map, with a familiar address punched into the search bar. The cold steel in my waistband sent a shiver up my spine. The house I shared with my wife was identified by a little dot in the center of the page.

"Where did they find this?"

"He had a desk on the train. Wilmington PD thought maybe the guy was stalking you. They reached out to Secret Service, who explained you were not their problem anymore."

"Not their problem," I said with a chortle.

"In about as many words."

"So, what, they fob it off on the FBI?"

Barack nodded. "And the FBI said it sounded like a Secret Service problem. After another back-and-forth, someone who used to work in the presidential detail reached me through one of my current agents. They thought I might have your number, I guess. I said I'd let you know myself, to see what you wanted to do. If anything."

That was the world we lived in now. Nobody wanted to take responsibility for anything anymore. Not even inside the highest levels of government.

Especially inside the highest levels of government.

"You could have called."

Barack shrugged. "It was a nice night for a drive."

"You also could have rung the doorbell."

"I was thinking about it," he said.

"Well, let us know you're coming next time, and we'll have a cold beer waiting."

I refolded the map and tried to give it back.

"That's a copy. Keep it."

I glanced back at the master bedroom window, where the TV was flickering. The thought that Finn would ever stalk me was beyond ludicrous. Still . . . "Is there any

21

indication Finn was part of . . . something larger?"

Barack shook his head. "Not ISIL, if that's what you're asking. The Service ran him through all the databases. Not a single red flag. No recent weapons purchases."

"Are there any reporters on this thing?"

"The accident — yes. The rest of the story — no. The police are sitting on the case until they hear from Steve."

"Steve?"

"You passed him at the edge of the woods."

"Secret Service," I said. "Friendly guy."

Barack shrugged. "He gets the job done."

Champ trotted to my side. I scratched him behind the ears. "Who else knows about the map?"

"An engineer turned it in to the cops, so it's passed through a couple of hands," Barack said. "There's a lieutenant working as the point person. Her detectives have started legwork on the case already. Plus two or three guys in the Service know. Too many people to make this thing disappear, if that's what you're thinking."

That is what I had been thinking, and Barack could see it on my face.

"What about his family?" I asked.

"They're planning the funeral. We've left

them in the dark about everything."

"Let's keep it that way, at least for now," I said. "I'm not asking for a cover-up. Just a little discretion. They don't need this. Let them make their peace first."

"If we hint that there's a national security interest at stake here, we can stop it from spilling into the papers. At least until after the funeral. In the meantime . . ."

"Yeah?"

"You should look into getting some private security. I just walked right up to your house. Your backyard motion light was out, too." He tossed a lightbulb to me. "You really ought to replace this with a compact fluorescent or an LED. They cost more up front but pay for themselves after just a few years."

"Thanks," I said.

I turned back to my house, then paused. The old bulb was, of course, from the motion light on the back porch. Of that much I was sure.

However, the socket was more than twelve feet above the porch. You couldn't reach it without a ladder. "Wait, how did you . . ."

I glanced over my shoulder, but no one was there. Barack had disappeared back into the inky darkness, same as he'd come, leav-

ing nothing behind but the stale smell of
smoke.

3

"Didn't hear you come to bed last night," Jill said.

I stumbled into the kitchen around half past nine, weary from a night of bad sleep. My mind had been on fire with questions about Finn Donnelly. Every time I finally started to drift off, some little noise outside would startle me awake. Several times, I wondered if I hadn't dreamed my entire encounter with Barack Obama.

The lingering scent of tobacco in my hair said otherwise.

Meanwhile, Jill looked beautiful and well-rested as always. She'd been up for who knew how many hours in the sunroom, enjoying her e-reader. She used to read paperbacks, the small kind they sold in grocery stores. Harlequins. A couple of years back, she'd switched to electronic books. Said she liked being able to adjust the size of the type, even though she missed all the shirtless men on the book covers. I could laugh along with this little joke, because I certainly didn't feel threatened. See, your Uncle Joe had something those men would never have: a Presidential Medal of Freedom.

"You fell asleep to the TV," I reminded her. "I didn't want to wake you."

She'd set out coffee and breakfast. The coffee was cold.

"Hmmmm," she said. She didn't glance up from her bodice ripper. Jill didn't know anything about Barack's visit, as far as I knew. I didn't plan on telling her that he'd stopped over. It was just better that way.

The morning paper was on the table. The above-the-fold story on the front page of the *News Journal* was much ado about nothing, as usual. More White House drama. The current administration knew how to do one thing right: If you wanted to push through an unpopular agenda with minimal resistance, distract the bastards. Do something every day to grab the headlines — something big, bold, and preferably stupid — thereby banishing the dull stories about how you were systematically dismantling the country to the back pages with the *Hagar* comics.

I flipped through the paper, pretending to

read the headlines and a paragraph or two of each story.

"Have you thought any more about the CPAP machine?" Jill asked.

"No," I said, dodging the question for the umpteenth time. My doctor had diagnosed me with mild sleep apnea. It could lead to sleep deprivation, which could explain why I'd been waking up later and later in the mornings. My doc had recommended a complicated gizmo that forced air up my nose while I slept. She showed me one of the devices in her office. It looked and sounded like Darth Vader's mask.

I returned to the newspaper. There was a small write-up on the train accident on the front page of the Local section, under the byline of the *News Journal*'s crime beat reporter:

MAN KILLED IN AMTRAK ACCIDENT
WILMINGTON, DE — A man was struck and killed by an Amtrak passenger train approximately a mile from Wilmington Station around 8:23 a.m. Wednesday morning.

Wilmington police identified the man as Finn Donnelly, 63, of Wilmington, Del. According to Amtrak officials, Donnelly was an Amtrak conductor but was off duty at the time of the incident. No passengers were injured.

All inbound and outbound trains were halted Wednesday morning as local authorities investigated. The National Transportation Safety Board has announced its own investigation into the matter, a routine procedure for all railroad accidents involving loss of life.

No further details were immediately available.

No mention of the map.

And no mention of Delaware's favorite son, Joseph R. Biden Jr.

I flipped to the obituaries. Finn's funeral was Friday. Tomorrow. They used to wait a couple of days before dumping you in the ground. These days, it seemed like they wanted to shuffle you off this mortal coil before your body was even cool.

I excused myself from the breakfast table. Champ followed me to my office, where I closed the door halfway — just enough to give me a warning if Jill busted in on me.

The *News Journal*'s story hadn't been updated online. Somehow Barack had managed to keep the lurid details under wraps . . . for now.

I didn't expect to hear from him again.

We'd had a great run together in office, but Barack had moved on to bigger and better things. He was too big for one country. He was too big for one best friend. He belonged to the world now. I told myself I was happy for him. But if that was really true, why couldn't I shake the feeling that I'd been dumped the day after graduation?

There was a knock at my office door. Champ's head perked up. Jill had changed out of her robe and into her black jogging pants and a Race for the Cure tee.

"I'm heading out for a run," she said.

Champ didn't move. He was too much like me — a walker at heart. Especially when the weather outside was as nasty as the devil's armpit.

For a split second, I considered telling my wife about Finn's accident. I couldn't remember if she'd ever met him, though, and there was no sense ruining her morning jog with such grim news. It could wait until she got back.

"Break a leg," I told her.

"You're always welcome to join me."

I waved goodbye, and she blew me a kiss.

Jill ran five miles every day, averaging nine and a half minutes a mile. I was more of a fourteen-minute-mile-on-a-treadmill sort of guy. Lately I'd been slowing down my pace.

Sometimes I'd quit early because I felt out of breath.

My doc said I was healthier than ninety percent of guys my age. Why didn't I feel it?

"What do you think, Champ? Should we go downstairs and walk a couple miles?"

He stared blankly at me. Some dogs can run on treadmills, but Champ wasn't one of them.

I tied on my running shoes. Normally, I'd use my time on the treadmill to think through whatever was troubling me. Getting the legs moving supposedly has a synergistic effect with brain synapses (that's what Malcolm Gladwell told me once). Today, however, I planned to watch some TV and zone out. I didn't need to think through my troubles, because I'd already decided on a course of action: I'd tell Jill about the accident, of course, but keep the information about Finn's map to myself. At least for the time being. It wasn't like he'd been found with a gun or anything. There was no reason to worry Jill. These past few weeks, she'd been enjoying her newfound ability to go running without a Secret Service escort. I didn't have a clue where we'd find private security that could keep pace with her.

Besides, Finn was dead. Everybody knows

that dead men can't hurt you.
Only the living can do that.

4

Just before eleven, I strolled into Earl's Hash House down on 8th and Washington in Quaker Hill. It was a classic diner, the kind that only served one type of coffee: black. If you ordered an orange mocha Frappuccino, you'd be given a side-eye that would make you wish you'd never been born. At one point, presumably, Earl's had been a new establishment, but nobody remembers when that was. It was old when I was a kid. It was even older now.

Some people probably said the same about Dan Capriotti.

He was waiting for me at the long counter. Dressed in a maroon leather jacket and blue jeans, the same outfit he'd been wearing since the early seventies. These days, his thick black hair was dyed and his sneakers were orthopedic. Otherwise, he looked much like he had the last time I'd seen him, more than a decade ago, right down to the dinged-up detective badge clipped to his belt loop. He'd called me that morning and said he had some information about the Donnelly case. Off the record.

I'd just finished my walk and was about to step into the shower. "If it's about the map —"

He interrupted me. "It's not about the map."

I didn't know many cops down at the station these days. There'd been major turnover while I'd been out of town as Wilmington tried (unsuccessfully) to shed its image as Murder Town, U.S.A. Fortunately Dan and I went way back. If only he'd been the one to find the map. He could have called me directly and saved Barack the trouble.

"You're here by yourself," Dan said, shaking my hand firmly. A cop handshake.

"My wife's got a class," I said.

"I meant no security. No Secret Service."

"I'm just a private citizen these days."

"You don't seem too nervous for someone who might have been in the crosshairs of a madman."

I glanced around. The guy behind the counter was busy at the register.

"Let's find someplace more private to talk," I said.

We took a red vinyl booth in the back. My

eyes flicked over the menu, which I knew by heart. Nothing ever changed inside these walls, which were plastered in graffitied dollar bills. I'd signed a few, once upon a time. They were still behind the counter somewhere.

There were only a few other people in the diner. Mostly the old geezers who showed up day after day for coffee and toast. They'd bicker about the day's news until they wore themselves out. I'd always seen myself becoming part of a crew like that someday. Me, Barack, W. Maybe Jimmy Carter, if he wasn't too busy peanut-farming.

The waitress stopped by to take our orders.

"Pie à la mode," I said. "Hold the pie, Deborah."

She'd heard the joke before. I still got a kick out of it. The good jokes never get old.

"One scoop of vanilla for the wise guy," she said. "And how 'bout you, hon?"

Dan tapped his coffee. "Just the worm dirt. I'm watching my figure."

After the waitress left, Dan leaned across the table. "So how well did you know this conductor?"

"I used to ride his line. I knew him well enough."

"Did you know what he was into?"

34

I raised an eyebrow.

"The toxicology results aren't back yet, Joe, but it's pretty likely he was high as a kite when the train hit him. He may have even been dead already. Now, the cause of death is listed as PENDING on the death certificate, but —"

"Hold up. You're saying he was on something? He didn't even drink, as far as I know."

Dan shrugged. "Maybe he didn't drink, but he definitely liked to party."

"I don't understand."

"We found heroin. A little baggie, in one of his pockets."

I fingered the rosary on my wrist. "That doesn't make a lick of sense. A sixty-three-year-old man with a wife and daughter doing heroin? When he knows he'll be tested as part of his job? And he's so close to retirement age?" I was trying to speak in a hushed voice, but was having a hard time. "I'll bet dollars to donuts you won't find a trace of drugs in his system."

"And if I were a betting man, I'd take you up on that offer. Just because he's been tested in the past doesn't mean a thing. All it takes is some back pain and a prescription for oxy. Two or three months later, they move on to something cheaper. And the only thing that's cheaper is heroin."

"When will you get the blood tests back?"

"Six to eight weeks."

"Could you expedite the testing?"

"That *is* the expedited time frame."

The waitress brought my ice cream and refilled Dan's coffee. I tried to make sense of what he'd told me. Heroin used to be the drug of choice for jazz musicians and beatniks. Not anymore. Opioid addiction was a growing problem while Barack and I were in office. By the time we realized how widespread the problem was, it was too late. It had reached epidemic proportions. It was a new reality that I still wasn't used to.

"This investigation is being handled personally by Lieutenant Esposito," Dan said.

"A good cop?"

"A little rough around the edges, but not as rough as I was. Word is she's in line for the chief's job, once he retires."

In all of Dan's years with the force, he had never been promoted above detective. He was effective, but he made more headlines for his unorthodox methods than for his busts. He reminded a lot of people of Dirty Harry. Which was only fitting, since there were rumors that Clint Eastwood had based his performance on Dan Capriotti.

He sipped his coffee. "Listen, Joe, we've

been friends for a long time. I know the paper with your address is hinky. I know you're concerned —"

"More befuddled than anything."

"Then I'll give it to you straight: forget the map for now. If this turns out to be anything more than a junkie passing out at the wrong place at the wrong time, I'll eat crow."

"Finn Donnelly was no junkie."

"I guess we'll see."

"You said Esposito's handling this personally? Should I get in touch with her directly if I have questions, or . . . ?"

Dan nearly sprayed coffee across the table. "That's the last thing you'd want to do. You're better off going through me. She isn't too happy about this whole thing, especially with Secret Service sniffing around."

Dan didn't sound happy, either. Local police didn't like it when the feds flew in and started throwing their weight around. Of course, the Secret Service wasn't actually running an investigation. That was just a smokescreen. I could have told Dan the truth, but I didn't want word to spread at the station that the "national security" storyline Barack and I had cooked up was an empty threat. At least not until after the

37

funeral. Then they could talk all they wanted.

"Thanks for meeting me, Dan. I wish I had something to share with you about the Service investigation, but that's above my pay grade. All I know is that they ran some checks on Finn, and they all came back clean."

"If they found something, could you even tell me?"

"If something's classified, they're not going to share it with me either. I'm just a private citizen." I paused. "By the way, I'm sure you or one of your coworkers has also talked to Finn's family. Do you know what they have to say about all of this?"

"A couple detectives has been in contact with the daughter, but we're keeping her in the dark. No one's mentioning the drugs or the map to your house."

"So the daughter doesn't know a thing. What about his wife?"

"Are you joking?"

"Swear on the grave of Jean Finnegan Biden, I haven't heard a thing. Did they split up?"

"It must have been a while since you last talked to Finn."

"Saw him briefly the last time I rode the Acela. Seven or eight weeks ago. We didn't get a chance to talk, though."

"Huh. She's still at the assisted-living facility."

"He never said a word about that."

"He didn't tell you about her stroke?"

"Not a word."

Dan set his coffee down. "She's paralyzed on her right side, and unresponsive. Even if there was a break in the storm — even if she was suddenly able say something as simple as 'yes' or 'no' — I doubt she could help us."

I told him I'd let him know if I heard anything from the Secret Service — some stray fact or insight that might help him tie up the case and earn brownie points with his boss. The look of weariness on his face, however, told me that he wasn't expecting a call. He was probably right about the map being nothing to worry about. If that was the only suspicious piece of evidence, I might have been able to put it out of my mind.

But Finn? Involved with drugs?

He was a teetotaler. Same as me.

Something wasn't right.

Martin Luther King Jr. said the moral arc of the universe was long and bent toward the side of justice. By the time the universe got to righting the wrongs in Wilmington, however, I feared that it would be too late — not just for Finn or the city, but for us all.

I left without touching my ice cream.

5

Inside the entrance of Baptist Manor was a large aquarium that stretched a good ten feet down the hall. Swimming inside the tank were dozens of goldfish, each its own spectacular color. Brilliant orange. Deep red. Shimmering blue. I'd been to Baptist Manor several times before, but this — the aquarium, the fish — was new. It was both mesmerizing and depressing. Like most of the residents, the fish wouldn't leave this place until they were belly-up.

"Can I help you, sir?"

The secretary at the registration desk was waving to me. Her face lit up when she recognized me. I'd seen that look before. She was starstruck.

If only women looked at me like that sixty years ago.

She gave me a visitor's badge and directed me to the third-floor medical ward.

I passed a room where twenty or so residents were lounging in front of a big-screen TV tuned to Fox News. Half were snoring. The other half, I assume, had advanced dementia — it was their only possible excuse for not changing the channel.

When I reached Darlene Donnelly's room, the door was open.

I rapped lightly and, hearing no voices, stepped inside.

There was a sheer curtain dividing the room. Darlene's bed was closest to the door. A much older woman was in the bed near the window. Both were asleep. This wasn't a nursing facility — it was a departure room. Neither person was hooked up to any heavy equipment, so I guess that was a positive sign. Still, I was reminded of my visit last summer to the National Zoo with my grand-kids. Two hours, and not a single animal awake. By the time we'd reached the exit, I'd been half asleep too.

On a nightstand beside Darlene's bed were dried flowers and sympathy cards. I pulled a chair to the bedside. I didn't try to wake her. There was no point. I'd learned more about her condition from a doctor who'd seen her back in January. He wasn't supposed to discuss it with me — HIPAA regulations and all that — but we went way back. Not only had Darlene's stroke left her

partially paralyzed, but she was also cata-
tonic. She could open her eyes, but her
thoughts were anybody's guess.

But I had hope.

Finn had had hope.

"He talked about you all the time," I told
her. I wanted to believe Darlene could
process what I was saying. The odds, of
course, were slim. "I've never known someone so in love with his own wife. I can only
imagine you felt the same way about him. It
breaks my heart, what's happened. It breaks
my heart. Your husband was a good man."

Behind me, a toilet flushed. I turned to
see a middle-aged man exiting the restroom.
His long black hair was slicked back into a
ponytail. It took him a moment to notice
me, and then he froze.

"Sorry, I didn't know anyone was here," I
said.

"No worries," he said, striding past me to
the other patient's bedside. He had great
long legs and stood a good six inches taller
than me. The sleeves of his flannel shirt
were rolled up, revealing a tattoo of a grinning skull with diamonds in its eyes. Back
in my day, the only people who got tattoos
were sailors. I had to remind myself that we
weren't back in my day anymore.

The man lifted a red leather-bound book

off the woman's bedside table.

I rose from my chair. "If you want to be alone for a few minutes, I can leave and come back. These curtains aren't much, are they?"

He looked me up and down. He was either trying to place me or size me up.

"Sorry to hear about her husband," he said finally. "Read about the accident in the paper."

"Thank you," I said. I didn't know what else to say, so that's all I said.

I lingered at the edge of the curtain for a moment, watching this man and the sleeping woman. I examined the book in his hand more closely. It was a Bible, the kind you find in hotel rooms. A Gideon Bible. The way it was beaten and worn told me it was well-used.

"Is that your mother?"

He looked at me, then at the woman in the bed. He shook his head. "I minister to the patients here. The forgotten ones. Their families may forget, but God never does." He checked his watch. "I'm sorry, I didn't realize the time. If you'll excuse me."

I put a hand on his shoulder on his way out. "It's Joe, by the way."

"Reggie."

We shook hands, and he left.

It was also time for me to say goodbye to Darlene. I told her I'd pray for her. I was also planning to donate what I could to make sure she got the care she deserved — a room of her own would be nice — but there wasn't any way I could magically make her better. Once the doctors are done with you, it's between you and God.

I was turning to leave when I spied the red leather Bible on the bedside table. The minister had accidentally left it behind.

I picked it up and started after him. The long-legged man wasn't in the hallway, so I stopped by the receptionist's desk near the elevators. She was busy tapping on her phone.

"There was a man here, ministering to the patients. Did you see which way he went?"

"A minister?" she said, without looking up. She had fair skin with freckles and strawberry-blonde hair. "We have a minister, but he's only here Sundays."

"This was a tall guy, with long hair."

"On this floor? I think I'd have noticed."

Her head was still buried in her phone.

"I didn't just dream him up. He was real." I waved the Bible. "This is real."

She looked up with a little half frown that highlighted her dimples. "You might try the front desk downstairs. Everyone that comes in the building has to check in."

The front desk was empty. I poked my head outside, but didn't see the man. I returned to the desk. While I was waiting for the receptionist to return, I glanced at the visitor's log. Nobody by the name of Reggie had signed in all day.

After a few minutes, the receptionist exited the women's restroom. When she saw me waiting at the desk, she hustled over and took her seat. "Sorry about that, Mr. Biden."

I handed her the Bible. "A man left this upstairs. Can you make sure it gets to the lost and found?"

"Oh!" she exclaimed. "Anything for you, Joe. Can I call you Joe?"

"Everybody does," I said, flashing my trademark grin. "Do you have security around here, by any chance?"

"There's a camera up there," she said, pointing to a black half sphere mounted on the ceiling. "But it's not hooked up. Why do you ask?"

"No reason."

As soon as I thanked her and turned for the door, I dropped my smile. I didn't know who the long-legged man was, but he wasn't there ministering to the patients. I doubted that he'd be back for the Bible. It was just a prop.

The man had mentioned Darlene's husband's accident, so he wasn't in the room at random. If Finn had been on drugs — and that was a big if — the man could have been a fellow hophead. Maybe he'd been there to toss the room, looking for something to sell so that he could score.

I'd spooked him, though.

Chances are he wouldn't risk a return visit.

I called Dan and left a message, telling him what had happened. "You'll want to get in touch with their daughter, see if anything was stolen. My guess is no, but Grace would be the one to ask. The security at this place has more holes than a pound of Swiss cheese. Let me know if I can help."

Dan didn't call back that night, so I went to bed thinking he didn't need me. Nobody seemed to want my help anymore. I got the impression that some people just thought I was too old. That I'd retired from public office and joined the Geezer Squad over at Earl's. I might have had an enlarged prostate, but I wasn't ready to sit around all day in a diner bitching about it. There were still a few miles left in this old clunker.

6

I wore my best black suit for Finn's service. The suit had seen far too many funerals over the years, but it did its job without complaining too much. When you reach my age, the endless succession of funerals becomes a blur. The only thing that ever changes is the name on the program.

There wasn't a cloud in the afternoon sky for the graveside service. A real crop duster of a thunderstorm had come through overnight. The air was still sticky, but it had cooled down a few degrees. It was baseball weather. A perfect day to sit by the lake and sip a virgin piña colada and really enjoy my semiretirement. Invite the family over. Fire up the George Foreman.

Instead, I was at the Wilmington and Brandywine Cemetery. Jill had her Friday summer class, so I was flying solo. She'd dropped me off and would pick me up on her way back home.

Besides Finn's daughter, there wasn't another familiar face among the two dozen mourners. I didn't recognize anyone from the years I'd spent riding the train. Not that you'd expect commuters to come out for a conductor's funeral. Not these days.

I took a seat in the very last row. This was about Finn, not former vice president Joe Biden.

The priest listed in the program was Father O'Hara. I'd met him once. Years ago. He'd been a young man then, and I suppose I had been too. The priest making his way to the head of the crowd was noticeably grayer. He walked with a slow gait, almost as if he carried some great burden on his back. It was difficult to believe he was the same man. As he took the podium, he nodded at me with recognition.

After Father O'Hara's opening remarks, Finn's sister delivered a short eulogy. A train rumbled past on the elevated tracks outside the cemetery. Not loud enough to drown her out, but distracting. It might have even been the same train that took Finn's life. Everyone else had to be thinking the same thing. Finn's sister sped up her delivery, plowing through her tears like they were nothing but light drizzle.

Father O'Hara retook the podium. As he

ran through his rehearsed lines — the Corinthians, the Psalms, the verses I recognized from too many other funerals — my attention waned. Father O'Hara wasn't known for his brevity of wit (nor his brevity, nor his wit). My eyes drifted to the nearest gravestones, searching for familiar names. Senator Richard Bassett, signer of the U.S. Constitution, was buried in the cemetery somewhere. So were a handful of other Delaware dignitaries from centuries past. War heroes, governors. Congressmen. Their weathered tombstones jutted at odd angles from the damp ground, making the cemetery look like a crooked smile filled with busted teeth. Despite its pedigree, the aging cemetery wasn't the proper burial place for a proud man like Finn. With its overgrown weeds and rusted gates, it wasn't the proper burial place for anyone anymore.

When a cemetery dies, where do you bury it?

After the service, I waited for the crowd to thin before approaching Finn's daughter. We'd never met in person, but I felt like I'd known her forever. Finn wasn't a storyteller, but he loved to show off photos of his family. The pictures did the talking for him. I'd watched Grace grow up through the years — from the hospital to kindergarten and finally high school graduation — all through the lens of a devoted father. Finn's wallet eventually became so thick with photos of his wife and daughter that he couldn't sit down on the damn thing.

Grace sported the same curly red hair I remembered from her high school photos. And the same toothy grin. The ivy tattoo peeking out of the neck of her pilgrim dress was new. Even though she'd done some growing up, she was still too young to be an orphan, with her father taken too soon and her mother all but gone.

As I approached, she whispered something to her aunt, who stepped aside to give us space. A motorcycle roared to life and tore out of the parking lot. It was loud enough to wake the dead, though the dead didn't seem to mind.

I reached out a hand to shake Grace's. "I was a friend of your father's," I said. Before I could say any more, she fell into my arms. I patted her back as she sobbed into my chest. "It's okay," I said, over and over. "It's okay."

Eventually, we broke apart. She wiped her eyes with a black handkerchief.

"How you holding up, kiddo?" I asked.

"He still has your bumper sticker on his car. He was so proud of you."

"Proud of *me*?"

"You were vice president."

I gave her a dismissive wave. "There's this old joke: A man had two sons. One went out to sea, and the other became vice president. Neither were heard from again."

She didn't laugh, but I caught the corner of her lips curling up slightly.

"What I'm trying to say is your dad was a train conductor. That's real responsibility right there. Never heard him complain once, in all the years I rode that train. I'm a better man for knowing your father. If he was proud of me, well, it goes both ways."

"It's nice to hear that," she said.

"I'm sorry about your mother, too. I stopped by to see her yesterday. If I'd known sooner . . ."

"Dad wanted people to remember her as she was, not what she'd become. He visited her every day, first in the hospital, and then when they moved her to the facility. He felt terrible moving her there, but he couldn't afford to keep her at home."

I gave her shoulder a squeeze. The road to recovery for stroke victims was long and uncertain. For a woman Darlene Donnelly's age, the road was even more perilous.

"I offered to drop out of college, to get a full-time job and contribute so we could bring her home, but Dad wouldn't hear of it."

Amtrak employees were supposed to have the best healthcare, straight from the United States government. Amtrak was a pseudo-private company, but I'd been one of the senators who'd fought for them to have the same healthcare plans other government employees had. Yet somewhere along the way, things had been diluted. It was no surprise that hospitals were booting patients out the door. The whole damn country's healthcare infrastructure was falling apart — everything Barack had built. Everything *we'd* built.

I placed a hand on Grace's shoulder. "Look at me," I said. Her tears were welling up again. "This isn't your fault."

Without meeting my eyes, she said, "It didn't matter how many hours of overtime he worked. In-home care was never going to be something he could afford. I'm not a finance major — I'm an English major — but even I knew it was a lost cause. Still, Dad believed until the end that he could swing it. There was a ray of light, how-ever . . ."

"A ray of light."

"It's kind of funny, in a sick way. I thought there was a chance Dad's life insurance

53

payout would cover the cost to bring Mom home. He had a small Amtrak policy that was enough to pay for the funeral. But he took out another policy on himself shortly after Mom's stroke. A million dollars. The lawyer my aunt hired is already saying the insurance company is trying to hold up the claim. They're looking for some way to prove that he took his own life. That he did this on purpose." Grace looked around the cemetery. "Who would do this on purpose?"

The lawyer was right, of course: the insurance company was going to fight the family's claim tooth and nail. The family would be forced to sue to get them to pay out. The insurance company would come back with its own findings — findings that could run counter to the medical examiner's report. I wondered, for the first time, if maybe Finn hadn't laid down in front of that train on purpose, to leave his family the life insurance money. It was just plausible enough . . .

Except that didn't explain everything. If he'd been planning to kill himself, why had he printed directions to my house? And why was there heroin in his pockets? The puzzle still had lots of missing pieces.

My mother had been big into puzzles.

I'd never had the patience for them.

What I really wanted to do was absorb

54

Grace's pain, but I knew it was an impossible task. Our pain is ours, and ours alone. All others can do is mitigate the damage.

And that's what I would do for her: mitigate the damage.

Grace didn't deserve to live with question marks surrounding her father's death. The moral arc of the universe bends toward justice, but sometimes the universe needs a little help. It was the reason I'd gone into public service. Now I felt a similar tug. Some grave injustice seemed to be brewing. I didn't have the faintest idea what I would do, but I couldn't just watch from the sidelines.

"Your father was a good man," I told Grace. "The insurance claims administrator didn't know him. Your family lawyer didn't know him, I'd bet. Not like you did. Not like I did."

I looked her in the eyes. Hopefully, she couldn't hear the traces of doubt in my voice. I was beginning to think that none of us knew the real Finn.

"I'm going to find the truth about your father," I promised. "I'm giving you my word as a Biden."

7

On the way to the parking lot, I passed two caretakers in green jumpsuits taking a break from their work. They were leaning against a great oak tree, chugging a couple of tall energy drinks. Nearby was a large hole in the earth and a pile of dirt. I nodded at them, and they returned the greeting. Once they finished, they'd probably take their shovels up the hill to bury my friend.

I pulled out my phone to call a car service. The cemetery was full of bad memories, and I didn't want to stay a second longer than I needed to. Too many souls, taken much too soon.

Before I could launch the app, I spied two men stepping out of a minivan. As we neared each other on the cemetery walkway, I could see they were both dressed in navy-blue Amtrak uniforms. One was the size of a water buffalo; the other was as thin as a railroad spike. The water buffalo was the

Wilmington station manager, Grant. We'd been tight once upon a time. In my Senate days, if I'd been running late for the train, I would give him a call and, magically, the 7:46 a.m. Acela would be held up until I arrived.

The railroad spike I didn't know.

"How's it going, Grant?" I said, shaking his hand.

"Helluva lot better than it's going for Finn."

"It's awful, just awful," I said.

The skinny guy glanced away. There were beads of sweat on his upper lip. Finn was Amtrak — part of my "extended family," as I liked to say. For these guys, though, Finn *was* family. Finn Donnelly's membership in the railworker brotherhood ran deep. His grandfather had been a railworker, dynamiting canyons and laying rail for the old Trans-Atlantic Coast line during the Great Depression. Finn's father had been a railworker as well, working the yards in Chicago for thirty-five years.

I looked up the pathway, following it with my eyes to the tent propped up over Finn's coffin. "The service was at two. It's over now, but there's some family left up there."

"We'll wait until they leave," Grant said. "Don't want to cause a scene."

57

"I'm sure it won't be a problem —"

"We'll wait."

I nodded. Grant probably knew Finn's family mostly through Finn's stories. When you know somebody secondhand, it can be a shock to the system to meet them in person. Especially if the link between you has been severed.

The skinny guy whispered something to Grant that I couldn't make out, and then he returned to the van. Grant didn't say anything.

"Your friend, he's . . ."

"An engineer," Grant said quickly. "Al."

Al. Alvin . . . Alvin Harrison. The engineer who'd been driving the train that hit Finn, according to the follow-up story I'd read in the *News Journal* earlier that morning. No wonder they wanted to avoid the family.

"How's he taking it?" I asked.

"How would you take it?"

I stared back at the man in the passenger seat of the minivan. Alvin looked broken, haunted. Even though he hadn't been responsible for Finn's being on the tracks, he was being put through the wringer just the same. It was impossible to say how many test tubes of blood had been drawn from him, how many interviews he'd been submitted to. While the rest of us were try-

ing to cope with losing Finn, Alvin was trying to cope with life under the microscope.
I knew a little something about living under
a microscope. Even if you've done nothing
wrong, it's easy to start believing you were
somehow to blame.

"Listen, Grant, you knew Finn better than
me. Ever get a sense that he was . . .
depressed?"

Grant narrowed his hawklike eyes. "You
think it was suicide."

"I'm sorry if I misspoke." I don't know
why I'd asked the question. I didn't need to
be digging around in other people's business. It's just that I'd made that promise to
Grace.

Grant said, "It's the first question people
ask when somebody steps in front of a train.
You know why?"

I shook my head.

"Because the answer is almost always yes,"
he said. "There are plenty of other ways to
kill yourself, but nothing's more final than
stepping in front of a train. Take some pills,
there's a chance you wake up. Hang yourself, someone could cut you down. But the
Acela Express doing one-fifty?"

I waited for him to continue. After a few
moments, he said, "Finn's wife was sick —
real sick. He never said a word to anyone.

59

Not a word. I imagine that takes a lot out of a man. Was he depressed? How could he not be?"

Losing family was enough to wreck you. If it didn't, there was a chance you'd already been wrecked.

"But he never would have killed himself," Grant said. "Not like that."

"How can you be so sure? You just said —"

"I said the man was depressed. Not in the right state of mind, or however you want to say it. That doesn't mean he would hurt a fellow railroad man. People who step in front of trains because it's the easy way out . . . they're not thinking about how their actions affect the engineer who's driving. It's not even on their radar. But Finn would have known. He wasn't going to burden anyone with his death. Not one of his own brothers or sisters at Amtrak."

"I killed him," a voice from behind us said.

Alvin had left the van. He was staring through me with dark eyes.

Those eyes scared me. I quickly glanced away.

"I was the one who killed him," he said. There was no inflection in his voice. "He was lying on the tracks. I should have seen him sooner. I should have —"

"No, Al, we've been over this," Grant said.

Alvin was shaking now. "I keep replaying it, over and over, trying to remember if I saw him twitch . . . Did he move, or was that just the rumbling of the tracks shaking his body? Was it —"

"Stop," Grant said. He braced Alvin by the shoulders. "There was nothing you could have done. Nothing. We don't know why he was on the tracks. We'll probably never know. You braked as hard as you could. If you'd braked any faster, the train could have derailed. Think about how many lives you *saved.*"

Alvin closed his eyes and tilted his head toward the sky.

Grant pulled me aside. "This was a bad idea. I should get him home. He's had a rough couple of days."

"I can imagine," I said, though of course I couldn't. Nobody could.

"You need a ride?" Grant asked.

I started to say no, but I sensed there was more Grant wanted to tell me. Or maybe that was just wishful thinking.

"Where you headed?"

"Dropping Al off, then I'm heading on down to the station to finish out my shift," Grant said. "I can drop you at your place or —"

"The station's fine."

"Catching a train somewhere?"

I climbed into the backseat. "Something like that."

He eyed me in the rearview mirror. Getting dropped off at the station wasn't going to get me any closer to home, but it might just net me another puzzle piece or two. I had more questions about Finn, questions that I thought Grant might be able to answer. On the drive to Alvin's, however, neither of us said another word on account of the shattered man sitting in the passenger seat. Alvin's quiet sobs filled the dead air. I kept waiting for Grant to turn the radio on, to drown out the haunted noises. He never did.

8

After we dropped off Alvin, Grant pulled over to the side of the road a mile or so from Wilmington Station and killed the engine. We were in the heart of a long-abandoned industrial district, parked in the shadow of the interstate running overhead. The area was so forgotten, it didn't even have a nickname. Razor wire lined the tops of the fences protecting the warehouses and parking lots, though there were holes in the chain-link everywhere I looked. Empty eyes watched us through broken windows. Come nightfall, the squatters would come out of hiding, dealing on the street corners and servicing johns in the alleys.

Grant didn't say a word. He didn't have to. I knew why we'd stopped. Behind the abandoned peanut-butter factory with the busted-out windows was the site of the accident. Finn had taken his final breaths just a hundred yards away from where we were sitting.

I stepped out of the van, but Grant didn't budge.

"You're not coming?"

He shook his head. "I'll wait here, if you don't mind. There's a cross and a bunch of flowers marking the spot, unless someone's taken them."

"Why would someone steal a cross?"

Grant shrugged. "Why does anyone steal anything?"

I don't think he'd been planning on driving to the scene of the crime, but maybe he was tired of me pestering him with questions. He knew a lot about the accident, including the drugs found on Finn. He didn't mention the map, and neither did I.

I crossed the deserted street. Wilmington was a uniquely situated shipping port, sitting as it did between two rivers that flowed into the Atlantic. The boom times were over long before my family moved to town, however. Thanks to Delaware's corporate-friendly tax code, Wilmington had successfully transformed itself into a white-collar town. Nevertheless, a permanent underclass persisted. The poor lived in slums on the other side of the interstate; the poorest of the poor lived right here, underneath the interstate. The police did regular sweeps, knocking down tents and arresting users for possession or prostitution, but they were fighting a losing war. The people who called this place home had already lost their self-respect. They had nothing else to lose.

There was an empty field between the street and the tracks. It was unkempt and overgrown. The weeds came up to my knees. I treaded carefully, because only God knew what I might accidentally step on. A used needle, a broken bottle. A baggie of heroin, fallen from the pocket of an Amtrak conductor.

There were two pairs of train tracks, side by side on the other side of a chain-link fence. The ones farthest from me were the tracks headed southwest to DC. For several decades, whenever Congress was in session, I passed through here nearly every day. When the train rounded the bend and sped up on the straightaway, my head was usually buried deep in the day's paper. If only I'd looked out the window, what human misery would I have seen? And would I have been able to do anything about it?

I found a hole in the fence and ducked through. It wasn't without difficulty. I felt a twinge in my back as I bent over. I hated to admit it, but I was getting older. And getting older sucked eggs. While I publicly debated the merits of running for office again, the thought of crisscrossing Iowa in a tour bus for the third time made me question my very sanity. I knew what Jill thought; I knew what my kids thought. Opinions are like elbows: everybody has one. Most have more than one. Could I do it again, though? And could I do it without Barack by my side?

Imagine what he'd say if he saw you here now. An old man with nothing better to do on a Friday afternoon than creep around some post-industrial wasteland. Are you doing this for Finn . . . or for yourself?

It was a good question. I didn't know exactly why I felt so compelled to see the crime scene in person. By now, the police and the transportation investigators had already picked it clean like shoppers ransacking a Walmart on Black Friday. Whatever the investigators hadn't picked up, the vultures did.

The only thing marking the spot was a crudely erected wooden cross, jutting out of the rocks a couple of paces from the tracks. The flowers Grant had mentioned were missing. The cross looked lonely, like a bare tree in the middle of a field in the dead of winter. There wasn't any yellow tape to preserve the scene of the accident, no chalk outline to mark the location of the body. Of course, they'd recovered the body from many different locations. Grim, but true.

I tried to imagine Finn coming to this particular spot. He'd squeezed through this hole in the fence, or another one nearby. Even if Finn hadn't been high on dope when the train hit him — even if he'd died of natural causes — he still had been down here for some unknown reason. He was a third-generation railroad man. He knew the dangers of the tracks. So why had he climbed through the fence?

The cross began to vibrate. It was almost imperceptible, but it was there. I turned to see the DC-bound Acela hurtling toward me. It was two hundred yards away but closing in fast. I hadn't heard it round the bend. Compared to diesel engines, the electric trains were eerily silent. If Finn had been passed out on the tracks, he wouldn't have stood a chance. By the time he felt the vibrating rails and heard the train, it would have been too late.

I crouched low and ducked back through the hole in the fence, bracing for the back strain again. Instead, there was a sharp pop in my left knee. My leg buckled out from under me and I went down hard, landing on my side. The train zipped past with a high-pitched whine. The ground rumbled for two seconds, jostling every molecule of my body right down to the silver fillings in my molars. And then all was still again.

I rolled onto my back and clutched my knee. In high school, I'd been a standout football player. I didn't have the arm strength to be quarterback or the long fingers to be a wide receiver, but I had the getaway sticks. I could tuck the ball and run. Senior year, I was the leading scorer. Senior year, I'd also banged up my left knee. Since then, it had been known to act up on occasion. I'd always been able to grit my teeth and bear it. This was the first time it had completely given up on me. If you can't trust your own body, what can you trust?

I didn't know what I was doing out here, crawling around a crime scene. As head of the executive branch, Barack held the top law-enforcement position in the country. I'd been his right-hand man. That didn't amount to a hill of beans when it came to actual police work. It was like asking Santa Claus to make you a toy train. That was a job best suited for his elves. The fat man in the red suit didn't know the first thing about sanding down wooden toys for good little girls and boys. I had no business here.

What would Barack say if he saw me out here, rolling around like a turtle on my back? We hadn't talked since his visit two nights ago. As far as I was concerned, nothing between us had changed. Yes, he'd kept his word and put the scare into the police department. The lurid details, as they were, hadn't hit the papers. For that I was grateful. But there was too much still unspoken between us. I wasn't about to send another errant text through the airwaves and see if I'd get a response. I was through being made to be the fool.

Eventually, I sat up and stretched out my leg. My black suit was covered with a thin layer of dust. There was a shiny grass stain on my elbow. I could stand on my knee, but I was walking with a limp as I returned to the van. If Grant noticed, he didn't say anything.

9

Wilmington Station's official name is the Joseph R. Biden Jr. Railroad Station, though nobody uses it. Everyone still calls it Wilmington Station, which just shows they shouldn't name places after people until they're dead.

Thing is, it isn't the only place in town bearing my name: the city also renamed a public pool after me — the Joseph R. Biden Jr. Aquatic Center, down at the corner of East 23rd and North Locust. It's a pretty poor neighborhood. I'd worked as a lifeguard at the pool while putting myself through college. The other lifeguards would ask me questions about race relations, because I was the only white guy many of them knew. We learned a lot from one another. One black lifeguard asked if I had a gasoline can he could borrow. He wanted to see his grandmom in North Carolina. "We can't stop at most gas stations down there," he'd said. The pool was where my commitment to civil rights began. I hadn't fully understood what black folks were up against until then. I would have felt better if they'd renamed the pool after Martin Luther King Jr. or a local black politician, but the neighborhood appreciated that I'd never turned my back on them. I'd never turned my back on anyone. It just wasn't something a Biden did.

And it wasn't something I could do to Finn.

The station was full of commuters. Rush hour was just beginning. I slipped through the crowd with my shades on, unnoticed, headed for the newsstand to grab a bottled water. Spending the afternoon outdoors in a black wool suit had left me thirstier than a dry road.

When it came to Finn's death, Grant said he was just as stumped as me. He had never seen signs that Finn did any drugs. Was it possible to hide addiction that well? Perhaps we were just too close to Finn to see the truth. Dan Capriotti had seen all the evidence firsthand and was convinced this was nothing more than an overdose. Could it really be that simple?

Maybe the truth was staring me right in the face.

Grant had said one interesting thing: he'd turned over the security tapes from the station to the Wilmington PD, but didn't think they would shed any light on the situation.

"Why's that?" I'd asked.

"We've got four cameras set up here, all of which record direct to VHS tapes that are older than some of the sneakers in my closet. The most they'd be able to see is Finn getting on and off that train for work the day before. Those tapes have been taped over so many times, it'd be a miracle if they could even make out any details through the grain."

Another victim of government belt-tightening. What else was new?

I believed Grant was right about the tapes. Even if there was crystal-clear digital footage of Finn the day before the accident, it wouldn't amount to a hill of beans. Grant knew that Finn was on time for work that day, and that he'd worked a full shift. There was nothing out of the ordinary, at least from his recollection.

There were still the next sixteen-odd hours to account for, which I was able to reconstruct from articles in the paper, what Dan told me, and Grant's story.

Finn had gone home, or maybe to visit his wife at Baptist Manor. Grace had been away at school. She had a place near campus with a couple of roommates. There wouldn't be any cell phone records to trace Finn's movements, because Finn didn't carry a cell phone. He was one of the last holdouts of our generation, I suspected. Hated the damn things with a passion. I hated them, too, but you couldn't deny how much they'd changed our lives. How much they'd changed the world. And yet I knew that even if he had been carrying a phone — even if we could trace his movements through the cell towers it pinged (a trick I'd seen on *Law and Order* more than once) — it would only beg more questions.

I limped past the shoeshine stand. The elevated chair was empty, but there was a dark-skinned man sitting hunched on a bench, counting cash inside a zippered money bag. A newsboy cap covered his eyes, but this was no newsboy. This was Greg McGovern, aka "the Mayor of Wilmington Station." He knew everyone who passed through the station with any regularity. If anything went on in his station, he knew about it.

I took a seat in his chair. The pain in my knee momentarily went away.

The Mayor didn't look up. "Be with you in a moment," he said, his voice crackling like an old record. The Mayor was my senior by at least a decade. It had been about that long since I'd seen him, too. The last couple of times, there'd been a young man shining shoes in his place. I'd sort of figured the Mayor had retired.

I'd figured wrong.

"Take your time," I replied.

He froze, and slowly met my eyes. His face was webbed with creases. "Amtrak Joe. Didn't expect to see you 'round here. How's the missus?"

"She's good. Still teaching."

The Mayor zippered his money pouch and hid it in a drawer. He didn't have any family. All he had were the commuters who passed the time with him in this worn-out chair. The cracked leather seat was badly in need of replacing, just as it had been on my first visit in the seventies. Back then, the Mayor had been a young man, just like me. The years had chewed us up and spit us out like tobacco.

He took one of my shoes in his hand. It was covered in dirt from the field. He didn't say anything as he got to work on it. He'd seen much worse in his day.

"Just came from Finn's service," I said.

"Uh-huh."

"You following the news?"

"I hear things," he said.

"Good things, or bad things?"

He shook his head. "Just things."

"The police say it was an accident. That Finn got high and stumbled onto the tracks."

"High on what? Life?"

"Heroin."

The Mayor paused, then resumed his work. "I never seen 'im take a drink," he said. "We played cards together, Saturday nights. Me, him, Alvin, Grant. Knew him as well as you can know anybody, I suppose."

"You hear anything interesting about him?"

"Interesting?"

"Yeah," I said. "I'm trying to figure out what happened. How he ended up out there on the tracks. Where the drugs came from."

He glanced from side to side without looking up at me, like he was scanning the crowd for somebody to rush in if he gave the wrong answer. He didn't trust me.

"If the police say he was on drugs, then it must be true," he said. He gave my shoes one last pat with his rag. "Sure was nice to see you again, Mr. Vice President."

"It's just Mr. Biden, now."

"I suppose it is. Anything else, Mr. Biden?"

He still had a smile on his face, but he'd shut down. He had every right in the world not to trust me. If I was coming off too much like a cop, it was because I didn't have the time for pleasantries.

I pulled my wallet out, but he waved me off. "This one's on the house."

My hand hesitated on a twenty, but I handed him a business card instead. Jill had designed them for me when we'd started our foundation, but I'd been slow to give them away. Too many strangers already had my number.

The Mayor fingered the card and glanced up at me.

"In case you guys need another card player sometime," I said.

"What do you play?"

"Gin rummy."

"Rummy," he repeated. "You any good?"

I grinned. "It's been so long, I can't remember."

He nodded, but I could tell from his skeptical expression that he was trying to figure me out. My mind was sharp as a switchblade. I remembered the last time I'd played gin rummy — just as I remembered the first time and every time in between. It was the only card game that had ever held my interest, because it was one of the few where memory and strategy weighed more than the luck of the draw.

I wasn't interested in playing cards, though. I was interested in getting to the bottom of this whole business with Finn. So far, I wasn't being quick to point fingers. That has a way of blowing up in your face. But I also wasn't going to dillydally. Dan Capriotti had made it clear that the Wilmington PD was content to sit back and wait for the toxicology results.

That wasn't good enough for me.

I grabbed a water bottle at the newsstand and joined the short line for the register. I didn't recognize the cashier. That happened a lot more nowadays than it used to. People moved around the country more, especially the younger generations. They followed their jobs, their hearts. Their intuition. Picking up roots was easier to do than putting them down. Of course, my family had moved from Pennsylvania to Delaware once upon a time. We'd been outsiders. As much as I liked to think of Wilmington as my town, it had been someone else's first. And someone else's before that, all the way back to the first known settlers, the Lenni Lenape Indians.

My phone buzzed with a text. It was Jill. She was going to be late. Could I find my own way home and thaw out the chicken, she wondered.

"Is that all?" a voice asked.

I looked up. "Oh, sorry," I told the girl at the register. "Just the water." As she was ringing it up, the flower bouquets on the counter caught my eye. "And one of those."

It was an impulse buy — an eighteen-dollar impulse buy. I couldn't identify any of the flowers. Heck, they could have been weeds for all I knew. But they were pretty and I wanted Jill to have them.

Outside, I fired up Uber. My ride would be there in seven minutes — it was rush hour, but it was also Wilmington. Traffic never got as bad as it did in DC, thank God. I texted Jill, telling her I was on my way home, and the chicken would be thawed in time for dinner at six.

A black Cadillac Escalade pulled up to the curb in front of me. The truck-sized SUV sat there, idling. Was my ride early? If there was an Uber sign on the dash, I had no way of knowing — I couldn't see anything through the heavily tinted windows.

Suppose this wasn't my ride. Suppose it was some enemy of the state, some deranged lunatic fixated on a former vice president. Suppose Finn wasn't the one who'd left the printout of my address behind on the

78

train . . .

My heart rate began to ratchet up. I had no Secret Service protection anymore. No private security. I didn't even have my pistol, because who brings a gun to a funeral? The vehicle just sat there, towering over me. There was nothing stopping a passenger from rolling down one of the windows and poking me full of holes. I was a sitting duck, with no wings to carry me away. I inhaled sharply and squeezed the bouquet tight. Water dripped out the bottom and onto the cement.

The tinted back window lowered.

"Need a lift?" Barack Obama asked.

10

I buckled myself into the seat across the aisle from Barack. There was one more row of seats behind us, all empty. The same talkative agent who'd been with Barack a few nights ago in my backyard was in the driver's seat fiddling with the air-conditioning. Barack's ever-present gaggle of aides and personal assistants were, once again, MIA. Couldn't say I missed them.

"I thought the funeral was earlier this afternoon," Barack said, eyeing the flowers.

"These are for Jill. I'm on my way home —"

"Those are lilies, Joe."

"So?"

"So it's a sympathy arrangement. The lily is a funeral flower. If you were going for romantic, you should have gone for roses."

The Escalade eased into traffic. I stared at the flowers in my hand. They looked like regular white flowers. "They had some red roses, but they were three times the price."

Barack made a little finger gun and pointed it at me. "That's why they're more romantic."

I sighed. Barack was right. He was always right.

"Anyway, I was headed home, and —"

He patted me on my knee, the good one. "We'll drop you off," he said.

I leaned forward between the seats and pointed to the approaching on-ramp. "You're better off avoiding the interstate this time of day, if you can. Stay on this road for another mile, until you hit the four-way stop. Turn left, and stay on Thirty East until you see the sign for the Christmas tree farm. Stinson's. It's closed during the summer, but if you ever need a Christmas tree, they grow 'em big and tall. Unless you're Jewish. Are you Jewish?"

"No, sir," Steve said.

"You ever had matzah ball soup?"

"He already has your address, Joe," Barack said, cutting in. "How do you think we got to your place earlier this week?"

I patted Steve on the shoulder, and he flinched slightly. Service agents were known to be a little jumpy. "Let me know if you need anything, pardner."

I leaned back in the seat. Barack stared at

me for a beat.

"You look like you've been playing football," he said.

My shoes were shined, but the rest of my suit was filthy. "I tripped. It's nothing, really."

"Hmmmm," Barack said. The president was always saying stuff like that to me: "Hrmph" and "Hrrrrrm." Occasionally, a "Harrrumph." Even after working together for eight years, I hadn't decoded the meanings behind them. Barack was, at times, a fortress. At other times, a glass case of emotion, as Will Ferrell would say.

"How do you like the Little Beast?"

I raised an eyebrow.

"My new ride," Barack said, patting his leather arm rest. His mood seemed much improved since Wednesday. He explained that the aftermarket-upgraded Escalade was as close to his armored presidential limos — the so-called Beasts — that Barack could buy on the open market. He'd had this one imported from Afghanistan. It had been his gift to himself, after completing the first draft of his presidential memoirs. When Michelle saw what he'd paid for it, she said, "You'd better have a couple more book ideas inside that thick skull of yours."

"I'm guessing it's not a coincidence that

you're in Delaware again," I said.

Barack leaned forward between the front seats. "Could we get a little privacy back here, Steve?"

The agent turned the radio up. It was a newer rock 'n' roll tune. I missed the stuff you could dance to: Buddy Holly, the Four Seasons. Not that I'd ever been much of a dancer. I'd been known to trip over my own feet, even when I wasn't on a dance floor.

"We saw you at the funeral," Barack said.

"You've been following me."

"We went to the cemetery to pay our respects."

"You didn't know Finn."

"I knew how much he meant to you," Barack said. "We were going to flag you down afterward and say hi, but Steve and I saw you get in that van. It was all white. Generic. Perfect for an afternoon kidnapping. After finding that map, we didn't want to take any chances."

"You followed me?"

"For your safety."

"I'm not a child, you know. You could have called me."

He sighed. "You're right, Joe. But I still think you should at least look into getting private security, like I suggested. If not for you, then for your family."

"Leave my family out of this," I snapped.

"Whoa, easy fella. It's me, your pal. Barry. I'm not some bad guy."

I unclenched my fists. I hadn't even been aware I'd been clenching them.

"I'm sorry," I said. "I don't even know who the bad guys are anymore."

"I'm sure Finn Donnelly wasn't a bad guy."

"You don't know that. I don't know that. Nobody knows that." I told Barack about my meeting with my detective friend, Dan Capriotti. "The department's working this as a possible overdose. The life insurance company is investigating it as a suicide. I don't know who to believe. There are some strange guys around —"

"Strange guys?"

"Ran into some druggie at the facility, where his wife is living. Probably nothing, but . . ." I shrugged. "Did you know they found heroin on Finn? Can you believe that?"

"I was going to let you know. We just found out today, when the lieutenant faxed the case files to us."

"You can stop doing that, you know."

"What?"

I rolled my eyes. "What you're doing. I know you think you're helping me, but I've got my own contact on the force. Dan will let me know if they find anything important. Finn may have been mixed up with some dangerous people. For all I know, he was on his way to see me. To ask for my help. Now, do I believe he was on drugs? There's nothing to say he wasn't. I think the truth is going to be more complex, but there's nothing you or your sunglass-wearing goons can do but get in the way. You're free to go back to Bali or Cape Town or wherever and work on your tan."

He stared at me with thin lips but didn't say anything. What did he expect? He seemingly wanted to pick up right where we'd left off, like no time had passed since we'd left Washington. To be fair, it was exactly what I'd wanted.

Except it wasn't. I'd expected we'd go out for drinks together. Maybe play a few holes, like in the line we'd been feeding to the press. Instead, we'd been reunited by tragedy. The specter of death hovered over us, poisoning the air we breathed. It didn't help that Barack was his usual impenetrable self.

What did he get out of spending his energy and resources on something like this? He hadn't known Finn. He was working an angle. I'd never known him to be under-handed, but his every move was choreographed. There was something about all of this that he wasn't sharing with me.

The suspicion had been gnawing at me since Barack's first visit.

It was gnawing at me even harder now.

I'd already come to the realization that the police might not be putting maximum effort into their investigation. Dan still hadn't returned my call from yesterday. The trouble was, I'd also realized I couldn't uncover the truth about Finn's death on my own. I wasn't a detective. I didn't know what questions to ask, or how to ask them.

But that didn't mean I needed Barack's help.

"There's no reason for you to get your hands dirty," I told Barack. "The last thing we need is the Secret Service or the FBI or the NSA or whoever you want to call in complicating things."

"Joe," he said. His voice was flatter than Kansas.

"I'm serious. If I know you, there'll be drones buzzing Wilmington within a week. This isn't a war zone. I don't want you to turn it into one."

"That's not fair."

"You and I are private citizens now. There's no way this ends well if we start swinging our dicks around —"

"Joe."

"Don't 'Joe' me," I said. "I'm serious."

"You're serious."

"As a heart-attack sandwich."

"Well," Barack said, "that's that, I guess."

For the rest of the way to my place, Barack busied himself on his BlackBerry. I stared out the window. There was more to refusing Barack's assistance than my hurt feelings. The story behind Finn's death was a time bomb. If and when it went off, there was no telling how many people would be affected by the blast. Keeping Barack — and Jill, and the rest of my family — as far away from my clumsy attempts to defuse it was the right thing to do. It was the smart thing to do.

It was a lie so well told, I almost believed it myself.

11

I punched the code on my garage keypad and the door lifted, revealing an empty parking space. I'd managed to beat Jill home. My shoulders relaxed. The last thing I wanted to do was answer a bunch of questions about why I was hitching rides from Barack Obama. She'd been on the receiving end of more than one rant about Barack. "Give him time," she'd said, again and again. "He just needs some time to himself."

Her explanation always made me laugh. *Time to himself?* He wasn't spending time alone, or even with his family. He was hanging around with an endless array of celebrities, holding open auditions for a new best friend. And now that he hadn't found one, he'd come crawling back to me. He didn't have the decency to beg for forgiveness, or even say those two magical words:

I'm sorry.

And was that too much to ask?

I gave the Escalade a little wave once the garage door was up. Barack and Steve had insisted on waiting in the driveway until I made it inside. I'd told them not to worry, that I didn't have my keys but I knew the six-digit code for the garage. They said, "Oh no, it's no big deal, we'll wait just to make sure."

Make sure of what? That I hadn't forgotten how to open my own garage door in my old age?

I didn't wait around to watch them leave.

Inside, I stripped off my suit. My knee was beginning to swell. There was no telling how much I'd damaged it. All I knew was that I was lucky I could stand after that fall. Damned lucky. Jill wasn't going to be happy with me. Even if I'd gotten her roses, they wouldn't have made up for the growing list of transgressions I was going to need to apologize for.

I limped through the kitchen in my undershirt and boxers. I was about to open the freezer door when I noticed the phone on the wall was blinking. I think we were the last people in Delaware with a landline. The world was changing, but I wasn't.

I picked up the handset. I figured it was probably Jill, with a reminder about the chicken. Or somebody risking an FCC fine to sell us cut-rate car insurance. But the message was from Selena Esposito. *Lieutenant* Selena Esposito.

A sales call would have been vastly preferable.

Esposito had the gravelly voice of a pack-a-day smoker. It was the first time I'd heard her voice, but it perfectly matched her reputation for being tough as a two-dollar steak. Her message said she wanted to "talk mano a mano." I didn't like the sound of that. Whatever she wanted, I had to nip it in the bud. I didn't want to see this whole thing spiral out of control.

When I called her back, she picked up on the first ring.

"Didn't think I'd hear from you so quickly," she said. "I wasn't sure I had the right number."

"It's me," I said.

"Do you have a few minutes?"

"I just returned from Finn Donnelly's funeral. I've got a minute or two."

"Good," she said. I heard the sound of paper rustling in the background. "I hear you met with Detective Capriotti yesterday."

"We didn't discuss the case, if that's what you're worried about. Just two old friends, meeting for coffee."

"Don't bullshit a bullshitter, Joe. You don't

drink coffee."

I didn't say anything. If you don't have anything good to say, keep your mouth shut. That's what Mama Biden always told me.

"This is my department. I'm in charge here. Not your friend Capriotti, or anyone else down here you might know from preschool."

"We're all on the same team."

She snorted. "I'm not going to let you or any of your Secret Service lackeys come through here and treat my detectives like errand boys. Now, Dan likes to show off — God knows that's why he wanted this case — but he's got a dozen other dead bodies in the morgue to deal with."

"The Secret Service aren't my . . ."

"They're not your *what*?"

I'd been about to say that they weren't my lackeys, but thought better of it. She obviously wasn't aware that Steve had been bugging her at Barack's behest, not mine. There was no love lost between Barack and me. That didn't mean I wanted to see him dragged any deeper into this mess.

"You have to understand, Finn and I were friends," I said, regaining my cool. I filled her in on the basics of our relationship, careful not to offer any unsolicited information. I had something of a reputation for being loose-lipped.

"You're friends with a lot of people, it sounds like," she said.

I ignored her. "Listen. A man lost his life here. All I want is to make sure justice is done. His wife is sick. His daughter is having a rough time handling this —"

"Every criminal has somebody who loves them," she said. "They're still criminals."

"Finn wasn't a criminal."

"Then what would you call someone with a Schedule One drug in their pocket? A hero?"

"Drug abuse is a disease. We need to stop treating addicts like violent offenders. He's not a hero, but it's disingenuous to call him a criminal."

"The law says differently, Joe."

She was right, of course — the law was the law. Barack and I hadn't done enough to change it. The changes we'd made were being rolled back by the new administration. It was almost like we'd never been in office.

"Fine," I said.

"Fine?"

"You're right. I'm letting my personal feelings get the better of me."

"So you're going to leave my boy alone. If you insist on wasting any more of his time, you're going to regret it."

But he *was the one that approached* me, I wanted to say. Except there was no point. She could make Dan's life hell if she wanted to.

I told her I'd have the Service go through the proper channels for any future requests. She didn't need to know that the Service's involvement here had been off the record. She didn't need to know I'd told Barack to drop it. "How's that sound to you?"

"You know what, Joe?"

"What's that?"

"You're a lot smarter than I thought you'd be."

"Was that a compliment?"

She hung up without answering. I stared out the picture window that looked onto the backyard and, beyond that, the lake. The surface of the water was as calm as a soul at rest. Part of me wondered if it wouldn't be in everyone's interest to just let Finn be.

The doorbell rang. Without thinking, I undid the deadbolt and swung open the door.

It was Steve.

"Forget something?" I asked. I was vaguely aware that I was in my skivvies, but didn't care. There were more important things on my mind.

"Your flowers, sir."

He held out the bouquet of lilies.

"Keep them," I said, slamming the door in his face. The shocked look on his face as the door swung closed was priceless.

My satisfaction, however, was short-lived.

He rang the doorbell again, and Champ barked.

I didn't want to answer it, because I was still pretty wound up. Not just about the stupid flowers. About everything. If Esposito had really put the clampdown on Dan, that meant I was frozen out of my backdoor into the department. I wasn't going to be able to convince her there was an ongoing Secret Service investigation for very long. The larger question was, why did I think I could piece together the puzzle of Finn's final hours any better than the police could? It was becoming obvious that Finn had gotten sucked under by the currents of something dark and powerful. Now I was swimming in those same murky waters. If I wasn't careful, the undertow would pull me down as well.

I could sense my frustration getting the better of me. If I opened the door again, I was either going to stammer out an apology to Steve . . . or slam it right back in his flat face. I just wanted to go upstairs, draw a bath, and soak my banged-up knee.

The doorbell rang again. Champ barked.

I took a deep breath. "Stay back," I told Champ, putting a leg between him and the door. I opened the door a crack.

It wasn't Steve this time. It was Barack.

We stood there in the doorway, Barack and me, staring into each other's eyes like a couple of gunslingers ready to face off at high noon. Except it was past five o'clock, I was in my boxers, and neither of us had a six-shooter.

"Aren't you going to invite me in?"

Slamming the door in Barack Obama's face wasn't an option. Or it was, but it wasn't one that I felt like exercising. It was the nuclear option.

I stepped aside. "Come on in, Mr. President."

He wiped his shoes off on the mat. Steve quickly followed, with the bouquet. Champ trotted behind them, sniffing at their pant legs.

Barack measured up the inside of our home with narrowed eyes. "Nice place you've got here, Joe."

We were in the entryway. All he could see of the interior were the twin spiraling staircases. It was a hollow compliment if I'd ever heard one.

"I'm going to put some clothes on. You two can head on to the living room," I said, pointing down the hall, "and make yourselves comfortable."

I threw on a navy bathrobe. I didn't have time to go through my closet looking for a clean pair of Dockers. There was still a chance I could get Barack and Steve out of the house before Jill came home.

When I returned downstairs, I found them sitting on the leather sofa in the living room. Barack was scratching behind Champ's ears. The dog had a blissed-out look.

"Very Hugh Hefner," Barack said when he spied my robe. "I like it."

I took a seat in the recliner. "I don't want to be a party pooper, but Jill's going to be home soon. If she sees you here, I'll catch hell for inviting guests over for dinner without telling her first. She's got dinner all planned out and —"

"We won't be staying long," Barack said. He didn't look me in the eye. "There's just something I wanted to say, that I didn't get to say to you in the car."

I crossed my arms. "If you're here to say you're sorry, that ship has sailed."

"Sorry for what?"

"Sorry for — for —" I stammered. I knew exactly what I wanted to say, but the words were stuck on the back of my tongue. "S-s-sorry for —"

Barack and Steve exchanged glances, and Barack threw his hands up. "What I wanted to say was that there's more."

"More what?"

"I'm not trying to scare you. I know you want to let the police handle this whole situation. I know you have the utmost respect for the boys in blue —"

"Just spit it out, man."

Barack turned to the agent sitting by his side. "The folder, Steve."

Steve was holding a manila folder behind the flowers, and started to hand it to Barack. I reached out across the coffee table and swiped it from them. Inside, there was a sheaf of eight-by-ten photographs. They were all shots of a house that looked like it had been ripped apart by a pit bull puppy on adrenaline shots.

I looked up at Barack. "I don't understand."

"That's Finn Donnelly's house," he said. "Of course, he hasn't lived there for a while."

"Where was he living?"

"A no-tell motel close to the railroad tracks," Barack said. "Finn never said anything about it? I thought he was part of your so-called second family."

"I say that about everyone at Amtrak," I said. "With Finn, it was a bit truer than with most. Finn started working at Amtrak the same year I started riding — 1972. I went to his wedding. I sent flowers to the hospital when his daughter was born. He didn't always work the train I rode, but I saw him more often than not for over three decades. I rode that line — the Metroliner — ten thousand times."

"You counted."

"Some journalist did. I just inflate the number by a thousand every time I tell the story."

"It's not a lie if you believe it," Barack said.

"Who said that? Some Marxist philosopher?"

"My father."

"Huh." I wasn't going to touch that one. I continued, "Anyway, I didn't know he'd moved out of his house. I didn't even know until this week that his wife was in the hospital. His daughter said he was keeping things private. I wished he'd reached out."

"That may have been why he had your address," Barack said. "He needed someone to talk to, or help him out with the bills. Some people are too proud for their own good. They should know it's not a sin to ask for help."

Barack's phone buzzed in his pocket. He ignored it and continued: "As I said, Finn

99

wasn't living in their family home."

"The house felt too big without his wife."

"That sounds about right," Barack said. "So a few months back Finn starts renting out their house to a young woman and her son."

"And the new tenants . . . they did this?" I asked, raising the pictures.

Barack shook his head. "The kid's a toddler, but it takes more than a toddler to do this. These people have been model tenants — paying their rent on time, keeping the yard under control. Last night, they went to Finn Donnelly's wake. When they came back, this was how they found the place. Somebody had forced open the back door with a crowbar, according to the officer who wrote the report."

"Anything missing?"

"Tough to say. Doesn't seem to be, though. If I had to hazard a guess, whoever broke in didn't have any clue that the house was being rented."

"Does his family know?"

"Finn's sister knows. So does the daughter. They're both staying in town, for the time being. A Holiday Inn Express."

"Nice hotels. Continental breakfast."

"So I've heard," Barack said.

"What's Lieutenant Esposito think?"

"She doesn't think it's connected to his death. There've been a number of break-ins during funerals and wakes recently. Criminals are scouring the obits for victims and striking when no one's home."

"I read something about those guys."

"As far as the Wilmington PD is concerned, this was just a run-of-the-mill burglary."

"But that's not what you believe."

"Nothing was stolen," Barack explained. "It's possible they were scared off in the middle of the job. That's what the PD is saying. But it's also possible they were searching for something they didn't find."

Very possible, I thought. I remembered the man in the nursing home, the one with the long hair, claiming to be ministering to the patients. He'd been snooping around for something, too. I tossed the folder onto the coffee table. "Why didn't you want to share these photos with me?"

"I worried I was being paranoid. While we were talking in the car, I realized that I shouldn't have had Steve follow you. It was out of line. It was wrong of me, and I'm sorry."

So he knows the words.

"But . . ."

"But after we dropped you off, I thought

101

about it some more. I couldn't shake the feeling that if I kept this from you and something happened, I wouldn't be able to live with myself. The last thing I wanted to do was scare you without reason. Having said that, I don't buy the idea that the burglary and your friend's death are uncon-nected."

I didn't buy it, either. I decided there was no harm in bringing Barack up to speed. "Detective Capriotti was pushing the over-dose angle hard yesterday. I would never say a bad word about our local boys in blue — especially Dan, who I've known forever and a lifetime — but something's been eat-ing at me and I haven't been able to put my finger on it. Until twenty minutes ago, that is."

"What happened twenty minutes ago?"

"I talked to Lieutenant Esposito. The reason she's taken over the case personally isn't because she's some sort of microman-ager. It's because she's worried we'll lead her detectives around town on a wild goose chase. She wants this case shut down. I'm sure her reasoning's on the up-and-up, too: the last thing the Wilmington Police Depart-ment needs is another case for their homi-cide backlog. A few years ago, they made national headlines by clearing just fifteen percent of all murders. That's below the Mendoza line."

"Mendoza?"

"It's a baseball thing," I said. "The department has improved, but not by much. They're not our only hope here, though. There's also the National Transportation Safety Board —"

"— who aren't even going to look at the burglary report," Barack interjected. "They're going to look at the engineer of the train, and the circumstances surrounding the accident, but that's it. We may be on our own here."

We? I almost said, but held my tongue. There was no "we," as far as I was concerned. On the other hand . . . I couldn't dismiss Barack's help. I didn't know why he was so interested in Finn Donnelly, or why he'd chosen now to take an interest in my life again. But Esposito had thrown a wrench into the gears: herself. Unless I was going to ask Dan to risk his job for me, I needed Barack . . . or at least the Secret Service. As long as Steve was willing to play along, I was, too.

"Has anyone checked out this motel room?" I asked. "The one where Finn was living."

"There's nothing in the reports Esposito

sent over," Barack said. "I would assume his family cleaned it out, but that's just an assumption."

"How many times have you checked out of a hotel and forgotten something in your room? I'm thinking under the bed or in a dresser drawer. You think you've got everything packed in your suitcase, but maybe you left your phone charger behind the nightstand . . ."

"He didn't have a cell phone. Last guy in America without one."

I threw up my hands. "I know that. I'm just saying, it might be worth checking out. We need some real evidence. Something to prove there's more going on here than it seems."

Barack didn't say anything.

"It's just an idea," I said. "If you have a better one . . . ?"

Barack shrugged, then turned to his agent. "Find a vase for those flowers, and then we'll head back into town. We're looking for a joint called the Heart of Wilmington Motel."

"Wait. You want to go there right now?" I asked. It was a question, but only sort of — I had the sinking feeling I already knew the answer.

"Is that going to be a problem?" Barack

asked. "I know Jill. She'll understand. Just call her and —"

"Let me get dressed," I said. Then, to Steve, I added, "There's a vase in the pantry, just off the side of the kitchen. I'm sure your GPS can show you the way."

I dragged myself upstairs and did a mental tally of the work I needed to finish over the weekend. There were a couple of emails sitting in my inbox that I'd been avoiding all week. One had to do with my new gig at the University of Pennsylvania; another was about the Biden Institute, the research and public policy institute I'd set up at my alma mater, the University of Delaware. All of it was going to have to wait.

My SIG called to me from the closet. We were heading into a dicey part of town, possibly past sundown. I hadn't felt unsafe beneath the interstate, but that was then. This was now. The Secret Service agent would be armed. Why shouldn't I be, too? I spun the dial on the safe, removed the SIG, and felt the gun's weight in my hand. Then I returned it. I realized I didn't *need* a gun. I *wanted* a gun. Instead I pulled out my Presidential Medal of Freedom.

It wasn't something you could wear every day, like a class ring. Truth be told, most people just ended up having their medals framed. I hadn't, because I knew it would be too painful to look at every day. It was a reminder of eight great years . . . eight wonderful, glorious years that seemed like a lifetime ago. I placed it on my desk.

I called Jill while I was getting dressed. It went straight to voicemail. In the kitchen, I scribbled out a note letting her know that I was out with Barack, and that I'd fill her in on the details later. I glanced up at the clock on the microwave. It was quarter 'til six already. The earliest we could make it downtown and back during rush hour would be eight or eight thirty. It was conceivable I wouldn't be home until nine — past our bedtime.

I signed my name. Then, underneath, as if it was an afterthought, I added, "Don't wait up for me."

13

Barack Obama and I were two fairly high-profile individuals, so it made sense that we should take some measures to conceal our identities. We couldn't risk causing a scene parading around town. There was already enough hoopla surrounding Finn's case. Despite this perfect logic on my part, Barack had a fit when he saw me emerge from the house. "What is that *thing* on your head?"

I touched the brim of my baseball cap. KISS MY BASS, it blared with all the subtlety of a trumpet in your ear. There was an embroidered bass on it, with its mouth open, ready to be reeled in.

"It's called a disguise," I said. "Here, I got you one, too." I handed him a maroon cap embroidered with a large letter *P.* "Phillies. Y'know, since you're a White Sox fan. No one will ever suspect it's you."

"Hmmmmmm," Barack said, staring at the cap.

I put on my aviator shades, then smiled. "What do you think?"

"Remember when you flew into Minnesota to interview for the V.P. slot?" he said. "We were so worried people would learn about the interview . . . and you showed up wearing a plain denim baseball cap and those same sunglasses you're wearing now."

"It was a different pair."

"Point is, nobody recognized you," he said. "But it wasn't because of your so-called disguise. It was because you were a senator from Delaware. Most people outside the Mid-Atlantic region don't even know where the Delaware state lines are."

"Most Delawareans don't know, either."

"I guess what I'm trying to say is whether we wear hats or welder's masks, it's going to be pretty difficult to avoid drawing attention. Plus, everybody's seen you in those glasses."

"You're saying I need to take them *off* to disguise myself," I said, whipping my Ray-Bans off. "How's that?"

Barack stared at me. "You look like Joe Biden either way."

"Forget it, then."

"No, no. Wear them if it makes you feel comfortable."

"And you'll wear the Phillies hat."

"We'll see," he said. "You ready to go, then?"

I dangled the extra key for my Challenger. She was sitting in the garage, begging to be let out of her cage. "Want to take my car?"

"What's wrong with the Little Beast?"

"We might not be able to avoid attention completely, but we can be smart about it. Think what will happen if we roll up any-where in that . . . thing. Pull into that motel parking lot, and people are going to stare."

"Says the guy who's dressed for a safari."

I glanced down at my sandals, blue chino shorts, and orange-and-yellow aloha shirt. Barack had gifted me the shirt one year for my birthday. I'd called it a Hawaiian shirt, and he'd told me not to call it that. He explained that in Hawaii, they were called aloha shirts.

"I can go back inside and change —"

Barack held up a hand. "We just waited twenty minutes for you to change, Joe." He nodded at the Escalade. "As for the Little Beast . . . you have to weigh the benefits here. The body's been reinforced with military-grade armor. Its windows can withstand armor-piercing bullets. The

109

shocks are so good, you can drive over a land mine and not spill your tea. Plus, there's a button you push, and it turns the exhaust into a flamethrower."

"Really?"

"No, but that's damn near the only thing it doesn't have."

I hit the button on my keychain and waited for the garage door to dramatically unveil my baby: my neon-green 2017 Dodge Challenger T/A. A throwback to the 1970s Trans-Am series muscle cars. "You weren't the only one who bought a new car."

Barack's eyes opened wide. "What'd you do with your Stingray?"

"It's at the beach house."

Barack pinched the spot between his eyes. He was trying to be nonchalant about my new muscle car, but I could tell he was itching to get in and go for a test drive. "Steve would never go for it."

Steve was leaning against the SUV in the driveway, staring intently at his wristwatch. He had two fingers to the left of his Adam's apple, feeling his pulse.

"There's plenty of room in back for Steve." I slipped into the driver's seat and started her up. She purred to life. A real beauty, no denying it. Over the sound of the engine, I shouted, "3.6-liter Pentastar VVT

110

V6 engine with an 8-speed Torque-Flite automatic transmission that really gets up and goes."

I gave her a little gas, and Barack jumped. "Turn it off," he said.

"When you get her on the open road, she flies like Christ on a bike."

"No way," Barack said. "There's no way."

I nodded toward the Little Beast. "What's the gas mileage on that thing?"

The Challenger was an old-school gas guzzler, a muscle car in a world of flab. Still, it had to get better mileage than Barack's armored SUV, which looked as if it drank gas like the Tweeter-in-Chief drank Diet Coke.

Barack sighed. I had backed him into a corner and used his own ethics against him — a cruel trick. A career politician's trick.

He said, "Where do you want us to park the Little Beast?"

If we parked it in the garage, there wouldn't be any room for Jill to pull in. Barack's SUV was so wide it would take up both spaces. If we parked the SUV in the driveway, neighbors might start whispering. It looked just enough like the old Beasts that someone might put two and two together. The last thing I wanted was a couple of Johnny Crabapples trying to do the math.

"There's a Walmart not far from here," I said. "Plenty of people park their Winnebagos there. It'll be fine."

"Why not here?"

"It just wouldn't be a good idea."

Barack stared at me. "Did you tell Jill you were going out with me?"

"It's none of her business who I go out with. I'm in the seventh decade of my life — I can do whatever I want. No one's the boss of me."

"I used to be your boss."

"The American people were our boss," I told him. "But things have changed."

He shook his head and wiped a bead of sweat from his brow. "Did you bring that heater you were packing the other night?"

I felt a twinge of embarrassment. Of course Barack knew I was a gun owner — I'd talked about my shotguns enough that he could probably tell you the make and model. But he wasn't talking about my shotguns.

"There've been reports of prowlers," I said. "You can't be too careful."

"You're right about that. A lot going on in this world. Even when it comes to friendly faces, it's hard to tell who to trust these days." He paused. "So you're bringing it?"

"I'm not bringing it."

112

He looked me steady in the eye, as if he was trying to assess whether I was lying or not. Finally satisfied, he fit the Phillies cap on his head. "Then let's go, Joe."

14

I swung the Challenger into the motel parking lot. There were around twenty rooms lined up in a row, with the main office situated in the middle. A half dozen cars, all nondescript jalopies. The very idea that Finn had lived the last few months of his life in this roach haven made me sick to my stomach. He'd been a proud government employee. He'd deserved better.

"Color TVs," Barack said, reading from the sign out front.

"Color TVs? That settles it," I said. "I'm getting us a room."

Steve piped up from the backseat: "If we're staying here, I'd like to check the rooms first for potential jackals. Run the plates in the parking lot —"

"We're not staying here," Barack said. "Joe was kidding."

I'd stayed in dumps like the Heart of Wilmington on my first campaign — for city

114

council. There was no way Barack and I would be staying here, not now that we'd reached an age where a good night's sleep was more refreshing than a lemonade.

"Which room was Finn's?" I asked.

"One-ten," Barack said.

I looked at Steve. "You're the one with the badge. Why don't you see if it's available for a quick look-see?"

"And leave you two here on your own?"

"You think we're going to drive off without you?" Barack asked.

"I'm concerned about your safety, Mr. President."

"We'll wait in the car," Barack said. "We'll lock the doors. If anybody so much as looks in our direction, we'll honk the horn. Then you come in guns a-blazing and save the day. You'll look like a hero. They'll give you a book deal."

"What would I do with a book deal?"

I took my glasses off and rubbed the bridge of my nose. The sun was beginning to set. The drive had taken twice as long as I'd expected, thanks to Steve's insistence that we stick to back roads. Apparently everything with Steve was going to take twice as long.

"I'll go," I said, unlocking my door.

Steve sighed rather dramatically. "Stay in

the car. I'll be right back." He left us, muttering something under his breath that sounded a lot like "Six weeks . . . six weeks . . . six weeks . . ."

I leaned close to Barack. "What happens in six weeks?"

"He's leaving for CAT training," Barack said. "The guy's been putting his body through hell the past six months, trying to get in shape. You can ask him all about it — he'll talk your ear off if you give him a chance."

"Huh."

"You know, it's his job to protect us," Barack said.

"It's his job to protect *you.*"

That shut Barack up.

If Steve graduated from the training program, he would join the Counter-Assault Team — an elite paramilitary squad of Service agents who provided the firepower in case of an attack on the president. Steve was on his way to the Show. No more time putzing around with has-beens like us.

Once Steve was inside the motel office, I swung open my door.

"Where are you going?" Barack asked.

"Cool your jets, I'm just stretching my legs."

I slammed the door and hobbled around

the car, trying to work out the kinks in my back. The kinks in my leg were going to need more work. The swelling around my knee looked worse than before. I'd obviously torn something, and I wasn't sure it would heal on its own. It hurt when I stretched my leg, and it hurt when I didn't stretch my leg. It needed ice and rest, neither of which I was likely to get anytime soon.

I returned to my seat and turned up the radio. All I heard was the faint voice of a preacher, fading in and out, sermonizing about heaven and hell. I had heard enough sermonizing at the service today. I turned off the radio.

"That's interesting," Barack said.

At first I thought he meant the radio program, but then I followed Barack's gaze to a woman standing at the door of a room. She was fumbling through her purse. The room number read 110. Finn's room. I didn't have a good view of her face, but I could see she had long blond hair pulled back into a ponytail that reached her waist.

"How do you think she uses the toilet?" I asked Barack.

"Excuse me?"

"With hair that long. She can't just sit down, or she'd dip it into the toilet. If she flips it to the side, it touches the floor."

"Forget her hair. She's trying to jimmy open the door."

I took a second look. My vision wasn't what it once was, but it appeared she was sliding a credit card alongside the door lock. The motel's doors had old-style keyholes, not magnetic card readers.

"She could be a guest," I said without conviction.

"Could be," Barack said.

"Then again, she could be the burglar who broke into the Donnellys' home during the wake."

"Could be."

"There's only one way to find out."

I opened my door.

"We should wait for Steve," Barack said, but it was too late. I was already out of the car. I wasn't waiting around for him. The Secret Service couldn't tell me what to do anymore.

Barack mumbled something and got out, too.

I took one look at his gray-flecked scalp and shook my head.

"What?" he whispered.

"Your cap," I said. I reached back into the car and handed Barack the Phillies hat. "Oh, and don't lose it — it's Jill's. She's a

Phillies fan. Don't ask me why."

Barack put it on, but when we turned back around it was too late. The woman was gone. Was she in the room, or had we spooked her?

Again: there was only one way to find out.

We approached the door to room 110, moving as stealthily as my bum knee would allow. Inside, the lights were out. The curtains were pulled shut. I put a hand on the knob and gave it a slight twist.

It wasn't locked.

Neither of us had a weapon. This was a minor problem. If somebody — the woman — had just broken into the room, this meant she was a criminal. And criminals carry guns. I wished I'd packed my pistol . . . but, then again, maybe it was a good thing I hadn't. If we really, truly ran into trouble, would I have been able to pull it out of my chino shorts without shooting off my family jewels? Barack would have a real field day if that ever happened.

Barack placed one of his oversized ears on the door. Political cartoonists had loved to mock Barack's elephant ears. If only they could see him now, using them for their God-intended purpose.

"What do you hear?" I whispered.

A pickup the size of a semi rumbled past

the motel.

"I don't hear a thing," Barack said after it had passed.

"Then I say we go in."

"Legally speaking, we're treading on some dangerous ground," Barack said. "This is breaking and entering."

"Even if the door's unlocked?"

Barack nodded.

"Damn it," I said. "I don't want to start another Watergate."

"We're not in the White House anymore. We're private citizens."

"And as private citizens . . ."

"It's still illegal."

"Even if the door's unlocked?"

"I already said —"

The door swung inward. I tumbled to the floor, and Barack tripped over me. We landed in a heap, a jumbled mess of arms and legs.

"Can I help you?"

I looked up. The lamps were off, but there was a thin beam of light coming from the bathroom, illuminating the room . . . just enough to see the curvaceous outline of a beautiful woman with damp hair down to her waist. She was wearing a white hotel towel. *Just* a white towel. Whatever Barack and I thought we'd seen her doing outside,

120

we'd obviously been wrong. I didn't imagine many burglars stopped to take showers during heists.

I tipped my hat to her. "Good evening, ma'am. We're, uh . . ."

"We were looking for the pool," Barack said, untwisting himself from me. "We appear to have taken a wrong turn."

The woman studied us for a moment. I might have been dressed for a pool, but there was no way Barack was going swimming in his navy suit.

"They didn't tell me there was a pool," the woman said with a hint of a southern accent.

"C'mon, Joe. We'll take it up with the front desk," Barack said. Then, to the woman, he added, "Sorry to have disturbed you."

She maintained the bewildered look on her face as we quietly backed out of the room.

"I can't believe you called me by my real name," I said in a hushed tone on our way back to the car.

"I don't think she recognized us," Barack said. "I mean, we have these great disguises."

"You're making fun of me."

Barack slapped me on the back. "She can

call all of her friends. She can post about it online. Who would ever believe her?"

I shrugged. "Yeah, you're right. Still, next time we run into trouble, we're using code names."

"Next time?" Barack asked. "What are you planning?"

I had only a vague idea of what we'd been coming here to do, and that vague idea was mostly hot air. We'd just busted in on some innocent woman because our imaginations had gotten the better of us. Neither of us said a word about it, though. We were too embarrassed. What was I planning next? Nothing, if I could help it.

We returned to the car. Steve stepped out of the lobby with a key in his hand attached to a small wooden keychain. I rolled down Barack's window.

"Let's make this quick," Steve said, passing the key to room 110 to Barack. "The night clerk said we can take a look around."

"What about the person in the room now?" Barack asked.

Steve looked confused. "No one's staying in the room now. It's supposed to be empty."

"Son of a buttermilk biscuit," I said, grimacing. "We got bamboozled."

15

It wasn't the first time I had been bamboo-zled. It wouldn't be the last. Still, I should have seen it coming: there wasn't a woman alive who'd take a shower in a motel room without locking the door first. She'd taken us for fools because we were a couple of fools. Especially when it came to the fairer sex. Barack and I were chivalrous to a fault. We should have trusted our instincts. Instead, we'd been flustered into doubting ourselves.

The woman was long gone by the time we returned to the room. She'd left the door swinging open and the towel hanging over the back of the chair.

The towel wasn't even wet.

"If you'll let me know what we're looking for, I can help," Steve offered. He turned on a lamp; it flickered for a moment before shorting out.

"This is the first time I've tossed a room

for evidence," I said, lifting one of the pillows off the bed as if I was looking for change left by the tooth fairy. "Fingerprints, I guess?"

"The fingerprints would have been wiped clean by the cleaning person," Barack said, holding one of the glasses up to the overhead light. "Although it looks like no one's cleaned anything in this room in twenty years. It would take us weeks to dust for prints."

"I left my fingerprint-dusting kit at home, so I guess it doesn't matter," I said.

"You have a fingerprint-dusting kit?" Barack asked.

I peeked underneath the bed. "The FBI gave them to everyone in Congress one year. A Christmas gift." It took longer than usual to get to my feet, on account of my knee. "Looks like they have a little mouse problem at this establishment."

"Find some mouse droppings?" Barack asked.

"Found a mouse," I said. "Just a little guy."

"You don't seem too surprised."

"For twenty-nine bucks a night, I'm surprised he wasn't bigger."

I opened and closed the drawers in the dresser, all of which, of course, were empty. They'd been cleaned out by Finn's family, then by housekeeping . . . and then, possibly, by the woman who'd given us the slip. Besides the bed and a ratty green sofa chair, the room was as bare as a newborn baby's bottom. There wasn't a safe in the closet. There wasn't even a closet. There was a nightstand, but no pad of paper or pen. That meant I couldn't try out that trick from TV, where the detective rubs a pencil over the top page to get an impression of whatever the criminal had written on the ripped-off page.

I opened the nightstand drawer. Finally, something: a Gideon Bible. The familiar mottled maroon imitation-leather hardback of the Bible that was in every hotel room in the country. The same type of Bible the tattooed man had left behind in Darlene's room. Not that this was any kind of connection. In fact, if the Bible had been missing from the drawer, *that* would have been something. This? This was nothing.

"Either of you ever met a Gideon?"

Barack shook his head. Steve, peeking through the curtains, said, "I got a cousin who's a Gideon."

"Really?" I said. "What's their angle?"

"Spreading the word of Christ."

"You know what their business model looks like?"

Steve pulled the curtains closed. "They pay for the Bibles with donations. That's all I know."

"It's just, I've never seen a Gideon church," I said. "I'd always wondered if Gideons even existed."

"My cousin exists," Steve said. "She lives in Cleveland."

Barack peered out from the bathroom. "Did anyone check the bed?"

"I checked *under* the bed," I said. "You actually want me to touch the sheets?"

"We're looking for anything Finn may have left behind."

"But the *sheets*?"

"Anything," Barack said.

I shuddered. At least Barack was taking the bathroom. I didn't want to think about what sad state *it* was in, but I could guess I'd been inside cleaner porta potties at political rallies.

The bedspread was pulled all the way up, with nice and tight corners. The way Jill made the bed. I pinched the top corner of the bedspread like I was picking up a dirty diaper and slowly peeled it back. I don't know what I expected to find — blood, a bullet hole. Maybe a dirty diaper. All of the above.

Fortunately, all I found was a bleached

white sheet. Not that it made me feel any better about the room. It was no place to pass an hour, let alone the final months of your life. *Dammit, Finn, if only you'd told me* . . .

Barack made his way out of the bathroom. He shook his head.

"It was worth a shot," I said, collapsing into the chair. To me, it was undeniable now that Finn had been part of something larger. We had nothing concrete to prove it to the cops, but there was at least one person sniffing around his trail. Possibly more, if the burglary and the break-in at the motel were two different parties. Two different *criminals.* Not to mention the hophead in Darlene's room. At the very least, Finn had been involved with the wrong sorts of people. At the worst . . . he'd *been* the wrong sort of people. Could he have been a criminal himself? And what mattered more: the truth, or preserving Finn's name?

I'd promised Grace Donnelly that I'd find out what happened to her father. I hadn't said what I'd do with that information once I found it.

"The chair's been moved."

I glanced up at Barack. "What did you say?"

"The chair," he said, pointing to where I

was sitting, "has been moved." He crossed the room and knelt down. He ran a hand over the carpet. "Recently, too. There are still indents here."

I raised myself out of the chair with only minimal wincing. The last thing I wanted was to worry Barack. He didn't know how bad my knee was, and I intended to keep it that way.

I bent down to tip the chair to see if there was something hidden underneath it, but Barack and Steve stepped in to do the heavy lifting. "Let us young bucks do it, Joe," Barack said.

They rolled it onto its back.

There was a twelve-by-twelve-inch section of carpet missing. The edges were frayed, as if it had been cut up with a serrated knife. The bare plywood was showing. There was a faint pink stain in the center.

My heart was beating fast, propelled by equal parts terror and excitement. None of us spoke.

16

I left a message on Lieutenant Esposito's voicemail, letting her know we needed to talk ASAP. Since it was past nine o'clock, I wasn't sure if we would hear from her until morning. Police had to sleep sometime. One assumed.

"No luck?" Barack said, reading the expression on my face.

I shook my head. "No answer."

Steve joined us in the car after returning the key to the front desk. The night clerk didn't have a clue about the mysterious woman. Not surprisingly, the unhelpful gentleman also claimed ignorance when asked about the missing square of carpet. "He thought someone might have taken it as a souvenir."

I laughed. "The only souvenirs people take home from places like this are bedbugs."

"I guess we're done here, then?" Steve said.

"We're waiting for Esposito's call," I said.

"A few minutes," Barack said, much to Steve's obvious distress. "We can wait a few minutes."

I nodded toward the room. "What do you think happened in there?"

"Somebody spilled something on the carpet," Steve said.

I glared at him in the rearview mirror. "No crap, Matlock."

"Cool down, you guys," Barack said. "Steve's right. All we know for sure is that something was spilled on the carpet."

"Blood," I said.

"We don't know that, Joe."

"Would you go to all that trouble to cover up a ketchup stain? No, you wouldn't. The woman wasn't in there long enough to cut the carpet up and move the chair, so we can forget about her for the moment. If there's even a chance that's Finn's blood in there . . ."

I had the scenario all worked out in my head already. There was something Detective Capriotti had said the other day that kept coming back to me: *He may have even been dead already.* I'd done a little googling and found that rigor mortis takes up to two

130

hours to set in. Medical examiners can't determine the exact time of death. All they can give you is an approximate timeframe. Being hit by a train would almost certainly muddy the waters further. If the faint pink stain on the plywood was indeed Finn's blood, it was possible that Finn hadn't died of a heart attack, or an overdose, or even suicide. He could have been murdered.

I picked my phone up. No calls. I would have heard it ring, but sometimes missed calls show up that don't ring, for whatever reason.

"Something happened in that room," I said. "Something awful. Even if it has nothing to do with Finn, the cops need to take a look."

Steve leaned between the seats. "Maybe it's the police who ripped up the carpet. Did you think of that? Maybe they took it to test whatever was on there."

"And left it out of the case file?"

"If it was a dead end, sure."

I swallowed hard. I was searching for a comeback, but he had a point. I'd gone so far down one road that I hadn't stopped to examine any other possibilities.

"You may have a point," I squeaked.

"I can't hear you," Steve said.

"I said it's possible, okay?"

Barack stuck a hand between us. "No need to raise your voice, Joe. We can all hear you just fine."

I placed both hands on the wheel to calm myself. "Steve's right. I'm sure the police have already checked all of this out. When Esposito calls back, it'll be to chew me a new asshole. And you know what? She'd be within her rights to do that. I'm a grown man. I can take it. But dammit, something's not right. Something stinks to high hell."

Barack placed a hand on my shoulder. "I understand you're frustrated, Joe. But we've already gone above and beyond. When you talk to the lieutenant, tell her about the woman we saw. Tell her about the missing carpet. If she's as good as everyone says she is, she'll do the right thing and put more detectives on this investigation. She'll connect the dots."

"If we'd had our heads screwed on straight, we could have caught that woman red-handed. Instead . . ."

"Say we realized she had broken into the room," Barack said. "What difference would it have really made? We couldn't have held her against her will."

"Steve could have. Isn't that right, Steve?"

He cleared his throat. "Technically, you're correct. If we witness a crime in progress,

Service agents are allowed to make an arrest without a warrant."

"See?" I tapped Barack on the arm.

"But I left my handcuffs in the Little Beast," Steve continued. "Speaking of which, we shouldn't leave her at the Walmart for too long. Renaissance won't be happy if anything happens to her baby."

I glanced at Barack. "Renaissance" was Michelle's Service code name.

"I thought the car was yours."

He didn't look at me. "The Little Beast is insured by that tiny Australian gecko," he said, holding his thumb and index finger a couple inches apart for Steve. "She'll be fine."

"It's a British gecko," I said.

Barack and Steve both stared at me.

"The insurance company mascot," I said. "He's British, not Australian."

Barack rubbed the fatigue from his eyes. "I just don't know about you sometimes, Joe. I just don't know."

I stuck my keys in the ignition. Besides my Challenger, there were only three cars and a pickup in the parking lot. Either the motel wasn't doing much business tonight, or most of its clientele arrived on foot. A hot-pillow joint like this, I guessed the latter.

Suddenly, a thought hit me like I'd just stuck a fork in a socket.

"What happened to Finn's car?" I asked Barack.

"The Wilmington PD found it here in the lot. The report doesn't say anything more than that. Could be in the impound."

"But Finn hasn't been formally suspected of a crime. The car wouldn't be evidence."

"Then it'd be towed," Barack said, pointing to the sign on the light pole closest to my car. WARNING, it read. UNAUTHORIZED VEHICLES WILL BE TOWED.

"Eventually," I said. "It'd be towed eventually."

"You don't think . . ."

I nodded. "If his family didn't pick it up, Finn's car could still be here."

Unfortunately, neither Barack nor I had any idea what Finn's car looked like. Steve checked with the front desk, but they said they didn't record license plates. The reason was easy to guess — it provided plausible deniability for any number of law enforcement requests. Such as this one.

If Lieutenant Esposito ever returned my call, I could ask if she had Finn's license plate number handy. Steve offered to have one of his pals at Service headquarters do a records search, but I was worried about raising flags.

We paced the lot. Barack had his hand on his chin, trying to get his gray matter to work overtime. I never picked up the hand-on-the-chin trick. Whenever I tried, I didn't look like I was thinking. I just looked confused.

"The pickup isn't his," I said. "We can cross that off the list."

"You're sure?" Barack asked.

"He lived in Riverside. That area's ninety percent black. He wouldn't last long with that Confederate flag on his license plate."

"Cross it off the list."

"And that one . . . that's a Virginia plate," I said, pointing to a newer Mini Cooper. "I don't see him as having registered with the Virginia DMV, unless he was leading some sort of double life."

"Plenty of addicts lead double lives."

"But most addicts don't register their cars in other states for the fun of it."

"So Occam's razor says it's not his car," Barack said.

"Occam?"

"William of Occam," he said. "An English philosopher who had a theory that the simplest answer was usually the correct one."

I nodded. I vaguely remembered the term

from my law school days — but only vaguely.

These eliminations left just two cars, both with dark-blue plates proclaiming Delaware the "First State." One was a Buick Century, the other a Ford Impala. Both looked to be from the last century. The last century . . .

Of course. I walked around back of the cars and examined their bumpers. "Found it," I said, patting the Buick Century on the trunk.

"Ridin' with Biden," Barack said, reading the faded bumper sticker. "Cute."

The driver's side door was locked. I peered into the backseat window. It was a mess of plastic to-go bags and empty Styrofoam cups. "Looks like he's been living out of his car."

"Looks like your car, actually," Barack said, peering into the front driver's side window. "Looks like someone beat us here, too." He reached for the passenger side door and opened it.

"Maybe he left it unlocked."

Barack ran a finger over the rim of the window, stopping at a scratch in the glass. "Someone jimmied the door. That's why it was unlocked. Not a clean job, though. A professional wouldn't have left marks like this."

I examined the scratches. "How do you know so much about jimmying car locks?"

"You've never locked your keys in your car?"

"That's what a towing company is for," I said.

"If you can afford Triple-A," Barack said. "If you're a high-schooler and you've spent all your money on Al Green records and six-packs, you've got to rely on other means. Like friends who boost cars."

I shook my head. We'd had very different adolescences, to say the least.

I popped the button for the trunk. While Barack searched in back, I checked out the glove compartment. I still didn't know what we were looking for, but the glove compartment was a bust. I found the car's registration and a yellowed manual that hadn't been cracked open since the Reagan administration. But no insurance card. Finn must have kept it in his wallet. I felt underneath the seats. Nothing there but used napkins.

I sighed. I hadn't been expecting to find a handwritten manifesto, but I'd hoped there'd be something. A secret laptop that he hadn't told anyone about, with files that showed what he was really up to. Anything to shed light on the mystery that his life had become.

137

Barack slammed the trunk shut, then knocked on the back window. I reached over and popped the lock.

"They don't make backseats like this anymore," he said, sliding in.

"They sure don't."

Backseats were where the action was, back in the day. There was one car — the Chevy I'd gotten for my sixteenth birthday — with a backseat as big as a king-size bed. I'd had big intentions of putting it to use, but I was too timid around girls to be much of a Romeo in high school.

The first time I'd gotten intimate in a car wasn't until several decades later, during the '88 campaign. Jill and I were in the parking lot of the Iowa State Fair, waiting on my Secret Service detail. I kissed my beautiful bride on the lips, and she kissed back with a little tongue. Before we knew it we were rounding first base in the backseat of a rental car while my personal aide kept tapping on the window to get our attention.

I got called out at second.

"How can someone live like this?" Barack asked. He was pawing through the trash on the floor behind me.

"Sometimes, you just forget to clean out your car," I said. "It's not a top priority for most people."

"Maybe you should make it a priority."

"Me?"

"Yes, you," Barack said. "It took me twenty minutes to clean out your car just so Steve would have a place to sit. I don't even want to think about what happens when you hit the road, windows open, and all that trash just starts flying up into the air. You're liable to cause an accident, driving around like that."

I hadn't taken the car out all summer. The garbage in the back was from the days I'd been going to the University of Pennsylvania campus for the spring semester, and it had always been raining. I didn't say any of this, though, because it wasn't any of Barack's business.

"Sorry that I don't have the Secret Service to vacuum my car out, like some people," I mumbled.

Barack went around to the passenger side. "You know, Joe —"

"What?" I said, daring him, taunting him to do his worst. To say something that couldn't be taken back. To say what he really thought of me: for once, to speak what was truly on his mind.

"— I think we're onto something here." Barack held up a Styrofoam cup with a Waffle Depot logo. "What does this look like to you?"

"A coffee cup."

"There's a dozen of these bad boys," he said. "Along with a bunch of to-go bags. Looks like, before work, he would stop at the Waffle Depot for coffee, and maybe a bite to eat."

I thought this over. Finn's shift began in the early morning, before the sun was up. There weren't many early-hour diners between the motel and Wilmington Station. There was, however, a Waffle Depot.

"Do you think he went there the day of the accident?" I asked.

Barack held up a receipt. "I know he went the day before, at least. Says here his server was named Tina."

"Maybe he said something. Maybe he was acting funny." I paused. "We could swing by, just for a bite. I haven't had anything since lunch. I'm so hungry I could eat the balls off a low-flying goose."

Barack started to say something, then stopped.

"Hey, Steve!" he shouted across the lot. "You like waffles?"

17

Except for the waitress and cook, the Waffle Depot was deserted. We sat in a booth in the far corner. All three of us had sunglasses on, both to disguise ourselves and to protect our eyes from the fluorescent lighting that lit the room like John Boehner's tanning bed. Our caps were pulled low.

"Are you sticking your gut out on purpose?" Barack said.

"Are you talking to me?" I asked.

"I wasn't talking to Steve. Steve has one percent body fat. Isn't that right, Steve?"

"One-half of one percent," he said.

"Is that healthy?" I asked.

Barack shrugged. The forty-fourth president was in pristine shape as well — not one-half of one percent body fat, but close enough for government work. He'd been out in the world, kayaking, parachuting, and (probably) kickboxing in underground fight clubs. Meanwhile I'd been at home, staring at the rowing machine in the basement and occasionally hopping on the treadmill.

Steve yawned. There were dark circles under his eyes.

Our waitress, a short woman with dark hair and a pierced nose, stopped by to take our orders. Her name, according to her name tag? Tina. She poured a coffee for Steve. Barack and I stuck with water.

Just before she turned, Barack told her she looked familiar. "You work the graveyard shift, right? I think I've seen you closer to breakfast before. Must be some long nights."

She smiled. "I thought I recognized you from somewhere. Not from here, but from . . . well, I shouldn't even say it out loud, it's kind of ridiculous. You just look like someone famous, that's all."

"Barack Obama?" he said with a smirk.

"You must hear that all the time." She stepped back and sized him up. "He's a little younger than you, though."

Barack's smirk dropped. "Maybe you can help me out. There was a guy in here Tuesday morning. Eating by himself. A white guy with white hair, a little taller than my friend here. That ring any bells?"

She shook her head. "I was busy from start to finish. It was all a blur. There was a wrestling show in town. Those guys have big appetites — triple, quadruple omelets. One of them destroyed the men's toilet. Just *destroyed* it."

"Which wrestler was it?" I asked.

Barack glared at me.

"Anyway," I said, "the guy that was in here. He comes here all the time. He's a conductor, for Amtrak."

"Oh!" she said. "Finn. Always sits at the counter, always orders decaf." Her face dropped. "Y'all cops or something?"

I realized that, yeah, we probably did look like cops. Three guys with short hair and sunglasses, two of us in suits. Me in the aloha shirt, looking an awful lot like Magnum P.I. Only thing missing was the mustache.

"Something like that," I said.

"Is Finn in some kind of trouble?"

Barack and I looked at each other. She hadn't heard about the accident.

"There was an incident," he said. "The railroad sent us. We're just talking to people. Nothing formal."

"I get it. You want to know if I could smell alcohol on his breath, or if he smelled like reefer." She leaned down. "Half the people who come in on my shift are coming here straight from the bars. Even worse on a Friday or Saturday night."

143

"Except tonight," I pointed out.

"It's still early," she said. "The bars don't close 'til two."

We all looked up at the clock. It was only half past ten. It felt much, much later.

"But Finn," she continued, "I would have noticed if there was anything funny about him. You can't walk around in a uniform smelling like liquor — it'd be like a pilot walking onto a plane with a bottle of Jack Daniels. People tend to notice those sorts of things."

"So what do you remember about him? Tuesday morning. Did he seem nervous?" Barack asked.

Tina shrugged. "Everybody's a little squirrelly these days, ain't they? I think we all got a little ADHD." Her eyes went to Steve, who was checking his pulse again. Barack asked if she'd seen Finn Wednesday morning, too, but she hadn't. Just the morning before the accident.

I asked, "You didn't happen to see him with a bag of —"

Barack kicked me hard under the table.

"I wasn't going to say heroin," I whispered through my teeth, though I don't think Barack — or anyone — heard me.

"He did have a bag," Tina said. "Now that you mention it, yeah. It was a black bag, you know, like for the gym —"

"A duffel bag?"

"That's right. He usually didn't bring nothing in, but that night he had this black duffel bag. Kept it real close by, too. Kind of strange, if you ask me. He coulda just left it in his car."

"In this neighborhood?" I asked.

"What's wrong with this neighborhood?"

"Nothing," I said quickly. "Nothing at all."

As soon as she left us, I turned excitedly to Barack. "A duffel bag. That's something, right?"

"It's not *nothing.* That doesn't, in and of itself, necessarily mean it's *something.*"

I pulled out my phone to call Esposito, but Barack told me to hold up. "The lieutenant hasn't called back. If she does call us, then we can ask her if they found a duffel bag near the tracks or at the motel. Until then, there's no point. If you call someone and leave a message, you wait for them to call you back. You don't keep calling, and calling, and calling, and leaving more messages." He paused, then added, pointedly: "Unless your goal is to annoy them."

Steve wasn't listening to us bicker. He was in another reality completely, a reality that I wished I could slip into.

Our waitress brought out our orders.

Barack and Steve had both ordered grilled chicken breasts. They weren't looking at their plates, however. They were staring in horror at my plate as I reached for the bottle of Heinz 57.

"Are there even hash browns under that mess?" Barack asked.

"I'm pretty sure," I said. My hash browns were — in the parlance of Waffle Depot — "hot and bothered" (i.e., covered with cheese, onion, diced ham, and jalapeño). Seven hundred and forty calories, all gristle and grease. This was what I'd been doing to myself for months now. Jill had caught me more than once eating Ben and Jerry's straight out of the pint, in my boxers and undershirt in the middle of the night. I only had the foggiest of memories of even getting out of bed. It wasn't sleepwalking, but it was something close to it.

"How can you eat all those carbs?" Steve said. It was good to see him slip back into our realm and make conversation, even if he was being a little snot.

"Calories are good for you," I said between massive bites. "They give you energy."

"*Caffeine* gives you energy."

I looked into his eyes, half-shaded by drooping eyelids, and then down at his coffee cup, which he'd just emptied for the third time in under twenty minutes. "And how's that working out for you?"

He didn't say anything.

While we were waiting for the check in silence, Steve stared deep into what was left of my shredded potatoes like he was looking at a Van Gogh. I was seriously beginning to worry about his state of mind. Could we trust him with his weapon?

"You're hungry," I told him. "Have the rest of my hash browns. A couple of extra calories isn't going to hurt you."

He picked up a fork and stuck it into the mess on my plate, tentatively, like he was poking a dead animal with a stick. He took one bite . . . and then another. Before I could tell him to slow down, the plate was empty. He even licked it clean. He seemed to spring to life afterward, but it didn't take a psychologist to know he was being eaten alive by guilt. He was an impressive physical specimen, I'd give him that. If swearing off carbs and being constantly run-down was the cost, though, I wasn't sure the trade-off would be worth it. Us old fogeys need a little padding. Otherwise our skin begins to hang in folds over our curtain-rod bones.

Barack noticed the dour look on my face.

"We'll get to the bottom of this thing. Don't worry."

"There's no way you can guarantee that," I said.

"I didn't guarantee it. I just have faith."

"Here comes the hopey-changey stuff," I said, affecting my best rural Alaskan accent.

"Don't go negative on me, Joe."

"We need to be realistic. What are we doing? What are we really doing here?"

"Right now, I'm visiting the little boys' room," Barack said, sliding out of the booth.

I was about to say I'd go with him, but Steve was already on his feet before I could get a word out. I was left there, my mouth hanging open like a schmuck.

"What's that, Joe?" Barack asked, straightening his suit jacket.

"Never mind," I muttered.

18

Barack picked up the tab, and I didn't argue. Afterward, we paused on the sidewalk outside the Waffle Depot. Mayflies started dive-bombing us from the fluorescent lights overhead. We tried swatting them away, but they had the numbers advantage. I wasn't ready to get in the car yet, though. Not until we'd charted a new plan of action.

Barack, chewing a post-meal Nicorette, had a different idea. "It's time to call it a night," he said.

"You think the bad guys are going to call it a night?"

"The *bad* guys?"

"What else would you call them? We've got people breaking into houses, into motels. Into nursing homes, for God's sake."

"They could all be part of one organization. Law enforcement, the mob . . . the Secret Service," Barack said, winking at Steve.

Steve did not wink back.

"Let's go through what we have so far," Barack continued. "We have a man on the tracks killed by an oncoming train. He has heroin in his pocket. We've got a missing square of carpet in his room. There's a duffel bag, which could be in evidence or even picked up by his family, for all we know. Is that it?"

"From everyone I've talked to, he didn't get high," I said. "I'm not ruling it out, I'm just saying I don't buy it. And we don't know for sure if he was killed by the train. He could have been dead already."

"An overdose or a heart attack," Barack said.

"Or . . ."

"Oh, for cripe's sake," Steve said under his breath. "Here it comes."

"You can't tell me foul play's not a possibility," I said.

Steve looked at Barack. "Permission to speak freely, sir."

"You don't need my permission."

Steve took a deep breath. "Okay. I think this has gone far enough. I was willing to indulge this little fantasy of playing detective, but that was before you disregarded my instructions and dove raw-dog into that motel room."

"There was a woman," I said.

"A woman who may have been a transient, or a prostitute. Or maybe a drug user looking for a place to shoot up. She may have been armed, in which case you both could be on gurneys right now — or, worse, on your way to the morgue. I can't guarantee your safety, Mr. President, if you continue on this . . . this *absurd* quest."

Steve was breathing heavy.

"Is this the carbs talking?" Barack asked.

Steve ignored him. He was on a roll. "If a torn-up patch of carpet is evidence of anything other than a spilled glass of red wine, I'll be surprised. Very surprised."

"That's not the sort of place you'd expect to find a wine drinker," I said. "You have to admit that."

Steve shot me a look of pure disbelief. "You're hung up on this, aren't you? Say it. Just say it: murder. You think someone killed him."

"I didn't say that. But it's one possibility. It's a possibility no one else has looked at, as far as I know."

"You know why? Because no one else has time for this nonsense. You have zero evidence of foul play. Bad things happen. Burglars break into houses. They break into motel rooms. People spill drinks. And you

151

know what it all means? Nothing."

I could feel my temperature rising. Steve knew exactly what buttons to push. Barack must have noticed I was about to blow because he stepped between us.

"This Lieutenant Esposito seems quite capable," Steve said. "She was in the National Guard. Served in Afghanistan. I don't have any reason not to trust her judgment." He pointed a finger at my chest. "You, on the other hand . . ."

"I'm just some old bag of bones who's seen too many episodes of *Law and Order*."

Barack threw up his hands to prevent us from going at each other. "That's enough. Steve's right — we need to call it a day. We're not done, though. Tomorrow's a new day. If the lieutenant gives us a hard time, we'll follow the leads wherever they take us. Finn was Joe's friend, and Joe is my friend. We don't abandon our friends just because the going gets rough. If that bothers you, Steve, perhaps you'd feel better if you were reassigned." He paused. "To Bo."

"I'd rather scoop up dog shit than clean up whatever mess you two make out of this 'investigation.' If anything happens to you — if you trip and skin your knee — that's a black mark on my record. It could mean another year on the ex-presidential protection detail." Steve was sweating like a sinner in church, but he couldn't stop. "Plus, what do you think Renaissance would say if she found out you were playing Sherlock?"

"She wouldn't say anything," Barack said sternly, "about something she doesn't know about. You don't report to her — you report to your supervisor. Tell him whatever you need to, but we're not going to discuss any of this with Mrs. Obama. Got that?"

"If she asks —"

"She won't."

"But if she does —"

"Correct me if I'm wrong, but your agency's motto is 'Worthy of Trust and Confidence,' " Barack said. "I'm not asking you to cover for me while I sneak Marilyn Monroe in the back door of the White House. I'm just asking for a little discretion. A little trust."

Steve started to object, but then grabbed his side.

"You okay, Steve?" I asked.

Steve put his other hand in front of his mouth. Before our eyes, his skin went pale and clammy. It looked like he was trying to contain Mount Vesuvius.

"The hash browns . . ." Steve croaked out.

"How you feeling, Joe?" Barack said.

Before I could answer, Steve doubled over

and hurled onto the sidewalk. Wet chunks splattered Barack's slacks. Barack and I both looked away. A man and woman were on their way into the restaurant, and Barack gave them a little wave. They picked up their pace.

When the awful retching noises finally stopped, we both turned to see if Steve was alive or dead. The Secret Service agent was wiping his mouth with the sleeve of his black jacket. He was mostly alive.

"Why don't you go clean up," Barack said.

"Can't . . . leave you . . . here . . . alone. Have to stay . . . within arm's length."

"Forget whatever they tell you in training," I said. "I say you're not getting in my car smelling like a Jersey sewer rat."

Steve made another uncomfortable gurgling noise. He dashed inside, leaving us on the sidewalk beside the puddle of upchuck.

"What a wet blanket," I said. "He can't even handle his hash browns. They're greasy, but c'mon."

"He's a good guy. But . . ."

"But?"

"But he's a third wheel. A classic third wheel."

I had a thought. It was a pretty wild idea, but Steve was on the verge of blowing our entire operation. "I can't work with this guy looking over my shoulder," I told Barack. "Telling me to be careful all the time. We're playing things safe, and all we've got so far is a fistful of nothing."

Barack smiled slyly. He knew where I was going. It was the same place he was going.

"You're a horrible person, Joe. A horrible, horrible person. What does the bro code say about leaving a wounded man behind?"

"I don't know," I said. "What does it say?"

"I don't know, either. I'm not even sure the bro code exists. But if it did, it would say if we're in pursuit of the greater good, we're well within our rights to drop any dead weight that's dragging us down."

We went back inside to the men's room, where we found Steve praying to the porcelain god. Barack slipped two hundred-dollar bills in Steve's pocket so that he could catch a ride back to the Walmart parking lot.

My heart was aflutter as we stepped outside. I couldn't believe we were ditching Barack's detail. It was a dangerous world, especially for politicians in the public eye. Especially for presidents. Especially for Barack, who had received more death threats than any other president in history. So many plots against him had been foiled — more than the public would ever know. More than I would ever know. Half those whackjobs probably thought he was still the president, or running some sort of "deep state" operation behind the scenes. I wasn't hip to all the latest ramblings of the black helicopter crowd, but there was one conspiracy theory that said Barack and I were both "lizard people" — half-alien half-human hybrids who'd infiltrated society and were secretly controlling the government. We were behind everything — terrorist attacks, natural disasters, even the interest rate. It was a comforting thought, that someone was in control of this chaotic world.

I didn't think I'd look very good with a tail, though.

"Let's go back to my place," I said, unlocking my door. "We have a guest room — it's made up like a ski lodge. There's a pair of skis and everything."

Barack stared at me over the top of the car. "That would be the first place Steve would look. We'd be busted before we even got to sleep."

"Fine. How about my vacation house on Rehoboth Beach?"

"That's the second place Steve would look," Barack said. "We need to brainstorm on this. What's the *last* place Steve would look?"

I didn't need to think long on this one.

"Zap-bam-bingo, I've got it."

"Don't say my house. Please don't say my house."

I shook my head. "I've got something even better."

19

We were dropped off at the Heart of Wilmington Motel by a taxi, which I paid for with cash. I wasn't happy about leaving my Challenger at the Waffle Depot. If Steve put out an APB for my car, however, we'd be nabbed just like that.

After the taxi peeled out, I turned and saw the sign.

NO VACANCY.

"You've got to be kidding me," I said under my breath. There were only eleven cars in the lot, including Finn's.

Barack slapped me on the back. "This type of motel, all we have to do is wait. Something will open up within the hour."

I dragged my feet to the front desk. Barack wasn't wrong, however. Within twenty minutes, a room opened up. I paid in cash. The clerk didn't ask for ID; he didn't even ask for a name.

The first thing I noticed when we entered

our room was that one of the beds was missing. Or rather there were two beds, but only one of them had a mattress.

"Did you book the honeymoon suite?" Barack asked.

"It's not funny," I said. I was tired and cranky, and didn't want to deal with a missing mattress.

"I'll call the front desk and get it straightened out," Barack said. "You can use the shower first."

I hit the bathroom and undressed. Under the harsh lights, my knee looked pretty gruesome — black and blue and swollen like a bloated corpse. How was I going to explain it to Jill? The best thing would be to do what I always did: tell her the truth, and do a little old-fashioned Catholic groveling for forgiveness.

And if my knee was gruesome, my face was an absolute horror show. The circles under my eyes. The creases on my forehead. The weight of the world was on my shoulders, and finally I was starting to slump.

What was I doing? Barack might have been in his prime, but I was past mine. No matter how loudly I proclaimed onstage to anyone who would listen that I was in perfect health, I couldn't ignore the effects of Father Time. I was starting to feel my age. It wasn't something I would ever admit aloud to another human being, not even Jill. I wouldn't even say a word of it to Champ. There was nothing embarrassing about getting older, but I wasn't having it.

Had Finn been on his way to see me? Did he think I could offer him protection? What could I do that the police couldn't? I hadn't been able to prevent his death. I wasn't the vice president anymore. I didn't have any formal authority. I was just an old man. I couldn't keep pace with the shady characters I'd encountered so far, either physically or mentally — and with my banged-up knee, I didn't have a snowball's chance in heck of running from them if they turned the tables and started pursuing us.

I wasn't the same man Finn had known all those years ago. The man Finn had known was a decade younger. The man Finn had known hadn't spent eight years fighting Tea Party maniacs hell-bent on obstructionism. Barack's hair had gone gray; mine was already white when we started. It was madness to think I could help Finn . . . but I wasn't sure I had much choice. Finn needed me. His family needed me.

But first, I needed sleep.

I flicked the light switch off and returned

to the motel bedroom. I would shower in the morning.

"Everything come out okay, Joe?" Barack asked.

"Just fine," I said. Barack liked to rib me about my age, mostly in the form of jokes. *Are you getting enough fiber, Joe? How's your prostate, Joe?* That sort of thing. Barack did that to everyone, though. He liked to "joke" with his close friends and aides, when in reality he was putting all of us down. It had never really bothered me. I liked to think of myself as good-humored by nature. But today I wasn't in the mood. I glared at Barack, warning him that he should back off or get socked.

I hadn't socked someone in almost seventy years.

I was sort of looking forward to it.

I fell onto the bed without pulling back the bedspread. The mattress was hard and unforgiving; the pillow felt like it was filled with wet sand. While Barack showered, I picked up the TV remote and realized the room was missing a television; there were some wires and cables poking out of the wall where a TV had once been mounted.

When Barack returned, he was dressed in a T-shirt and gym shorts. Barack hadn't let himself go to the birds — I'd already known

161

this, having watched several of his little "adventure" videos. He was all muscle and bone. He gave new meaning to the phrase "dad bod." I realized I was staring and quickly looked away.

"Are you going to make room for me?" Barack asked.

I inched over to one side, leaving him half the bed, which wasn't much. My left arm dangled over the edge and touched the floor.

Barack slid in next to me. "I called the front desk, but they didn't have a spare mattress. Unless you want to wait for another room, this is it."

"Did they say what happened to the other one?"

"You don't want to know," Barack said. "You *really* don't want to know."

He turned off the bedside lamp.

We lay in the dark, side by side, each of us half off the bed, staring at the ceiling. We could hear the steady gentle thumping of a bedframe, knocking against the wall in the room next door. After a few minutes, the bedframe went silent. A woman cried out in ecstasy. Barack and I started giggling like a couple of kids.

When we caught our breath, I was too worked up to sleep.

"POTUS, SCOTUS, or FLOTUS," I said.

Barack turned to me. "What's that?"

"It's a game we used to play in the Senate, while we were waiting out overnight filibusters. I name three women, and you say who you'd like as your —"

"— POTUS, SCOTUS, or FLOTUS."

"You got it."

"So give me the names."

"Nancy Pelosi, Elizabeth Warren, and Hillary Clinton."

There was a long pause.

"Give me three different names," Barack said.

"Sorry, I can't change the rules."

"It's a little demeaning to women. Who came up with this game, Strom Thurmond?"

"Hey now, Strom may not have been Pope Francis, but he wasn't sexist."

"He was racist, Joe."

"The correct term is 'segregationist.' "

"Oh," Barack said, staring at the ceiling. "That's so much better."

"You're avoiding the question. POTUS, SCOTUS, or FLOTUS. Nancy Pelosi, Elizabeth —"

"Hillary for POTUS. Elizabeth for SCOTUS. Nancy for FLOTUS."

I stared at him, incredulous.

"Nancy for FLOTUS? Not Elizabeth Warren? You're insane."

"Elizabeth Warren is the youngest of the three. That's why I'd seat her on the Supreme Court. You know age was the primary reason they tapped Gorsuch."

"Fine. But Hillary as POTUS? You're joking, right?"

"Are you still bitter about the whole election?"

"I could have beat that short-fingered clown in the general, Barack, I could have —"

"Goodnight, Joe."

I sighed. "Goodnight, Barack."

I closed my eyes and tried to sleep, but couldn't get Hillary's face out of my head. I knew the direction the country had taken wasn't her fault. I also knew that, if I'd run, I would be sleeping in the White House instead of the Heart of Wilmington hotel.

I cracked an eye and saw that Barack was still awake, staring at the ceiling. I finally looked up, too, and saw that he was watching a cockroach run back and forth, like a swimmer doing laps in a pool.

"You ever think about running again?" I asked him.

"For president?"

"For anything," I said. "Senate."

"Michelle would kill me in my sleep."

"Be serious."

"I am," Barack said. "She said she'd smother me with a pillow. Even showed me which one she'd use."

"Fine," I said. "But you still didn't answer me. You ever think about it? Forget if you'd actually do it. You have to think about it, sometimes."

"I think about a lot of things," Barack said. "I don't like to talk about them."

"Bad thoughts?"

"Bad thoughts, good thoughts."

"You see a shrink?"

"You think I need to?"

I snorted.

"I'm a man, Joe," Barack said. "Sometimes, a man has thoughts that he shouldn't. Or, let me rephrase that: a lot of times, a man has thoughts that he shouldn't. You can't control your thoughts. You can only control your actions." He paused. "You're thinking about running, aren't you?"

"I think about a lot of things, too. But, yeah. That's one of them."

"What does your heart tell you?"

"That I was put on this earth to serve, and by God that's what I've done. The question is, when is it enough?"

Barack took a deep breath, then exhaled. "It's never enough. I'd give away every dollar I have — and I practically do, some years — to fix what's wrong with our country. To fix what's wrong with the world."

"But like you said, it's never enough," I said. "So why do we keep doing it?"

"To make a difference," Barack said.

"And have we?

"Made a difference?"

"Yeah," I said. "Have we made a difference?"

He closed his eyes. "I don't know, Joe. I just don't know."

20

The next morning, I woke from my deepest sleep in a long time. I felt like a much younger man. Reinvigorated. I stretched my arms wide and found the other side of the bed empty.

"Rise and shine, sleepyhead," Barack said. He was buttoning his suit jacket in front of the full-length mirror on the back of the bathroom door. One button, then two. Then one again. His suit — the same one he'd worn yesterday, a Martin Greenfield — looked cleaned and pressed.

Barack must have noticed my shocked expression. "There's a laundry service next door. Had them freshen my joint up. I wasn't going to walk around with hash brown chunks on my lapels. Your clothes are on the chair."

I wiped the cobwebs from my eyes and sat up. "Why didn't you wake me? When's checkout?"

Barack raised his palms. "Relax, Joe. We have plenty of time. It's not even ten."

I rolled out of bed. Immediately, my knee buckled under me, and Barack rushed to steady me.

"I'm okay," I said, a lie if either of us had ever heard one. I held myself up with a hand on the chair. "We don't have time to lollygag around. A man's reputation —"

"— is on the line," Barack said. His voice was cool, calm, collected. Vintage Barack Obama. Meanwhile, I was panicked and blustering — vintage Joe Biden.

I sighed. We were falling back into our old familiar ways.

"What's the plan?" I asked, getting dressed.

Barack narrowed his eyes. "The plan?"

"For breakfast," I said.

"There's no continental breakfast, if that's what you're asking."

I checked my phone. There was a missed call at two in the morning from a 302 area code. Esposito's home number, possibly? I dialed it back. The phone rang and rang but never went to voicemail.

"Dammit." It was a little early in the morning for curse words, but these were extraordinary circumstances. "I assume Steve called you. How's he taking things?"

"Pretty well, all things considered. He did lose the forty-fourth president of the United States."

"That reminds me. I need to call Jill and let her know I'm not lying dead in a ditch somewhere."

"One presumes that would have made national news," Barack said.

"Oh, don't give me that. You've already talked to Michelle, haven't you?"

"I texted her last night. I told her I was staying at your place. She thinks we're having a sleepover. As long as she doesn't talk to Jill, we're okay."

I groaned. "You want me to tell Jill I stayed the night at your place?"

"What the wives don't know won't hurt them. And as long as we keep our stories straight and don't get caught, our wives won't hurt *us*."

My stomach growled. Either I was hungry again, or my body just couldn't take any more stress. Jill and I had a fabulous relationship . . . but it was a relationship built on trust. I was about to break her trust. I knew it was for the greater good, but it still made me queasy.

I called her. At first I thought I'd gotten a reprieve, as the phone rang four times without an answer. But no. Just before it should have gone to voicemail, she picked up.

"I was out gardening," she said. "What'd you want?"

She should have been frantic with worry, but her voice was surprisingly calm. If anything, she was maybe a little irritated — as if she thought she'd finally gotten me out of the house, and now I wasn't willing to leave her alone.

"I stayed at Barack's last night," I said. "He was in town for the funeral, and we went back to DC for a nightcap. Stayed up late talking about old times. The usual stuff that guys do."

"Oh!" she said. "What's their guest room like?"

I had no idea what his guest room looked like. Not only that, but I had no idea what the inside of his kitchen, or living room, or any other part of his DC house looked like. I only had the vaguest notion, really, of what neighborhood the Obamas lived in.

"I stayed with Barack in the master bedroom," I said. "Michelle was out of town, and Barack didn't want to sleep alone."

Jill laughed on the other end. "I'm sure you did." She paused. "Did you need something?"

"I was worried that you'd be worried."

"If you were lying dead in a ditch some-where, I'm sure I'd have heard about it by now," she said. "It'd be all over CNN."

Barack was sitting on the edge of the bed with a smirk when I hung up.

"What?" I said.

"I didn't say anything."

I undid the chain lock on the door and looked over my shoulder. I had my wallet, I had my phone . . . whatever else I left behind, the maid could keep. If there was a maid.

"Where are we headed?" Barack asked.

"First, to the nearest fast-food joint for breakfast. And then . . . well, I haven't thought that far in advance."

"As long as they have green tea, I'm fine with wherever."

I opened the door. The sunlight blinded me at first, and I covered my eyes with my hands. I'd forgotten my Ray-Bans — if I remembered right, they were on the bath-room sink. However, I didn't need to see what was in front of me to know what was there. I heard it — the unmistakable, filling-rattling growl of a 1,500-horsepower engine. The Little Beast.

Barack handed me my sunglasses. With my eyes shielded, I could see the five-foot-eight figure standing beside the open back

door, his mirrored shades reflecting as much
sunlight as the metallic hood ornament. His
face was as stoic as ever.

"Who's hungry?" Steve asked.

21

We were sitting in the McDonald's parking lot when my phone rang. It was the 302 number again.

"This is Joe. Who's this?"

"It's the Mayor. I'm at a pay phone, so I don't have much time. I didn't want to say too much yesterday, because you never know who's listening. You dig me?"

"Yeah," I said, stepping out of the car to take the call. I needed to walk off the two Egg McMuffins I'd obliterated.

"I told you about our card games, but what I didn't tell you was that Finn had stopped coming to them. I think he knew that we knew he'd become mixed up in something bad."

"Drugs?"

"I don't know the specifics. He kept quiet about it. But we could all tell he was hiding something. At first we thought it might have something to do with his wife down at

173

Baptist Manor, because he never said a word about her being sick, even though we all knew it. But it wasn't that. Like I said, we didn't have any idea of what exactly he'd become mixed up in. What we did know was that it was nothing good. The last time he was over for cards, we got a look at the inside of his wallet. We're not high stakes. When he pulled a few bills out, though, we all saw the cash he was sitting on."

"You're saying he was loaded."

"Like a mother," the Mayor said.

"Maybe he just cashed out his savings . . ."

"Or something else. None of us said a word then, but later on we talked. Alvin swore he didn't know nothing."

"Alvin Harrison?"

"His engineer, yeah. Anyway, Finn had too much cash for somebody in his situation, with a sick wife and a daughter in school. Maybe if he worked in a cash business, like I do, it would make sense."

"Maybe."

"But later on, when I went to use one of the tens I'd won that night, I noticed something about it. It was dirty."

"All cash is dirty," I said. In fact, I once read that ninety percent of all U.S. currency tested positive for cocaine. You don't want to know how much tests positive for fecal matter.

"I don't just mean dirty, I mean *dirty*. There was a tiny highlighter mark in the corner of the bill. It had been marked by a cop, or the FBI. I wouldn't bet my life on it, but I'm pretty sure it was drug money."

"You think he was on heroin?" I asked.

"If you're getting high, the cash usually flows out of your wallet, not the other way around. Plus, I seen enough people doped up in my time to know what it looks like. You can't hide that faraway look in your eyes."

"Have you told the police any of this?"

The laugh at the other end was so loud and shrill I had to hold my phone away from my ear. "Stop by next time you're in the station," he said, "but don't mention this conversation, because it never happened."

It wasn't until I'd hung up that something hit me. Something the Mayor said . . . *Alvin Harrison. His engineer.*

His engineer.

Of course. Alvin was the engineer Finn worked in tandem with on the 7:46 a.m. Acela Express. I knew he'd been driving the train that hit Finn, but hadn't put two and two together. I should have realized earlier that he was also the same engineer who'd worked beside Finn every day. No wonder he was so shaken by the accident. Finn hadn't just been a coworker. Finn had been Alvin's closest coworker.

I returned to the backseat and told Barack what I'd learned from the Mayor. Barack listened from the front passenger seat, watching me in the rearview. He was on his third package of apple slices, which were the only things on the McDonald's menu he'd found acceptable. Steve pretended not to listen to us, but I could tell he was interested. He'd been surprisingly nonchalant about our ditching him last night. We all agreed to let bygones be bygones. There was too much on the line for personal feelings to get in the way.

I didn't have Alvin's phone number but I didn't need it. I knew where he lived because Grant and I had dropped him off at his apartment. "Start the car," I told Steve. "We need to talk to the engineer."

Barack craned around to see if I was serious. "You sure we shouldn't wait for Esposito?"

"The cops and the transportation board have raked this guy's chestnuts over the open fire. But if there's even the slightest chance he's holding something back, who's he going to talk to? Another cop, or Amtrak Joe?"

"You make an excellent point."

"Maybe they haven't asked the right questions. He knows something. He has to. Two men work that closely for that long, they're bound to open up to each other. They're bound to forge a close bond."

"Hey, Steve, that sounds like us, right?" Barack said, patting Steve on the back.

Steve started the car. I leaned back in my seat and closed my eyes. We started backing up, then abruptly stopped.

"We have company," Barack said.

I opened my eyes. Red and blue lights were flashing in the rearview mirror. A police car was blocking our exit; on either side of us were more police cars. We were boxed in.

"Nobody has anything illegal, do they?" I asked. "No guns, no . . ."

"We're clean," Barack said.

"No marijuana cigarettes? I know that stuff is legal in DC now, but this isn't DC."

"They're called joints, Joe," Barack said. "And, no, I don't have any on me. I left all my pot back in my man cave."

Before I could ask if he was kidding — he'd never said a word about having a man cave before — there was a tap on Steve's window. It was Esposito. She wasn't smiling.

22

Steve rolled down his window, but he didn't say a word. His hands were at ten and two on the wheel, just like we all learned in driver's ed. Esposito glanced at the well-dressed man in the passenger seat. Her eyes went wide when she realized this was Barack Hussein Obama, but she quickly regained her cool.

She spied me in the back. "So it's true, huh? Y'all really are best friends?"

"Something like that," I said.

Barack glanced in the mirror at me. It looked like he wanted to say something, but it wasn't the time or the place.

I cleared my throat. "We're on our way to the golf course."

Esposito scanned the endless blue sky. "Supposed to be a storm coming."

"They say you're more likely to hit a hole in one than get hit by lightning."

"I don't play golf, so I wouldn't know,"

she said, shifting her belt. "But I'm not here to talk sports." She rested a forearm on the open window and leaned in, encroaching on Steve's personal space. He didn't flinch. "You guys know that I put my best detectives on Mr. Donnelly's case — at great cost to the city, I should add. We're under siege. We don't have the manpower to assign detectives willy-nilly. But apparently that's not enough, because I get a voicemail last night saying we need to talk. A voicemail that says you 'found something.' You're damn right we need to talk."

"Well," I stammered, "the motel where he was staying —"

"What did you find?"

"There's a section of carpet missing in his room. Someone ripped it up, but there's a bloodstain on the floor underneath. Thought you could send someone over to test it."

"A bloodstain."

"And his car is still there."

She crossed her arms. "And what did you find in his car? Another bloodstain?"

I started to sputter something about Styrofoam cups, but she cut me off. "I'll tell you what you found: nothing. It's the same thing we found. And you know why we found nothing? Because there's nothing to find. One of my detectives noticed the missing carpet. Called out forensics. Whatever the stain was, we'll never know — it was treated with oxygen bleach. Now before you run with that, we checked the housekeeping supply closet and found gallons of oxygen bleach. Somebody made a mess. Somebody else cleaned it up. Nobody that worked there knew how long the carpet had been ripped up, even. It's not enough to build a case on."

"But when you consider the break-in at Finn's home —"

She cut me off. "We apprehended the burglars responsible, the ones who hit up homes while people were away at funerals. They're a couple of real lowlifes."

"Did they confess?"

"They will. We're still building our case. In the meantime, they're not going anywhere." She shifted her belt. "Listen, I understand if you're still spooked by the map with the address on it. But unless your buddies at the Secret Service have any evidence they're withholding from us, the case is all but closed."

"What happens if the toxicology results show he wasn't on drugs?"

"Then he had a heart attack or a stroke. Perhaps he took his own life. Unless somebody steps forward with a firsthand account of his final hours, we may never know why he was out there, and what really happened." She paused, then added, "I've seen this a thousand times."

"Mysterious deaths?"

She shook her head. "This. What you're doing. You're trying to piece together meaning from randomness. It's a path with no end. You're going down a dark road. I've seen families spend years and years looking for meaning in a loved one's death. They get the idea from TV shows that every death is a crime, and that crimes are solved over the course of an hour with commercial breaks in between. That's not real life. This is."

"I hear what you're saying. But —"

"It's better if we all move on," she said. "For you *and* Finn's family. Enjoy the day. Maybe you can get a few holes in before the rain begins."

"We'll try," I croaked.

After the cops left, I turned to Barack. "You have a man cave?"

Barack rolled his eyes. "Boy, you weren't kidding about her. What's her deal?"

"She's a Republican."

"Seriously."

"I get the feeling she's trying to divert us

182

for some other reason. That she knows more than she's telling us. And maybe covering something up."

"It's a possibility," Barack said. "The other angle is that she's being straight with us. That she has seen friends and family get obsessed with cases before and refuse to let go."

"If she knew what we knew —"

"You could have told her about the woman in the motel room," Barack said. "You didn't. You could have mentioned the duffel bag. You didn't."

"We never found a shred of evidence to directly tie the woman to Finn. And the duffel bag? I'm not sure it would matter. Esposito has her mind made up. All the evidence in the world won't be enough to get her off her ass. Dan has probably been reassigned to traffic control for a few weeks. And if he's not, I'm not sure if he'll risk his job to help me again. And I wouldn't ask him to, either."

Barack didn't dispute this. I knew he'd already come to the same conclusions.

"I have a bad feeling about all of this," I said.

"You didn't before?" Steve asked.

"Nobody asked you," I snipped.

Barack folded the newspaper he'd been

skimming. "Step back and look at what we have so far, Joe. Nothing we've found even remotely ties together. I can see that. I think you can too. What if Esposito is right? What if we're just trying to piece together a bunch of random events? The reason we haven't found anything to tie them together could be because *they don't tie together.* There's no hard evidence, because there isn't some vast conspiracy."

"People don't just die for no reason."

"I'm not saying they do," Barack said. "I'm just saying we may be trying to assign meaning where meaning doesn't exist. If we wait for the toxicology results to be returned, we may have a better picture of what happened."

"If we wait that long, this thing will have blown up in the papers. Somebody's bound to leak the details. The map, the heroin . . ."

"They will," Barack said. "But it will blow over. The news cycle is getting shorter and shorter. There are plenty of more important things going on. People will talk, and then they'll forget about it twenty-four hours later."

I stared sharp daggers at him. "For me, this is the most important thing going on. For Grace Donnelly, this is the most important thing going on."

"Chill, Joe. I didn't mean it that way."

I sighed. "As a man of faith, I refuse to believe in coincidences. It's either God's plan, or someone else's. And I don't think God has anything to do with what's happening in this town."

Barack kept his own religious beliefs closely guarded, but I could tell by the look in his eyes that I'd struck a chord. I gave Steve the address of Alvin Harrison to punch into the GPS. If anybody knew what was really going on with Finn Donnelly, it would be Alvin.

"Are you sure this is a good idea?" Barack asked.

"The only bad ideas are the ones that don't work."

He didn't say a word. He knew, same as me, that even if we were on the wrong path, we were too far along to turn back now.

___

23

Alvin Harrison lived in Brandywine Hills in northern Wilmington. The neighborhood was resplendent with old-world charm. Most of the homes were built in the thirties and forties, before the suburban boom kicked in and everything started looking like copies of copies. Beautiful, historic stone houses lined the streets of the hilltop neighborhood. Even the streets were old-timey, with author names like Byron, Milton, and Hawthorne.

We parked around the corner from Alvin's apartment building, in front of an elementary schoolyard. There were three kids shooting hoops. Otherwise the neighborhood was dead. There weren't many cars on the street. Nobody was out walking their dogs or jogging on the sidewalks. Everyone was probably still out to brunch.

Barack began to open his door, but I held up a palm. "This guy's been through a lot.

What do you think is going to happen if the Secret Service comes knocking on his door?"

"Steve can wait in the car," Barack offered.

"And let you guys slip away again?" Steve said.

"What would you do if I just ran for it?" Barack said. "I mean, if I just took off — zoom, down the sidewalk. Led you on a footrace through the middle of town."

"I'd chase you."

"You couldn't keep up," Barack said.

"Don't try me."

Barack smirked. "If you couldn't catch me, what would you do? Shoot out my kneecaps? That would be worse than losing me."

Steve did not look amused. Then again, he never looked amused.

"Let him be," I said. "He spent half the night sleeping on the floor of a Waffle Depot bathroom. I think he's been through enough."

Barack relented and agreed to sit this one out with Steve. I didn't blame him for wanting to run for it, to be free for just a few minutes. Unless the Obamas hired their own private security, they would be under Service protection for the rest of their lives.

They would never know the simple pleasures of, say, going grocery shopping without an escort. Of course, Jill did all the grocery shopping in our family, but I imagined it was a simple pleasure. Maybe I'd go with her sometime to find out.

Alvin Harrison lived in a two-story brick apartment complex. Unlike the street names, there was nothing quaint about his building. Someone had just plopped a pile of bricks down in the middle of all the Mid-Atlantic charm. Judging by the rusted guardrails and faded everything, whoever had built it had also forgotten about it.

I scanned a row of mailboxes near the staircase. When Grant dropped Alvin off at the complex, I hadn't seen which apartment he'd gone into. That's where the mailboxes came in. "Harrison" was penciled in under 23.

I slipped on my Ray-Bans and climbed the stairs, which zigzagged up the side of the building. The sky was bright and sunny, with no signs of the clouds the lieutenant had warned us about.

When I reached the second floor of apartments, my knee was killing me. I wondered if I couldn't get an injection to temporarily kill the pain. Sports stars did that all the time. A cortisone shot, I think is what they call it. Unfortunately, it would take too long to find a doctor who could shoot me up on a weekend. I wasn't about to burden emergency room staff with my sorry behind.

I pounded once on Alvin's door. Before I could knock a second time, it swung inward a few inches. It hadn't been shut all the way.

"Hello?" I called out. "Alvin?"

No answer.

"Anybody home? It's . . . Joe. Amtrak Joe."

No answer.

I pushed the door open a little wider, just enough so I could get a better look inside. There weren't any lights on, and the blinds were pulled shut. I could see the back of a couch from where I was standing.

A fat orange tabby rubbed up against my leg.

"Hey there, little . . . er, big guy," I said.

The cat had to weigh twenty pounds. It circled my legs, brushing against me, making little whimpering noises like a hungry dog. I reached down to pet it, and the cat hissed at me before scampering back into the apartment.

"Nice to meet you, too," I said.

Alvin didn't appear to be home, but the open door had me on edge. I stepped inside the apartment, calling Alvin's name. The cat whined again, louder this time. The fat bastard was sitting on the floor beside the couch, next to an orange prescription bottle.

And a shoe. I stepped closer and saw there was a leg in the shoe. And the leg was attached to a person, and the person was sprawled out on the shag rug.

Alvin was dead.

24

When I returned to the Escalade, it was locked. *Barack probably stepped out for a coffin nail.* He rarely smoked around me because he knew my views on tobacco. I'd always detested cigarettes, even before I launched the cancer moonshot.

"S!"

I whipped my head around at the sound of Barack's voice. He hadn't gotten very far. He was playing basketball with the three boys we'd seen earlier. Steve was watching from the edge of the court. Barack had removed his jacket, and his shirt sleeves were rolled up. Back in the White House, this always meant it was time for serious business. But right now, he was playing basketball with a group of third- and fourth-graders.

"Where's your baseball cap?" I hissed.

"You don't wear baseball caps when you're shooting hoops," he said.

One of the boys, a skinny kid with curly hair, shot a basket. It went through the hoop — actually the rim, because there wasn't much left of the hoop — and bounced away. Another boy chased it down.

"*E!*" the curly-haired boy screamed.

Barack fist-bumped him. "Nice shooting, kid. Keep it up and you could be the next Michael Jordan."

The boy scrunched up his face. "I don't want to make shoes, I want to play basketball."

"Look him up on the YouTubes."

The other boy tossed the ball to Barack. "Another round?"

Barack told them he'd be back sometime to stump for Delaware's Democratic candidates. "Your parents are all registered to vote, right?"

I tugged at his sleeve. "We've got a situation," I whispered. "Alvin is D-E-A —"

"We'll see you kids later!" Barack said, waving to them. Steve gave them one last glare for good measure and trailed us back to the SUV.

Barack unrolled his sleeves and buttoned his cuffs. "Those kids were like ten years old, Joe. They know how to spell."

"Sorry, I'm a little out of sorts." I told Barack the whole story. Steve sat up front, listening intently. Or maybe he was napping behind those sunglasses.

"And you're sure Alvin was dead?" Barack said. "Sometimes, the pulse can be so faint that you can't feel it on the wrist or neck."

"He was blue as a Smurf."

"Okay, okay," Barack said. "We need to figure out what to do. Let me think . . ."

"It's obvious what we do," I said. "Call the cops."

Barack was doing that pyramid thing with his fingers pressed up to his lips, which meant the wheels in his brain were spinning. As if they ever stopped spinning.

"Did you feed the cat?" Barack asked.

"You're worried about the cat?"

"I'm just trying to cover all of our bases. If you fed the cat, your fingerprints might be on the cabinets or the food bowl."

"I didn't touch anything, not even to feed the cat. He's big enough as it is. On my way out, I wiped my fingerprints off the door knob and got the H-E-double hockey sticks out of there."

"Good," Barack said. "Let's find a pay phone and call it in."

"That's going to be a little difficult to do," I said.

"Pay phones are kind of a rarity these days. We'll find one, though."

I crossed my arms. "That's not what I'm talking about. You've been spotted here. Those kids are probably telling their parents right now, or Twittering to their friends."

"Who's going to believe them?"

"Who's going to believe them?" I growled. "Esposito, for starters. She knows you're in town. If she hears some kids bragging that they played ball with the ex-commander-in-chief a block away from a crime scene connected to Finn, she'll put two and two together."

"By the time Esposito realizes we were in the vicinity of the crime scene, we'll be long gone. We've not broken any laws. I don't think we're going to be hauled off down to the local precinct and questioned. Can you imagine the negative press? Esposito will need time to build a case, and the city board isn't going to let her drag us in without a very, very good reason. By that time, we should either know what's going on or . . ."

Or we'll be victims, I thought. I could tell Barack thought the same thing, but he wasn't willing to say it. Neither of us was. We didn't know what kind of a mess we were getting into, or how deep the roots of the conspiracy went. But make no mistake: there was a conspiracy, all right.

It wasn't like we hadn't found ourselves in

194

strange waters and persevered before. Barack had battled the Clinton machine to capture the Democratic Party's nomination in 2008. Together, we'd fought our way to the White House against a Republican Party that called Barack every bad name in the book. We were out in the middle of the sea right now, in uncharted waters, with no life-jackets. We were paddling with our hands and feet to stay alive. We didn't know which direction to swim, because we didn't know where land was. And yet it all felt very familiar. Still, I had to wonder: with this much chum in the water, how soon before we drew the attention of the sharks?

25

As I stepped into the gas station, the bells on the door handle jingled. The clerk on duty had a handheld plastic fan blowing in her face. She stared at me for a beat, and then went back to watching the fan.

I made a beeline for the men's room and did my business. As I dried my hands, I read the descriptions of the various papa-stoppers for sale in the restroom vending machine. The big metal case on the wall promised all variety of sensual seductions, from glow-in-the-dark rubbers to studded Tinglers ("for her pleasure"). Take your pick. Just three quarters apiece. I had three quarters, but I wasn't going to blow them on a Tingler.

Outside the restroom, there was a pay phone. It was the fifth gas station we'd stopped at looking for one. I was beginning to think it would have been easier to contact the police via carrier pigeon. I fingered the rosary around my wrist and prayed to Mary that the phone wasn't out of service.

I inserted the coins. When the third quarter clunked down, I heard the dial tone. Who says Jesus doesn't answer small prayers? All you have to do is ask His mother.

I dialed the main police number. No sense tying up 911. Alvin didn't need EMTs. He needed a forensic pathologist.

A woman answered: "Wilmington PD."

"I'd like to report an overdose. A death."

"Okay."

"Do you want the address?"

"Hold on, let me get a pencil," she said with a sigh. "Okay, you said someone overdosed? Heroin, pills . . . ?"

"There was a bottle of pills. I didn't read it."

"Is the victim breathing?"

"He's dead. I already told you — he's dead. So, no, he's not breathing. Dead men don't breathe."

"What's your name?"

"Joe . . . Tingler."

"Okay, Joe. Are you with the victim now?"

"He's back at his apartment."

"The victim's apartment?"

"Yeah, the dead guy. His name is Alvin Harrison. He lives at the Brandywine Hills

197

Apartments. Number twenty-three."

"Okay. Where are you now, Joe?"

I hung up. Stay on the phone too long, and they can trace the call. Heck, the name of the gas station probably showed up on her caller ID. I figured she'd send a unit to Alvin's apartment first. They might check up on the gas station caller later, but "Joe Tingler" would be on the road by then.

I returned to the car.

"It's done," I said.

"Did you get my protein bar?" Barack asked.

I fumbled for the health bar I'd purchased inside the mini-mart.

Barack accepted it with a skeptical look. "Hmm."

"Hmm what?" I asked.

"Nothing. It's just — this protein blend is pretty low quality. Look at the label. Hydro-lyzed collagen? That won't give you a full spectrum of amino acids."

"So what are you saying? Did I just waste four dollars on a candy bar?"

Sensing my irritation, Barack unwrapped the bar and took a bite. If the taste bothered him, he was careful to hide it. "Is something bothering you, Joe?"

"You mean, besides the mounting body count?"

"Fair enough."

"Here's a crazy idea that just popped into my head: maybe we have it wrong. He was a sixty-something guy, on the verge of retirement, right? Let's say he found something out about Amtrak — they've been cutting corners on passenger safety. That would also explain why he was on his way to see me. He was a whistleblower, and I was the only person he could trust. He had a bunch of documents, so he packed them up and carried them with him. But someone knew. Someone up high. They killed him, then made it look like an overdose."

"Corporate espionage."

"Why not?"

"I hate to burst your bubble, but it's just too far-fetched," Barack said. "And this is coming from someone who knows state secrets that would scare Ellen straight." He paused, but neither Steve nor I laughed. "It was a joke. Sexual orientation is biological in nature, determined by your DNA, meaning it would be impossible to —"

"I get it," I said.

"Do you really think Finn was a whistleblower?"

I sighed. "No. It's just some fantasy. What's really bothering me is what I'm going to do if I find out Finn wasn't some innocent victim. Marked bills, a gym bag filled with who knows what . . . I keep telling myself that there's a man's reputation on the line, but maybe that man isn't Finn. Maybe that man is me. What happens if I find out Finn wasn't a good guy? What does that say about me?"

Before Barack could answer, my phone started buzzing.

It was Grace. She was sobbing.

"Is everything okay?" I asked.

"Two men just showed up with a warrant. They're going through the house right now."

"Cops?"

"No," she said. "DEA."

26

The Donnellys' home was located in Riverside, one of the roughest neighborhoods in Wilmington. Finn and Darlene had purchased the house in the early seventies, in what was then a post-war community of Irish immigrants. After the nearby Eastlake projects closed, its residents — and problems — spilled over into Riverside. Most of their Irish Catholic neighbors packed up and headed to the suburbs. Not the Donnellys. That wasn't Finn's style.

By the time I arrived, the DEA had already split. The woman and child who'd been staying at the Donnellys' house were also long gone, spooked off by the break-in earlier in the week.

"How long will you be staying in town?" I asked Grace. She was busy stuffing clothes back into a dresser. There was no sense folding them. Everything was headed for the Goodwill, she told me.

"I'll be in Wilmington the next week or so, while we get Dad's affairs settled. All the bills paid up. Aunt Jessop and I were cleaning the house, getting it in shape so we could list it — and then the DEA came through here and trashed everything. I sent her back to the hotel for now."

"I'm sorry you have to deal with this. Did they take anything?"

She shook her head. "I know you used to be a lawyer. I couldn't get ahold of the family's attorney, so I just thought . . . I'm sorry to drag you into this. I didn't know who else to call."

"You did the right thing."

"I don't understand. What would the Drug Enforcement Agency want with my father?"

I'd read over the warrant already. The Donnellys' address was indeed listed as the target. The property to be seized, however, was simply listed as anything "illegal to be possessed" or "material evidence to be used in a subsequent criminal prosecution." Boilerplate text. Still, I recognized the judge who'd signed off on it. The document appeared legit.

"Let's head into the living room," I said. "We need to talk."

She offered me something to drink —

water, tea, coffee? Barack and Steve were waiting down the street in the Escalade. They could wait a little longer.

"Warm milk, if you have it," I said.

I took a seat on the couch. She joined me a few minutes later.

"Thanks," I said, taking the milk. I took a sip — a small one, just to judge how hot it was. Instead, I found myself doing my best not to gag. It was the perfect temperature. Not too cold, not too hot. Something was off, though. "Is this . . . skim?" I asked.

"Almond milk," she said. "Is that all right?"

I forced a smile. "Perfect."

I set the mug on the side table. In as plain terms as I could, I explained to her what the police had found in her father's pocket. She listened to me, stone-faced, as I told her there was more — a map, with my address on it. That my working theory was that Finn may have had a drug problem and needed my help. I didn't believe for a second that Finn actually did drugs, but what else did the evidence point to?

I didn't say anything about the carpet with the possible blood stains. I stuck to the known facts. And I most definitely didn't say anything about my other theory: foul play. I didn't want her to lose herself down the same mad road I was on. Not until I knew for sure. Hope was one thing; false hope was another.

"What do the police believe?" she asked.

"You'd have to ask them," I said.

"They didn't tell me any of this."

"Think back to when they talked to you. Did they take a statement?"

She shook her head. "The only cop I've spoken to is Detective Caprese."

"Capriotti?"

"That's it. Detective Capriotti."

I sighed. "It may be my fault."

Her eyes went wide.

"Not what happened to your father, but why they've kept you in the dark. The part about my address made it to the Secret Service somehow, and I told them to keep a lid on it. I knew the kind of headlines it would generate. I wanted your family to be able to say goodbye without fighting off reporters left and right. I thought the police would at least ask you about any substance abuse in your father's past."

"They may have talked to my aunt," she conceded.

I rubbed my forehead. Trying to work out the kinks in my brain.

"There wasn't any, you know. Any substance abuse in his past," Grace said. "He

204

never even took a —"

"— drink. I know." I placed a hand on her shoulder. "This has to be a shock."

"It doesn't feel real."

And it never will, I thought. *You just learn to live with the feeling.*

We stared across the room at the barren walls. When Finn had rented out the house, he'd apparently pulled everything down. All their paintings. There were still a few personal things left, like a metal train on the mantel.

Grace caught me eyeing it.

"Dad was the third railroad worker in our family. The first conductor. It was his life." She wiped a tear away. "I thought sometimes that he would have been happier with a son, because a boy might have been more into trains. It sounds silly, because I know it's not true."

"He was so excited to have a child, especially a daughter. He told me that himself. He called you his little miracle."

She laughed. "That's because it took them twenty years of trying."

"Practice makes perfect."

The edge of her lips curled up. "When I was thirteen, he asked me what I wanted to be when I grew up. I said, 'Anything, so long as it doesn't have to do with effing trains.' I

205

was a little rebellious."

"Just a tad."

"I was thirteen, but I could see the future. Trains were on their way out. They'd been on their way out since the first Model T rolled off the assembly line. I wasn't going to jump on board a sinking ship."

Then she excused herself, and I thought about what she'd said. America had been built with trains. That was a long time ago. The steam train was a relic. Passenger light rail was the future. Or at least it should have been. Every year, fewer and fewer people were on board with the dream. High-speed trains worked in Europe and Japan, but America was a different beast. Without government funding, passenger trains were money-losers. What Americans didn't realize was that without government funding, so were highways and any other form of transportation, public or private.

When she returned from the bathroom, I thanked her for the almond milk that I hadn't touched. She walked me to the door. "Before I leave, I was wondering, did the cops return a duffel bag to you? It might have been with your father's stuff at the motel. A waitress down at the Waffle Depot mentioned it to me, and it's been bugging me ever since. I'm sure it's nothing."

Grace shook her head. "Dad had a suit-case at the motel, but that was it. Haven't seen a duffel bag around here, either. If it was his, it's missing, just like his watch."

"His pocket watch?"

She nodded. "The police didn't find it at the scene of the accident. He never went anywhere without it. We assumed it had been stolen out of his room. It could have been in the duffel bag." She shrugged. "Maybe the duffel bag was stolen, and the watch was in there?"

"Maybe," I said. I didn't want to say any more. "Listen, I should be going. I'll see if I can figure out the deal with the warrant. In the meantime, stay with your aunt at the hotel, if you can. This house has already been broken into once —"

Through the window slats, I could see a woman walking up the driveway. She had a fine figure, but that's not the first thing I noticed. What really caught my eye was her waist-length blond hair, pulled back into a ponytail, swinging behind her as she ap-proached the door.

27

I pushed Grace up against the wall, behind the door.

"What are you doing?" she asked.

I shushed her with a finger to my lips. How the woman out front had slipped past Barack, I had no idea. Surely he would have recognized her from the Heart of Wilmington. This time, she was wearing a bit more than a towel — a white pantsuit and stiletto heels. But it was her.

The woman's heels click-clacked on the steps, and the doorbell rang.

Grace and I stood silent, flattened against the wall.

The doorbell rang again.

I looked around for something that I could use as a weapon. No coat rack, no umbrella stand, nothing. I removed one of my sandals. I wasn't planning to attack the woman — I'd never hit a woman in my life — but I had to be ready if she went on the offensive.

She'd broken into the motel room. If she tried breaking into the Donnellys' home . . .

The doorbell rang again. She wasn't giving up.

"See what she wants," I whispered to Grace.

"I don't understand —"

"Just open the door. I won't let anything bad happen." I raised my sandal with both hands, ready to swing it like a baseball bat.

Grace undid the deadbolt and opened the door a crack. "Can I help you?"

The woman's voice was low and muffled, and I couldn't make out a word. Whoever she was, she wasn't selling Girl Scout cookies. They only sell them January through March.

"Come in," Grace said, opening the door wide and pinning me against the wall.

The woman stepped inside. I couldn't see her, but I could smell her. The cloying scent of strawberries and bananas filled the room. I recognized her perfume as one I'd bought for Jill many years back. She never wore it, thank God.

Grace started to close the door, and the woman removed her coat. She turned to look for a coat rack and instead came face to face with me — a man with a raised sandal, prepared to swing away.

209

She hurled her suit jacket. It caught me right in the face and everything went dark. I dropped my sandal, scrambling to pull off the jacket, but I wasn't fast enough. The woman started beating me like a piñata. I threw up my hands, shielding my face. Grace was shouting something I couldn't understand. I pulled away the suit jacket just in time to see the pointed heel of a black stiletto coming at me. It cracked me on the cheekbone. Remarkably, I stood my ground, bracing myself against the wall. One more whack of that heel and I knew I'd be licked for sure.

"You again!" the woman said. She lowered her heel, but didn't put it back on. Not yet.

Grace stepped between us and handed me a business card. "This is Abbey."

I read the card. "Abbey Todd. Corporate Risk Investigator, Delmar Investigations. Medical claims, property claims . . . and life insurance claims."

28

I pressed the package of frozen vegetables to my face. The chill went down to the bone. She'd gotten me good. Too bad I couldn't ice my wounded ego.

We were sitting on opposite sides of the couch, a wide gulf between us. My almond milk sat untouched on the table next to me.

"Perhaps it would be best if Mr. Biden and I talked in private," Abbey said.

"I'm not leaving you two alone," Grace said. "Not until somebody tells me what that" — and here she pointed to the door — "was all about."

"Mistaken identity," I said.

"Who *were* you going to hit with your shoe?" Grace asked.

"It's complicated."

Abbey glanced over at me. "It's not very complicated, is it, Mr. Biden? Would you like me to leave so you can explain to Ms. Donnelly what you were doing at her father's motel room the night of the funeral?"

"What's she talking about, Joe?"

I sighed. "I didn't want to get into this — not today — but we might as well. I don't believe what happened to your father was an accident. I don't believe that he in any way voluntarily stepped onto those tracks, high or otherwise. I believe he may have been — What I mean to say is, I believe something . . . untoward may have happened to him."

Grace threw her hands over her mouth.

Well, that certainly sucked the air out of the room.

"Do the police know about your theory?" Abbey asked. "The transportation board has already wrapped their investigation. They've cleared Amtrak of any wrongdoing. The engineer didn't hit him intentionally. Calculating the speed of the train and the amount of time he would have had to brake — there's just no way anyone could have done a better job of braking. That doesn't sound like murder to me."

"Finn didn't kill himself."

"I never said he did."

"I know how your type operate," I said.

"Frankly, Mr. Biden, I don't believe you know my type."

There wasn't anything I could say to that.

"I'm still investigating," she said.

"You're a liar. You're hiding something. I know when I'm being lied to."

"It's funny you should bring that up."

"Guys," Grace said. "Please."

Abbey toyed with the end of her ponytail. "If you want to know what I was doing at the motel the other night, I'll tell you. It's no big secret. I'm a private investigator. Most of my clients are insurance companies, and they hire me to investigate suspected fraud. And before you ask — every time a claim has to be paid, the insurance company suspects fraud. That's just the way the industry works."

I switched the frozen vegetables from my left hand to my right. It was a California vegetable medley. Carrots, broccoli, and cauliflower.

Three of my least favorites.

Abbey continued: "In the case of an accident like this, I'm interviewing witnesses. Family. Friends. Anyone who can clue me in to the victim's state of mind. I also look for physical evidence."

"Like a note," I said. *A suicide note.*

She nodded. "In the event of a victim taking their own life, a third of the time there will be a note. Lately, people have been leaving them online, so that makes things easier

213

for us. Paper notes have a way of getting lost. Families want to hush things up, especially if there's insurance money on the line."

"I can't believe you think we would do something like that," Grace said.

"I don't believe anything until I have evidence that I'm confident will hold up in civil court. I'm not some amateur sleuthing around on a whim." She smiled icily, but made a point of not looking at me. "I was at the motel as part of my routine investigative process. Many deaths occur at motels — if I told you the number, you'd never stay in one again — and there's always a pad of paper on the desk or nightstand. Sometimes in the drawer. Rub a pencil over it, and you can see the impression of the last thing someone wrote before tearing the top sheet off."

"That really works?" I asked, dumbfounded.

"You think Raymond Chandler just plucked it out of thin air?" she said. "In this case, there was no notepad. There weren't notepads in any of the rooms. It was a dead end."

"If you'd just handed me your card at the motel, instead of pulling a fast one . . ."

"I wanted to play things close to the

chest," she said. "So to speak."

I looked away. We didn't need to get into the state of undress Barack and I had found her in.

Grace picked up my still-full mug and took it into the kitchen. Abbey and I sat in silence again. I felt rotten, like I'd been caught by a truancy officer skipping class to watch a double feature at the Comerford on Wyoming Avenue.

When Grace returned, I stood up. "Where do you want the vegetables?"

"Keep them," she said flatly. I'd broken her trust. There was nothing I could say to patch things up.

29

The Little Beast was still parked two doors down from the Donnellys'. The front passenger-side door was locked. I waited a few seconds for Steve to unlock it. When I didn't hear the automatic door click, I shielded my eyes and peered through the pitch-black window.

Empty.

I'd left Steve specific instructions to *not* leave it unattended. He didn't know what happened to unattended vehicles in this area. I did.

A couple of black teenagers with low-slung pants were sitting on a porch behind me. They were passing a cigarette back and forth. I was pretty sure it wasn't tobacco. They were staring at me, trying to figure me out. For the first time, I wondered if my bright aloha shirt wasn't as inconspicuous as I'd thought. It didn't scream "Joe Biden." But it was definitely screaming.

"How you kids doing?" I said.

They didn't respond.

"Joe!"

Barack waved from halfway down the block. He had a Big Gulp cup. Steve was carrying a takeout bag.

"That guy was trying to break into your car," one of the teen boys shouted to them. The kid could have been fifteen or sixteen. His hands were buried in the pockets of his hoodie.

Barack handed them each five bucks. "Thanks for watching it. But I know this guy. We're cool." Barack had the keys, and he unlocked the doors. "Get in, Joe."

I was opening the passenger door when a polished Ford Charger rounded the corner. I tensed up as it rolled slowly down the street, rims spinning. I could feel the bass pumping from the speakers rattling my fillings. It reached the intersection and sped off.

"Is there something bothering you, Joe?" Barack asked.

I didn't have a racist bone in my body. But I did have a healthy fear of ending up in the crossfires of a gang shootout. I'd been in war zones before, but many of them paled in comparison to Riverside. Though the neighborhood had a relatively small foot-

print, it accounted for a hugely dispropor-
tionate amount of violent crime in the city.

I stammered out a few sounds that only
vaguely resembled words, trying to find
some way to articulate my concerns about
the area without coming across as a bigoted
crank. Before I completely embarrassed
myself, he mercifully cut in.

"Chill. Anyone messes with you, they're
messing with me. And I've got two words
for you: predator drones."

He hopped in back.

"The DEA warrant looked legit," I said,
sliding into the front seat. "I don't know
what to do about that just yet. I hadn't
expected another agency to get involved."

"They don't go after low-level users."

"We could get in touch with them. If they
were sharing information with the Wilmington PD, we should have heard about it."

"Esposito's trying to brush us off," Barack
said. "Maybe she's giving them the cold
shoulder too."

"Dan would know . . . except I'm not going to reach out to him until we know more.
He might not help us anyway."

"If he's your friend, he'll find a way. That's
what friends do."

I ran a hand through my hair. I was due
for a trim soon.

"I did learn that Grace hasn't seen the duffel bag," I said. "Oh, and there's a watch missing, too."

"Expensive?"

"Doubt it," I said. "Finn never went for the flashy ones. The cheap ones, they don't last that long, so he was always buying a new one every couple of years. I don't know what his last one looked like."

Steve started the SUV. Its 6.2-liter V8 roared to life.

"So the Amtrak workers, they all buy their own watches?" Barack asked.

"You think Mariano Rivera would take the mound with a glove that wasn't his?" I said. "Back in the day, the railroads required engineers and conductors to carry them. They had to be accurate and reliable — there were watch inspectors who checked everything out, even. These days, they can use whatever watch they like, as long as it's in good working condition and displays the time down to the second. Lot of conductors go for vintage pocket watches. Most engineers use wristwatches."

"You sure know a lot about trains."

"I don't know jack squat about trains. I know a lot about Amtrak. There's a big difference. I'm not a foamer, for Pete's sake."

"Speak English, Joe."

"A rail fan," I said. "A foamer. It's usually not a complimentary term. They're also called trainspotters, railnuts. Hoggers."

"Hoggers?"

"Don't you start, Barack."

A tight-lipped smile spread across his face.

"You guys get me something to eat?" I asked.

"Those vegetables not fill you up?" Steve asked.

Even he was giving me a hard time now.

I squeezed the bag in my hand. It was thawing out, and dripping into my lap. "About that . . ."

I explained the strange encounter and handed the woman's business card to Steve, who called in a request for a background check on her. Just to be safe.

"You've got a little bruising under your eye," Barack said.

That's what happens when you take a sandal to a stiletto fight, I thought. I rummaged through the fast-food bag. Whatever grilled chicken breasts they'd gotten for themselves were long gone. They'd saved me three breaded chicken fingers.

"No dipping sauce?" I asked.

"There's ketchup in there," Barack said. "They had barbecue sauce, but I know you can't handle anything hotter than honey

220

mustard."

I told Steve to start the car.

"Where are we going?" Barack asked. "Off to interview a witness? Examine a crime scene? Shake down some heavies?"

I shook my head. "We're going to get me some danged barbecue sauce."

30

I found what I was looking for at the gas station's condiment bar, next to the rack of wieners and taquitos. I pumped a whole coffee cup full of Mad Mark's Southern Pit Viper Extract BBQ Sauce. It was a deep burgundy, loaded with pepper flakes. My taste buds burned at the sight of it. Then I grabbed some water for Steve and joined Barack at the counter.

He was waiting with a bottled green tea. He had his back to the counter and his cap down, trying to play it cool so he wouldn't be recognized. The girl at the counter was reading a paperback thriller, oblivious to the fact that the forty-fourth president of the United States was leaning back on an elbow right in front of her.

If Barack was hidden in plain sight, I was practically invisible. Older Delawareans knew me, but the younger generation — and transplants — usually looked right past me.

The only vice presidents anyone recognized were the ones who had gone on to become president. And Al Gore, who had drawn attention to himself with a beard big enough to have its own Zip code. With the five o'clock shadows Barack and I were sporting today, we were well on our way to looking like a couple of hippies too.

Barack stared at my cup. "What are you trying to prove, Joe?"

I pointedly ignored him.

"Hot one out," I announced, tossing a five spot on the counter. Barack rolled his eyes — he wanted to get in and out as quickly as possible. However, I was a Delawarean. And Delawareans make small talk.

The girl looked out the window. "Global warming," she said with a shrug.

"Actually, it's more of a gradual process than that," Barack said, suddenly interested in our conversation. "That's why we prefer the term 'climate change.' What you'll see is a degree or two warming over the next fifty years, which will be enough to cause the sea levels to rise ten feet. When that happens —"

"Is that coffee?" the girl asked, pointing to my cup.

"Barbecue sauce."

"I have to charge you the same as a coffee."

"Whatever. Oh, and add his drink, too," I said, motioning to the green tea.

I took my change and left Barack at the counter. He was sketching out a diagram on the back of a napkin, trying to explain the complexities of climate change to somebody who probably couldn't count to twenty without taking off her shoes.

"What's taking him so long?" Steve asked, as I slid into the passenger seat and set the barbecue sauce in the cup holder between us.

"He's giving a seminar on global warming."

Steve sighed. "We're going to be here a while. What do I owe you for the water?"

"Don't worry about it," I said.

The pump stopped. Steve hopped out to take care of things. I snuck a look at the gas pump, curious about the cost of filling the Little Beast. I saw the dollar amount and nearly choked on my tongue. It was more than the GDP of Rhode Island.

Steve returned with the receipt.

"I hope you get reimbursed for that," I said.

"I've got the president's card," he said, flashing a platinum Visa.

A motorcycle rolled in a couple pumps behind us, on the opposite side. Normally I wouldn't have noticed, but Steve was watching the bike intently in the side mirror. Steve was always watching — watching this, watching that. Movement caught his eye; lack of movement caught his eye. He was a good agent.

"You don't remember me, do you?" Steve asked.

"From Wednesday night?"

"From your first term. I was on your detail."

I wracked my brain to place him, to no luck. I never forgot a face. Secret Service agents, however, were always hiding behind their same sunglasses and same haircuts and same suits and same attitudes.

"I'm sorry. Were you on my detail long?"

"Close to eight months," he said. "You were kind of a jerk."

"To you?"

"To all of us."

I'd heard the criticism before. Agents had complained — anonymously — to the press about my detachment. They also complained about my swimming habits. Apparently, not everyone wanted to see the vice president sans trunks.

"I'm sorry if I gave you a hard time."

"I didn't care," he said. "I don't care."

"But you brought it up."

His eyes flicked to the rearview mirror.

"I'm the son of a car dealer from Scranton," I said. "Having a security detail wasn't the most comfortable thing in the world for me."

"For what it's worth, following someone around twenty-four-seven isn't the most comfortable thing in the world for us, either."

"I get that. It's just not how I was raised. I wasn't brought up to think I was better than anyone else. Nobody deserves special treatment."

"The vice president and his family deserve special treatment."

Other protectees were warmer with the agents assigned to protect them. Nobody made friends with their detail, but they treated them like human beings. Not human shields.

"I was afraid of getting too close," I said. "Not to you personally, but to all the agents. I couldn't put a name and a face with somebody I knew might be tasked with taking a bullet for me. I'd never be able to live with the guilt. I'd rather take the bullet. It'd be easier to live with."

"Or die with."

"Or that."

We sat in silence. I could still see Barack inside at the register, talking animatedly with his hands. The woman behind the counter was, for her part, transfixed. Give him five minutes, and Barack could have an atheist singing hymns.

"We shouldn't hang around here much longer," Steve said.

I turned to look for flashing lights in the distance, but there weren't any. We'd stopped at a gas station on the edge of town, where the city turned into country. I'd become increasingly paranoid that Esposito would catch up to us sooner rather than later.

The biker was still fueling his Harley. He turned to the side, and I caught a brief glimpse of the large patch covering the back of his leather vest. A giant skull with diamond eyes. The skull was grinning, a dagger between its teeth. Beneath it were the words MURDER TOWN. The chapter location. The club's name at the top of the vest was obscured by the biker's hair.

"I've seen that skull before," I said.

"The skull?" Steve said, adjusting the mirror. The guy had turned back around. Steve would have to wait to get a look for himself.

"The one on the back of his vest. The guy

in Darlene's room had a tattoo just like it."

"You mean the minister?"

"He wasn't a minister."

The biker was fiddling with the pump. They make you jump through so many hoops these days just to fill your tank. *Is this a debit card? Would you like a car wash? How about a ninety-nine-cent coffee? How about some flipping gas?*

"He hasn't been following us," Steve said.

"How would you know?"

"I'd know." The guy glanced in our direction, then looked away. "I'm going inside to get Renegade."

"You recognize the patch?"

"We've had training on motorcycle clubs. I can't place the design, but it looks familiar. There aren't many with chapters in Wilmington. Climb over here and take the wheel. Meet us out back."

Before I could protest, Steve was on his way into the gas station. What I really wanted to happen was for him to detain the biker. See what we could learn about that skull. See if he was in a motorcycle club with the other guy, the guy who wasn't a minister. Unfortunately, Steve had other plans.

I crawled into the driver's seat and turned the key. The Little Beast roared to life.

Out of the corner of my eye, I saw Steve emerge from the employee entrance. A beat later, Barack exited behind his human shield. Unfortunately, Steve was a foot too short to be one hundred percent effective, so Barack had to crouch.

"Let's see what you can do," I said, putting the pedal to the metal. The Little Beast lurched forward and my head hit the seat back. I pumped the brakes and threw the SUV into reverse in one neat little motion, then spun around toward the employee entrance. I skidded to a stop just inches from backing over Steve and Barack and turning them into gas station hot-dog meat.

Steve threw the door open and they tumbled into the backseat. The biker rolled past us and stopped at the road. He threw a lingering look in our direction. The windows were tinted so I knew he couldn't see me, but he was staring me down nonetheless. He shouted something that I couldn't hear, and gave me a one-fingered salute before tearing off down the two-lane highway.

You're not getting away that easy, I thought.

I stepped on the gas, and we rocketed in reverse. The SUV seemed to pull out from under me, and my head jerked forward. The Little Beast plowed into an air station before

I found the brakes. We screeched to a stop.

We sat there for a moment in silence. All three of us were breathing heavy. Air escaped the broken hose somewhere under the vehicle with a high-pitched hiss.

I collected myself as best I could, threw the gear shift into drive, and stepped on the gas like my wife was in labor.

31

I heard the sound of Steve checking the chamber on his gun. I looked in the rearview to see if he was planning to lean out the window and pop off at the biker to blow his tires out, but he'd already reholstered the weapon.

"Everybody buckled up back there?" I shouted.

"I strongly advise you to pull over," Steve said.

"And let this guy get away?"

"Yes."

I snorted. "Not a chance."

We were heading northwest out of Wilmington on Route 52. The countryside passed by in a blur as we followed close behind the biker, who was zipping in and out of traffic. He must have thought it would be easier to lose us on the country road, rather than the tight grid of downtown or the bumper-to-bumper traffic on the interstate. Fortunately, there was one thing the biker hadn't counted on: weekend drivers.

We passed a pickup that was doing fifty-five in a fifty-five. Clearly a sociopath. Maybe in Middle America it was acceptable to drive the speed limit, but not on the coast. If you weren't doing at least ten over, you were liable to be run off the road. In Delaware, speeding wasn't breaking the law; it was self-preservation.

Barack leaned between the seats. I could tell he was trying to get a look at the speedometer. The needle was fluttering between eighty and eighty-five. No matter how hard I pressed the pedal, the Beast wouldn't go any faster. The motorcycle topped out at the same speed, so we were locked in step with each other.

"Listen, I know he flipped you off. But this is madness. It was just a middle finger. It's not worth getting into an accident."

"He knows us. He knows that we know who he is."

"And who is he?" Barack asked.

"I don't know his name, but I know that skull on his back. His club has something to do with Finn. And he's just flaunting it in our faces. He was mocking us back there."

"He's not going to pull over, that much is

obvious. What are you planning to do?"

I didn't say anything.

"How are we on gas?" Barack said.

The tank was three-quarters full and he knew it. "If you want to drive, you're more than welcome to."

"You're doing a great job, Joe."

"You mean that?"

"Could I give you a suggestion, though?"

I shook my head.

Barack ignored me. "You might want to move your hands down a notch. Ten and two used to be the recommendation, but experts now say nine and three are better. In a crash, the airbag can break your wrists if your hands are too high on the wheel."

"That what they teach you at Harvard Driving School?"

He didn't take the bait. I waited for him to look away, and then I slipped my hands down the wheel to nine and three.

The motorcycle whipped around a mid-sized sedan with Vermont plates, and I did the same, keeping pace. As we passed the sedan, I caught glimpse of a small tuft of white hair poking out above the bottom of the window. The driver's head was so low, it was a miracle he could see. A pair of bony hands hung from the steering wheel like Halloween decorations.

"Everybody wave to Bernie," I said.

Nobody laughed at my joke.

Developed lands segued into fields and farms. Weekend drivers loved driving past fields for some reason. There wasn't much to see right now. The corn was barely a foot high. Other crops hadn't started poking up yet. The biker occasionally checked us out in his side mirror, but didn't slow. Which one of us was going to make a mistake first?

"You know what the official state beverage is?" I said out loud. There was no answer from the back. "Give up? I'll tell you: it's milk. Milk is the official state beverage of Delaware."

"Fascinating," Barack said.

"I know, right?" I said, glancing in the rearview to see if he was rolling his eyes.

He wasn't.

"Cow," Steve said.

I looked at Steve. "Yeah, though we've got goats in Delaware, too. You know what gets me, though? Almond milk. It's not milk, it's more like juice. Just call it almond *juice* —"

"Cow!" Steve and Barack screamed, pointing through the windshield.

My eyes returned to the road just in time to see a large black-spotted dairy cow in the middle of our lane. In the opposite lane was a semi, coming right toward us. I pumped

234

the brakes and spun the wheel hard to the right, praying silently to Saint Francis that we wouldn't crash.

My prayer must have gone to Saint Francis's voicemail.

We skidded around the cow, which had a very nonchalant look on its face, given the situation. The antilock-braking system kicked in and prevented the brakes from locking up and sending us ass over teacup, but it couldn't prevent us from diving headfirst into the ditch.

The Little Beast rocketed up the opposite embankment. We tore through a barbed-wire fence like it was nothing more than party streamers, and then we were in a field. The car rocked back and forth over the uneven dirt, going slower and slower until finally rolling to a stop. That's the last thing I remembered before blacking out.

32

When I came to, I was still in the driver's
seat. My eyes were burning — not due to
an injury, but due to the barbeque sauce
that had splattered all over the dash. Steve
was slumped over in the back, blood trick-
ling down the side of his face. Barack's seat
was empty.

I stumbled outside. The smell of burnt
rubber filled my nostrils. There were deep
scars in the field from the tires, all the way
back to the road. The Escalade had left fifty-
foot-long black skid marks on the highway.
We'd come to a stop just short of a herd of
cattle, which hadn't taken much notice of
us. I counted twelve of them, in addition to
the cow that had somehow wandered onto
the highway. A baker's dozen.

I heard the trunk slam shut.

"Barack?"

He peeked around the corner of the car.
"You're awake. I was just coming to check

on you."

He was holding a first-aid kit. "I'm fine," I said.

"You sure? You hit the steering wheel pretty hard."

I touched my forehead and found a knot. I didn't remember going headfirst into the wheel, but I must have.

"You feeling nauseous? Brain fog?"

"Not any worse than usual," I said.

"You're making jokes, so you can't be too out of it," Barack said. He opened the rear driver's-side door.

Now that the smell of burnt rubber was dissipating, another smell took over. I looked down at my feet. I was inches away from a pile of manure. We were in the middle of a fecal minefield.

Barack peered back at me. "Oh, and watch your step."

"I've been on farms before," I said.

We both had. A couple of summers, we'd spent more time in Iowa than in Washington. That was what you had to do if you wanted to win the first-in-the-nation caucus. My only regret was that with all the cows I'd milked in the state fair over the years, I'd never won the state Democratic Party's nomination for president. Never even came close. At least there'd been ice cream.

I peeked over Barack's shoulder. Steve was awake, but he didn't look good. There was a glassy look in his eyes. Steve wasn't an agent, I realized. He was a human being. A human being in pain. He hadn't asked to be dragged along on this quixotic quest. He'd only come along because he didn't want a black mark on his record, not when he was so close to getting a spot on the presidential Counter-Assault Team. We'd taken advantage of him, and he didn't deserve this.

Still, he should have been wearing his seatbelt.

Barack carefully wrapped gauze around Steve's head. "There's a cut along his hairline. The scalp bleeds more readily than any other part of the body. Except for arteries, of course."

"Of course," I said, though I had no idea what he was talking about. Barack didn't have any medical training, as far as I knew. But his brain absorbed everything. If it came down to it, I had faith that he could deliver a baby. Maybe even perform a circumcision.

"He's definitely got a concussion, but what worries me is internal bleeding. He wasn't buckled in. He flew into the back of your seat pretty hard."

Steve squinted at me. "Was it the Russians?"

"The Russians?" I asked, squeezing his hand. It was cold and sweaty.

"They're trying to tamper with the election. We have to stop them."

Barack frowned at me.

"What happened?" Steve asked. "They won, didn't they?"

"We were chasing a biker," I told him. "Do you remember that?"

Steve coughed into his hand. There was fresh blood in his cough. "The Marauders."

"Have you called the meat wagon?" I asked Barack.

"There isn't an ambulance in Delaware that could make it through the mud in this field. Don't think they're going to land a helicopter here, either, least not without some trouble. We'll take him ourselves, as long as the Little Beast starts."

"Sounds like a plan," I said.

"That's because it *is* a plan, Joe."

"The Marauders," Steve said again.

Barack shook his head. "Hand me the keys, Joe. We need to get on the road."

It was his car, so that was fine by me. Or it was his wife's, actually. Despite everything I'd driven it through, the Little Beast wasn't in bad shape. It was bulletproof and, apparently, barbed-wire-proof. At least I hadn't hit the cow. No car is cow-proof.

"The Marauders," I said, trying the word out on my tongue. Steve wasn't talking about the Russians. He was drifting in and out of lucidity, but he was trying to tell us something. *The Marauders* . . .

I snapped my fingers. "The MC."

"We don't have time to talk hip-hop," Barack said. "The keys —"

"Not an MC, an *MC*. Motorcycle club. The Marauders."

Steve started to nod, but winced. He grabbed his ribs. He was trying to tough it out, but it was hard to hide his pain. He was a soldier . . . but even the best soldiers can go down. His eyes kept wandering, never stopping long enough to focus. He was fading fast. The last thing he said before passing out was, "Are those cows?"

33

After we dropped off Steve at the nearest hospital, Barack pulled into a nondescript garage and parked in the basement, the last spot in a long line of cars. There was a thin layer of water on the cement. Either there was nowhere for it to drain, or it was so thick with motor oil and sludge that it couldn't move.

"This is all my fault," I said. "I'm the one who got us into this mess. I'm the one who couldn't handle the car."

Barack didn't look at me. He was behind the wheel now. "You're being too hard on yourself, Joe."

"Am I wrong?"

"About which part?"

"Any of it," I said.

"I shouldn't have let you drive in the first place. The Little Beast takes some getting used to."

"How many fields have you driven her into?"

"Zero."

I felt a yawn coming on and covered my mouth. I was able to avoid it, but my energy was flagging. The car chase had gotten my heart rate up. Adrenaline was coursing through my body. Everything felt electric. My fingertips were tingling, abuzz with energy. And then I crashed. In more ways than one.

A boat of a car crept past us. An olive-green 1973 Cadillac Fleetwood. It stopped, then backed up into a space directly behind us. I watched over my shoulder as it flashed its headlights — once, twice. Three times.

That was the signal.

Barack and I stepped out and slipped into the backseat of the Fleetwood.

Detective Capriotti didn't turn around.

"Thanks for meeting us," I said. "I wouldn't have called if it wasn't important. Should we drive somewhere . . . ?"

"I've already been put on traffic duty for a week. I could be fired just for talking to you. Let alone, I didn't know you were going to bring . . . *him*."

"Sorry," I said. "Dan, this is Barack. Barack, Dan."

They shook hands between the front seats.

Neither man smiled.

"We need your help," I said.

"I'm wondering if I haven't helped you enough already. I told you what we found in your friend's pockets because I thought you'd appreciate it. The lieutenant gets a call an hour ago from Finn Donnelly's daughter, who's all pissed off that we kept it from her. Now where do you suppose she learned about the drugs, Joe?"

"She's family. I assumed she knew."

"I told you she didn't. Or are you forgetting things in your old age?"

"I thought . . . ." My voice trailed off. "It doesn't matter now."

"I'm not finished. A couple of days ago, I get a call from *you*. Telling me I need to check up on some guy you thought might be snooping around Finn's wife's room. Nobody there knew anything about some minister —"

"He wasn't a minister."

"First he was, then he wasn't. Do you hear yourself? This is paranoia." He shook his head. "Then there's this."

Dan unfolded a paper and passed it back to me. It was a sketch of the actor Richard Gere.

"I don't understand," I said.

"We got a call about ten thirty this morning," Dan said. "Alvin Harrison died of an overdose. Oxy, from the looks of it."

I tried to look shocked, but I couldn't fool Dan.

He continued, "A neighbor described a suspicious character snooping around Alvin's apartment. She's one of those ladies who watches everything out her window. You know the type. Anyway, the only problem is, she's not quite all there. Mentally, if you know what I mean. The description she gave the sketch artist was quite detailed, though." He paused for effect. "You wouldn't happen to know anything about Alvin's death, would you?"

Barack examined the drawing, and then me.

Back and forth.

He bit his lip.

"Talk to Richard Gere," I said, handing the paper back to Dan. "He's from Philly. He could have been in town. You never know."

"So this is how it's going to be, Joe?"

"I didn't call you to discuss Alvin Harrison," I said. "I need to know if you know anything about the Marauders."

"The outlaw biker gang. You want to let me know what's going on?"

"Not particularly," I said.

"I hope this doesn't have anything to do with Finn Donnelly."

"If I say it does, are you going to tell me off?"

"You want my help, I need to know where this is coming from. There's no connection between the Marauders and your friend."

"The Marauders aren't involved in the drug trade?"

Dan shrugged. "I'm not a narcotics detective, but their name pops up now and again. Marijuana. Guns, I guess. The usual outlaw biker stuff."

"And you don't shut them down?"

"We have to pick and choose our battles, Joe. Half of this city is high on something right now. Should we just start kicking in doors without warrants? Unless they start trouble, we keep out of their business."

"You're saying because they're white, you don't hassle them," Barack said.

"You don't know me," Dan snapped.

I felt a tension headache coming on. It could have been the aftereffects of the concussion. It could have had nothing to do with the concussion.

I said, "The guy I ran into at Baptist Manor the other day was part of their club. Finn wasn't, obviously — he didn't even own a bike — but maybe he hung with them. Maybe they're the ones who sold him his dope."

Dan laughed. "What are you going to do, arrest them by yourself?"

"We're not stupid," I said.

"Could have fooled me. These people call themselves one-percenters. As in, they're the one percent of bikers who live outside the law. They don't dick around, Joe. They're a bunch of bad hombres. You can't just walk in there and start asking questions. They'd cut you to ribbons. Here's what I'll do: I'll ask around in narcotics, discreetly. Won't let them know it's related to Finn Donnelly, because I don't want to catch hell with the boss. But I'll see if there's any heroin activity surrounding this group. If not, I want you to drop this thing. I mean it."

"That's not up to me. It's the Secret Service's investigation."

Barack nodded slowly.

"I don't see how heroin trafficking falls under their jurisdiction," Dan said. "So Finn printed off a paper with your address. I get that. But if you were truly afraid for your life, you'd be in a bunker right now. Both of you. Instead, you're driving around without a single agent in sight. What am I supposed to make of that?"

"It's a national security —"

"Don't feed me that bull, Joe. How long we known each other? Long enough to know each other's tells."

"What's my tell?"

"If someone's tipping their pitches, you don't let 'em know what their tell is. You're a baseball man. You should know that."

"And you should know I'm being straight with you, dammit," I growled.

Another long pause. Then Dan said, "Write this down."

He gave me the address of the clubhouse where the Marauders operated. He started his car and we got out without another word. It was only after we returned to our vehicle that I realized I hadn't thanked him. My headache had come on fast and strong, and I had no time for niceties. If we made it through the weekend in one piece, I'd send him a thank-you card.

34

We stopped at the Waffle Depot to switch cars. I was relieved to discover my Challenger had made it through the night without being stolen.

Next, we stopped at Wilmington Station. At the ticket booth, I bought two one-way tickets on the next DC-bound train. The silver-haired octogenarian working the booth recognized me . . . which was exactly what I was hoping for. We chatted for a minute or two about our grandkids, who were about the same age. On my way out the door I waved to a few passengers who gave me "the look." Even shook a couple of hands. A teenaged girl with a red ribbon in her hair raised her camera phone, and I gave her my most vice-presidential grin. She pursed her lips and winked. She removed the ribbon to let her hair down and made another face. It took me longer than it should have to realize she wasn't taking my picture — she was taking her own.

The Mayor nodded to me, but we didn't speak.

Outside, I tore up the train tickets and dropped them in a trash can.

Barack was sitting in the passenger seat of the Challenger with his cap low over his face. "I was beginning to worry you got lost in there," he said. "What took you so long?"

"I can't exactly walk into the Joseph R. Biden Jr. Railroad Station without attracting a crowd."

"Nobody calls it that," Barack pointed out.

"Tonight they will. I made a scene," I said. "I did everything but kiss a baby. If Esposito or her goons look for us, the trail is going to lead them to Washington — and then it's going to go cold as Des Moines in January."

"Unless she's better at her job than you think."

"I thought we were both in on this plan."

"I'm just saying, I doubt it's going to fool her. She's being groomed to be the next chief of police for a reason, and it's certainly not on account of her charming personality."

I slapped the wheel with both hands. "Next time, I'd appreciate it if you could voice your objections *before* I spend two hundred bucks on useless tickets."

249

"It might work," Barack said, but there was a discernable lack of conviction in his voice.

I shook my head. "You know, this is where it all began."

"Inauguration Day," Barack said. "How cold was the wind chill? Ten degrees, wasn't it?"

"I meant before that. My first run for president."

The station was where I'd announced my campaign, back in 1987. I rode an Amtrak train rebranded the "Biden Express" with my family from Wilmington down to DC. After a decade and a half in the Senate, I was ready for a bigger challenge. Little did I know that the bigger challenge wouldn't be the primary race (which I would unceremoniously quit), but a pair of cranial aneurysms that would leave me on death's door. I'd had my last rites read.

"You really want to follow up this lead, about the motorcycle club?" Barack asked. "Do you know anything about biker gangs, beyond what you've seen on cable TV?"

"I used to ride."

"Really?" he asked with disbelief.

"I had a life before I went into politics. Wasn't in a club, or one of these outlaw groups, but I had a bike."

"I believe you. But we need to seriously think about how far we're going to go. The body count is rising. Steve is in the hospital. And let's not forget that you got whooped by some woman swinging her shoe."

"She's an Amazon," I said. "Seven foot tall."

"If she's the same woman from the motel, she wasn't that tall."

"She was in heels this afternoon. Flats the other night."

"Regardless, you're in rough shape. And I'm not even going to mention that knee that's been hobbling you this whole time, or the concussion you sustained this afternoon."

"You think that was my first concussion? Ha."

"We need to think about the bigger picture here, Joe. What's more important? Solving this mystery, or your health? A lot of people are counting on you. Maybe more than you realize."

"This isn't about the future," I said. "This is about right now."

Barack didn't say anything.

I continued, "Remember what you said, when our poll numbers started to dip in 2008? Things were starting to swing McCain's way. If the election tipped in his favor, we'd be dead in the water. Our whole strategy was built on maintaining that sense of inevitability — that sense that this was your time. America was ready for a black president. If there was even a sliver of doubt in people's minds, it would open the door wide. 'I knew America wasn't ready,' the doubters would say. 'I knew he was too young, too cocky, too black.' After Axe read the poll numbers showing the Straight Talk Express pulling neck and neck with us, doubt started to creep into that room. And what was it you said?"

Barack looked up and to the left, no doubt replaying that day in his head. He didn't have to repeat what he'd said, though, because I knew every word:

Things have been easy so far. They're not going to stay that way. The path to victory isn't a straight one. There are going to be ups and downs, twists and turns. There will be times when we all wonder what the hell we were thinking. That's doubt. You know what the opposite of doubt is? It's not certainty, because nothing in this life is certain. The opposite of doubt is hope. I'm not talking about blind optimism; I'm not talking about wishful idealism. I'm talking about that stubborn thing inside each and every one of us that insists something better awaits us as long as we have the courage to keep fighting.

"As long as you have hope," he said, repeating his words from that day, "you're still in the game."

"And when you lose it?" I asked, echoing a field organizer's question.

"You can't lose it. Hope never dies." He looked down at his hands. "We were younger then."

"Not by much. You're younger now than I was then."

"I'm not talking about the years."

"We had eight years," I said. "It wasn't easy."

"I never expected it to be."

"Together, though . . . together we got it done."

He focused on some faraway point.

I wiped my nose with my sleeve. I was getting the sniffles. Maybe the start of a summer cold. I was all too aware that, at my age, that could mean a joyride in a pine box.

"Forget about 2008, and 2012, and 2016," I said. "Forget about everything we did, and everything we didn't do. Forget about our successes and our failures. Focus on this one thing, right here. This is it. This is our chance to make a difference. A real difference."

I put a hand on his shoulder. For once, he

didn't shrug it off or make a joke out of it. "I don't exactly know what happened between us at the end, but it's water under the bridge. You got that? We're out of our element here —"

"We're not even on the periodic table."

"All the more reason to harness whatever hope is left inside us. What do you say? Can we do this?"

"Yes." A thin smile spread on his face. "Yes we can."

35

The Marauders' clubhouse was located about half a mile from the Heart of Wilmington Motel. We'd driven past it twice this weekend without a second glance; it was an anonymous concrete fortress. The windows were boarded up. There was no signage anywhere, no address number. The parking lot was cracked and empty. The building had, once upon a time, been a strip club. There was more discreet parking out back. That was where we'd find the motorcycles, I guessed.

Barack and I parked in the lot of the pawn shop next door. There were two pickup trucks next to us, which gave us some small cover as we scoped out the clubhouse. The last time I'd been inside a hockshop had been back in college. These days, pawn stores were being replaced by check-cashing joints and payday-loan emporiums that had no qualms about taking advantage of the struggling American consumer during times of hardship.

"Guns, gold, jewelry, and DVDs," Barack said, reading the window signage. "The story of America. All that's missing are the Bibles."

"I've never heard of someone pawning a Bible," I said. "Where I come from, you can lose your home, your kids, your wife, and the clothes off your back . . . but the one thing you hold onto is the Holy Bible."

"This *is* where you come from, Joe."

He was half right. Though this wasn't a neighborhood I'd ever spent time in, Wilmington was where I'd lived for most of the past sixty-plus years. My formative years, however, had happened in Scranton. It was where my ancestors were; it was where my roots were. Can a man claim more than one hometown?

I flipped the visor up. "Let's go next door and get this over with."

"Remember, it's just you and me now. We don't have any backup. We don't have any weapons. If anyone's in there, they're going to be armed to the teeth. So we should figure out how we're going to play this before we just bust through the front door like a two-man SWAT team. Speaking of which, it would take a lot more than a shoulder to knock that door in."

The front door was steel. It could have been a foot thick for all we knew. Neither Barack nor I was on the guest list. There was, however, an alley that ran between the clubhouse and the pawn store. "We'll go around back. There's more than one way in and out. Once we're inside, we'll ask some questions. There's our plan. See how easy that was?"

Barack frowned. "Without a court order, it might be difficult to get them to co-operate. They're called *outlaw* biker gangs for a reason."

"I'll open my wallet if I have to. And if that doesn't work . . ."

I cracked my knuckles.

"You're getting worked up, Joe. If you walk in there angry, you're going to encounter nothing but hostility. Let's just sit here in the car for a few minutes and breathe deeply. Okay?"

"I'll breathe deeply when this is over," I said, throwing my door open.

"Wait," Barack said, reaching for me.

It was too late, though. I was done waiting.

This time, Barack didn't follow me.

Behind the clubhouse, two dozen motor-cycles were lined up against the building.

All that chrome shone brightly under the midday sun.

I slipped on my Ray-Bans.

There was, as I'd suspected, a back door for deliveries. A little wooden ramp led up to it. The door was steel, same as the front, with one difference: it was propped open with a keg. The country twang of Kenny Rogers drifted out of the open door. The sun cast my shadow behind me, and there wasn't enough light coming from within the building to see beyond the opening.

I took a deep breath.

The Irish in me told me to barge in and make a scene, but Barack was right. We were both unarmed. My "plan" wasn't a plan at all. It was bullheaded and reckless. As soon as I put one sandal inside the clubhouse, I would be crossing a line that I couldn't uncross. The longer I thought it over, the more I realized just how far in over our heads we were. Barack and I weren't detectives. We weren't even politicians anymore. We should have known better than to go around poking bulls. One of us was liable to get gored.

On the other hand, there was something to be said for just going for it. Thinking was overrated. Even the best-laid plans could fail. Just ask Hillary.

I stepped through the open door. Inside the clubhouse was pitch-black. I couldn't see a thing, including my own nose. It took me a second to figure out that was because of my sunglasses.

Once I took them off, I could see better. Funny how that works.

There weren't any lights on, but there was a little sunlight coming in from the open door behind me. Enough to recognize I was in a kitchen. Dishes were stacked high in a sink. It didn't look like anyone had cooked in here since the Cold War.

I found a door on the far wall and opened it a crack . . .

You know that scene in movies where the out-of-place guy struts into the honky-tonk, and the music stops playing and everyone looks up and there's that long moment of uncomfortable silence?

That's not how it happens in real life.

In real life, the music keeps playing. That uncomfortable moment is stretched out even longer as you wait for someone to unplug the jukebox. Not that I mind Kenny Rogers, but when you've got two-dozen bikers pointing guns at your face, the last thing you want to hear is all that talk about knowing when to walk away and when to run. It doesn't matter how fast you are. Even if my knee had been one hundred percent, it's impossible to outrun a hailstorm of bullets.

36

"That's the guy I was telling you about," one of the bikers said. His southern accent was thicker than Grandma Biden's turkey gravy. I recognized him as the speed demon who'd led us on the chase through the country. He was armed with only a pool cue, but I didn't doubt he could break me seven ways 'til next Sunday.

I raised my hands in surrender. "If I could just say one thing —"

I heard a couple of safeties click off, so I shut up. I was outnumbered and outgunned. Even if Barack had followed me in — even if Steve was still with us, and not lying in a hospital bed — we would have been outnumbered and outgunned. The Marauders weren't your typical motorcycle club composed of weekend riders. They were a gang. Judging by the array of high-powered weaponry on display, they also apparently didn't realize that fully automatic weapons had been banned in the U.S. since 1986. Dan had tried to warn me. I'd been foolish to ignore him.

The speed demon stepped up to my face. He reeked of marijuana. Despite the pungent odor, I didn't flinch. Criminals were like dogs: they could smell fear. They could also smell urine, which was sure to leak down my leg at the first loud noise.

"You nearly backed right into me, just as I was pulling out of the gas station," he said. He was still wearing his black motorcycle helmet, which looked like something out of a World War I documentary. "You were driving like a madman. You chased me halfway to Pennsylvania. There's no telling how many accidents you almost caused."

"Backed into you? I didn't even see you!"

"Exactly," he said.

As much as it pained me to admit it, he was probably right. I'd backed up the Escalade without first adjusting the rearview or side mirrors.

"You were following us first," I said. "That's why you were there. Admit it."

"Why would I follow you?"

"Because of who I am."

"And who are you?"

"The vice president of the United States." I paused. "Former vice president."

262

The bikers looked around at one another. There was a lot of shrugging and head shaking. The Marauders weren't exactly my target demo, but they couldn't be that clueless . . . could they?

"Vice President Biden. I was your state's senator for thirty-six years."

Still no recognition.

With a heavy thud, a body landed on the floor beside me. The Marauders' skull logo grinned up at me from the back of the man's vest.

"Keep moving," a deep voice boomed from behind me.

The guy on the ground wasn't dead. Just dazed. He scrambled to his feet and stumbled toward the pool table, which he caught for support.

Barack put an arm around my shoulder. "How you doin', Joe?"

The speed demon who'd been in my face stared blankly at the president. Then he glanced back at his friend, then to the president again. Barack had a sawed-off shotgun balanced casually on his shoulder.

"Where'd you get the hardware?" I whispered to Barack.

He nodded at the biker clinging to the pool table. "This fool set it down while he was smoking out back. I picked it up just as he was returning to the kitchen door."

A machete clanked on the floor. The bikers had all lowered their weapons.

"Looks like you all know who my pal is," I said with authority.

"He's the guy who killed Bin Laden," one of the bikers blurted.

They all nodded in agreement. The awe in their eyes was, frankly, embarrassing.

"Actually, SEAL Team Six —" I started to say, but Barack cut me off with a stiff pat on the back.

"— is waiting outside, in case there's any trouble," he finished. "If we're not out of here within ten minutes, two dozen trained killers are going to bust in here and shoot this place up like they've got video-game cheat codes. Am I making myself clear?"

A few guys nodded. A couple "yessir'd" him under their breath. They may have been outlaws, but I'd seen more than one U.S. military insignia on their vests.

"We're looking for somebody," Barack said, pacing the room. "Somebody with a tattoo on their forearm."

The bikers looked at one another. There were a few muffled laughs. There were very few Marauders in the clubhouse who didn't have tattoos on their forearms.

"A skull tattoo," I said. "The club logo."

Barack continued to walk the room, inspecting forearms. I scanned the clubhouse from side to side, but didn't see the man who'd been in Darlene Donnelly's room. He was the key to all of this, I was sure. He probably wasn't the only one involved with the drug trade — if so, we'd be back. But we couldn't interrogate them all at once. We may have had the upper hand momentarily, but somebody was going to point out the obvious: Barack Obama wasn't commander in chief anymore, and there was no way SEAL Team Six was waiting outside. Right now, however, most of the bikers were too high on reefer or drunk on whiskey to think clearly. We'd interrupted quite the party.

Out of the corner of my eye, I caught a biker inching behind one of his buddies. I couldn't see his face, but I could see the tangle of long hair. Barack followed my eyes and strolled casually over to the man.

"Turn around," Barack ordered. I'd never seen the president quite like this. He'd had a life before I met him, though. Biographies had been written about him; he'd even penned a few books about himself. They left out more than they revealed. I wondered if anyone would ever truly know the complete Barack Obama. I wondered if even Barack Obama would ever know the real

Barack Obama.

When the biker didn't comply, Barack dragged him out from behind his buddy and spun him around. Barack held the guy's forearm out for me, showing off the tattoo. "This the guy?"

I didn't need to see the tattoo; I recognized his face.

I nodded.

Barack gave him a shove, and the faux minister stumbled into the middle of the clubhouse. "Does anyone know this clown's name?"

"T-Swizzle," the speed demon said.

Barack arched an eyebrow. "T-Swizzle?"

"It's Taylor Swift's nickname."

"I know, I have daughters," Barack said. He tossed a pair of handcuffs to T-Swizzle. "Put these on."

Barack had pilfered the silver bracelets from Steve before we dropped him off.

The poor guy looked around at his friends expectantly, waiting for them to step in and prevent him from being hauled away. Nobody would meet his eyes. Loyalty extended only so far in the criminal world.

37

The man who'd given me the slip at Baptist Manor sat trembling in a folding chair. We were a couple of miles from the Lake House, in a storage unit I rented month-to-month. The rest of the facility was pretty empty — nobody wanted to dig around in their old forgotten boxes of memories on a sunny Saturday afternoon. Lucky break for us. Not so much for T-Swizzle. That meant there was no one besides me and Barack to hear his desperate pleas: "I don't know any Finn Donnelly. You have me confused with some other guy. You have to let me go, because if I go to jail then I'll never become a patch-wearing member —"

I told him to shut up. He was only digging himself deeper.

"Freedom of speech," he spat back. "I got freedom of speech."

I said, "If you don't shut up, that hole you're digging is going to be your grave," and I'm not sure who looked more surprised, T-Swizzle or Barack. I'd been thinking about that line for a while and was secretly thrilled I'd finally gotten to use it. I tried not to show my excitement. The time for fun and games had long passed.

T-Swizzle's full name was Taylor Brownsford, according to the driver's license in his wallet. We'd also found something else in his jeans: a pocket watch. Finn's pocket watch. There was no debating it. Even in a world where facts seemed to matter less and less, any idiot could tell whose watch it was from the inscription on the back: TO FINN — FORTY YEARS — LOVE, YOUR DARLENE.

The watch was the first piece of physical evidence that directly tied the Marauders to Finn Donnelly. If there'd been any question about what we were going to do with Taylor — hand him over to Dan or Esposito for interrogation, or grill him ourselves — the pocket watch had sealed his fate. I wasn't going to let him plead the fifth. I wasn't going to let him slip through my fingers.

Barack and I stepped outside. I kept one eye on our captive, but so far he hadn't made any attempts to escape.

"What's that?" I asked Barack. He was grinning at a framed 8-by-10 he'd found inside the storage unit. He showed me the photo, an image of me and him jogging around the White House in dress shirts and ties. It was part of a promotion for one of Michelle's get-off-your-fat-ass campaigns. "This was from your office in Washington," Barack said.

I snatched it from him. "Quit playing around. We need to lay some ground rules."

"Good cop, bad cop?"

"I'm not playing, Barack. This is serious. Rule one: no torture."

He rolled his eyes, just as I'd known he would. "I can't believe you'd think I would resort to enhanced interrogation techniques, Joe. The U.S. crossed the line after 9/11 — that's not a road I want to go down again."

"Just remember, you don't judge a man's character by what he does when things are easy. You judge him by what he does when they're hard."

"Another of your mother's famous sayings?"

I shook my head. "That's one of yours."

He thought I was being patronizing. What he didn't realize was that I was trying to lay the ground rules for myself. I didn't see how we were going to get out of this situation. We were beyond pretending that Barack wasn't Barack, or playing silly games with ball caps hiding our faces.

I didn't care. I just needed Taylor to spill the baked beans.

"That's all you have? One rule?" Barack asked.

"Unless you have any."

He shook his head, and we returned to our captive. Barack pulled the garage door shut behind us. We had cleared out a little space in the center of the unit by stacking boxes around us to the ceiling, and that's where the biker was sitting. A single bulb lit the space, which was littered with mouse droppings and spiderwebs.

"You're looking at hard time," I told him. He was slumped over in the chair. "You were in Darlene Donnelly's room. There's video evidence," I fibbed. "You can't deny it. Stop pretending like I'm some confused old man."

"Why are you doing this?"

"Why are we doing this?" I said, spitting his words back in his face. "Because you're the scum of the earth! The lowest of the low!" I paused to catch my breath. "Finn was my friend. First I find you in his wife's nursing home. And now we find this in your pocket."

I held up Finn's pocket watch. It was enclosed in a pewter case decorated with a reproduction of the Saint Benedict medal.

Taylor was silent.

"The guy with the beard and the robes," I said, pointing out the embossed figure in the center of the medal. The robed man was holding a cross in one hand and a book in the other — *The Rule of Saint Benedict.* "He's a Catholic saint. See the words running around the circle?"

I knew the inscription by heart, even if I couldn't pronounce the words: *Eius in obitu nostro praesentia muniamur.*

"It translates to, 'May his presence protect us in the hour of our death.' Do you know what time it is, Taylor?"

He was on the verge of tears.

"You'd better start beating your gums," I said.

And talk he did.

38

"I was returning the watch," Taylor Brownsford said.

"To Finn's wife?"

He nodded. "I found it down by the tracks. Where Finn was hit by the train."

"What were you doing down there? Looting the crime scene?"

"If I tell you the truth, can you promise I won't get in trouble?"

"No," Barack said.

The biker sighed. "I was shooting smack, all right? I bought it from a street dealer down in the old warehouse district."

"What's your dealer's name?"

"There's not one guy. You just drive up — or ride up, in my case — and pull to a stop. Keep your car running. Don't park. Somebody will come out. Hand them the money, and they spit out a balloon."

I recoiled at the image. A balloon full of dope, covered in someone's spit. I didn't want to hear any more, but I had to keep pressing him, no matter how disgusting the details. These hopheads had seen plenty worse. They shot dope with dirty needles. A little spit wouldn't make them bat an eyelash.

"Keep talking," I said. "You decided, what, to shoot up by the tracks?"

Taylor shook his head. "I don't usually shoot by the tracks. But I needed a fix, so I rode for a couple of blocks until I found an empty lot. That's where I found the pocket watch. At first I thought it was neat, but then I saw the inscription. I heard about what happened. I might be a junkie, but I'm no thief."

"And you knew Finn's wife was in the nursing home."

"It was on the TV."

"Which channel?"

"How should I know?"

I looked at Barack to see if he was buying any of this. Darlene Donnelly hadn't been mentioned by name in any of the newspaper reports that I'd read. I might have believed him if he said he'd read her name in the obituaries.

"When's the last time you had a fix?" Barack asked.

"A couple hours."

"Where's your rig?"

"Why would I tell you? You think I'm stupid?"

"No," Barack said, "but I think you're a liar." He twisted the biker's arm. Since Taylor's hands were still cuffed, his elbow bent into a painful-looking position. Barack held it there.

"You're hurting me," Taylor whined.

"Where are your track marks?"

"My track marks?"

Barack let go of him.

I got right down in the biker's face. "Now I want you to go back to the beginning of your story, and tell us the truth this time. No baloney, mister."

"You can't do this," he protested. "I have rights."

"Not where we'll take you if you don't come clean," Barack said. "I hear Gitmo's nice this time of year."

The biker's face went white. "What? You can't be serious. I'm an American! I'm —"

We were interrupted by a ringing phone. Barack and Taylor both looked in my direction, as if it was my phone making the racket. But I'd turned my phone on vibrate.

It rang again.

And again.

And again.

"Are you going to answer that, Joe?" Barack asked.

I pulled my phone out. "It's not —"

It was my phone. Oops.

UNKNOWN CALLER.

The Mayor, calling from a pay phone again?

"Hello," I answered, using the deepest voice I could muster.

"Hello, Mr. Biden," said a distorted voice.

"There's no Mr. Biden here. This is Joe . . . Tingler."

"Tingler?" Barack whispered.

I covered the mouthpiece and shooed him away. "Who's this?"

"The answers you seek are within reach," the caller said. It was impossible to tell if it was a man or woman through the distortion. "There's an ice cream stand on the Riverwalk. Be there in one hour. Alone."

"Who should I be looking for?"

"You'll recognize me. But leave the police and Secret Service out of this. If you try anything funny, you'll never get what you want."

"And what do I want?"

"Justice," the voice said, and the caller hung up before I could ask what in the Sam Hill they were blabbing about. They hadn't

275

mentioned Finn Donnelly. They didn't have to.

My hands were shaking. I was angry — angry with the possibility of walking into a trap. Angry with the entire city, which was falling apart all around us. Angry with the world.

"We need to go," I told Barack.

"Now?"

"Now."

We headed for the door.

"Um, guys?" Taylor said. "Aren't you forgetting something?"

We turned around. The biker was still in the chair in the middle of the room, hands cuffed in his lap. Taylor was staring at us like a dog waiting for a treat.

"You're right," Barack said. "We did forget something."

Taylor watched with eager eyes as Barack returned for him. Instead of freeing him, however, Barack clocked the side of his head with the butt of the shotgun. The biker sat there, dazed for a second or two. Then his eyes rolled back and he fell to the side off the chair, like a tree axed by a lumberjack.

I was breathing heavy. If we'd been straddling the legal fence until this point, we were now completely on the other side.

Barack slid into the passenger seat of my

Challenger. "We'll be back after we're finished. Until then, he can sleep it off."

I pulled out of the lot, tugging my visor down to keep the glare of the setting sun out of my eyes. After a few minutes on the road, Barack turned to me. "Joe Tingler."

"What?" I said.

"Are we using codenames now? Because if we are, you need a better one."

"Joe Tingler sounds cool."

"You've never been interested in being cool," Barack said. "We're a couple of politicians. We're as square as it gets."

"Oh, cut it. You're like the coolest guy I know. That's no bullshit. It doesn't even have anything to do with you being black."

Barack's eyes grew wide. "I'm going to pretend you didn't say that."

"The part about you being black or —"

"Just keep your eyes on the road."

39

Wilmington's Riverfront district sat along the banks of the Christina River. The Christina was more of a flooded culvert than a river, but nobody could argue its serene beauty. The Riverfront dated to the 1990s and represented Wilmington's last successful attempt at gentrification. There were a few condos and town homes for the young set. There was a smattering of hip bars and restaurants, meant to draw the suburbanites downtown. The multimillion-dollar revitalization project had been propped up by the city's taxpayers, who were still paying for it.

The crown jewel of the district was the Riverwalk, a brightly lit paved path that followed the riverbank. I couldn't remember the last time I'd gone for a walk down here with Jill. Apart from some live acoustic music coming from one of the bars, the Riverwalk was quiet. Foot traffic was light. A few geese waddled on the water's edge, squawking at Barack and me as we passed. They were probably used to getting fed by visitors. We had nothing to give them.

A couple out for a late-night jog trotted past without another look. At my suggestion, we'd upgraded our undercover duds. I'd ducked into a mall for a change of clothes. Barack's biceps stretched out the arm holes in his Tapout T-shirt. My zippered hoodie hung off my shoulders like a towel on a rack. We also had new caps, sneakers, and oversized shorts.

Barack wasn't too happy with what I'd picked out for him. "We're crossing our fingers that Joe Q. Public doesn't recognize us dressed up like idiots, but that our mystery caller does."

"We're not dressed like idiots, we're dressed like teenagers."

"There's a difference?"

The lights were on at the minor league baseball stadium to our right. "Want to watch a few pitches through the outfield fence?" I asked Barack. "We've got some time to kill."

"Come down to DC," he said. "The Nationals are on a tear this year."

"I'm not sold on the Nats' bullpen."

"Everybody's got a weakness," Barack said. "You just have to find it."

"You've got a weakness?" I said.

He didn't answer.

I glanced at my watch. Some forty minutes had passed since I'd spoken to the anonymous caller.

"You should head back to the car," I told Barack. "My phone says the ice cream stand is just ahead. I'm supposed to come alone."

"You don't want me to hang back by the trees?"

The trees were all new growth. They'd been planted twenty years ago. Barack may have been thin, but even he would have a hard time hiding out in the scrawny woods.

"I can take care of myself," I said. "I'll be safe. Promise."

Barack eyed me suspiciously. "You have an idea of who this is."

The caller said I'd recognize them, so I was assuming we'd met before. Of course, the distorted voice didn't give me much to go on. Dan was on my short list, but we'd already met him once today. He'd said he wouldn't be helping us again. Also on the short list was the insurance fraud investigator, Abbey Todd. But her identity had checked out, and I didn't see what else she could do for me. My money was on either Lieutenant Esposito or one of the DEA agents.

Regardless of the caller's identity, I wasn't armed. I was headed up shit creek without a paddle. If Barack had any backup plans, he hadn't shared them. Which surprised me, if I'm being honest. Barack was a man of action, but he rarely did anything without thinking it over thoroughly first. The maddening part of his process was that he never shared what he was thinking with anyone, including those closest to him. That included me. I flew by the seat of my pants — when I dropped a new policy objective in one of my speeches, it wasn't because I'd thought it over for days or weeks without telling anyone. It was because the idea just popped into my mind, and gosh darn it, I was going to say what was on my mind, even if it cost me votes.

A thick cloud cover had moved in. I could tell just by the ozone in the air that a storm was on the way. The change in weather had also brought humidity so thick you could bottle it and sell it on the street corner. That was Delaware during the summer. If you didn't like it, just do what everyone else did: Complain. Incessantly. It was a beloved pastime in the First State.

I wasn't sweating, though. I should have been. Maybe I was retaining water because of the heat. The scary thing was, I hadn't hit the men's room all day. That wasn't a good sign for a fella whose prostate sends him to the restroom every hour most nights.

I sent Barack on his way. He disappeared back toward the car. I was all alone. If I ran into trouble, I'd call him. Or 911. Or both. Cell phones give you the illusion of protection, but are no real help if things really get rough. Same as guns. Most gunfights are over within seconds. There is rarely enough time for a victim to pull their piece. There's something powerful about the illusion of protection, though. Something comforting.

I eyed every stranger who passed me, looking for some sign that they were the caller who'd promised me the one thing that had been eluding me. *Justice.* I hadn't told Barack about the caller's promise. The word was so vague as to be meaningless. And besides, justice meant different things to different people.

Like a mirage in the desert, an ice cream stand materialized just ahead. A sign announced PEE-WEE PENGUIN'S ICE CREAM IGLOO in rainbow-colored letters. There was a mascot, too: a friendly-looking penguin with a scarf and stocking cap, holding an ice cream cone. Another sign promised: SEVEN FLAVORS AND TOPPINGS.

Let's just say it was no Baskin-Robbins.

I joined a line of half a dozen adults and a handful of kids. There were no mysterious lurkers in the trees nearby. In fact, I was probably the most mysterious person around, since I was still wearing my sunglasses. The sun was on its last legs, and the streetlights along the Riverwalk had already kicked on.

The bug-eyed teenager in the window leaned out to take my order. "Nice shades," he said. Something about the way he said it told me he was ribbing me.

"One scoop, chocolate chip." I cracked my wallet. "Waffle cone."

"I've got this," a woman's voice said from behind me.

I turned my head.

Abbey Todd.

I instinctively flinched. My body remembered what she'd done to it earlier. I relaxed, however, when I saw that she didn't have any high heels in her hands. She was wearing flats now. Her long hair was gone — it had been a wig all along, I realized. Clever girl.

She paid for my cone and we headed down the pathway. The old industrial district's streetlights were visible upriver. We were a mile away from where this whole thing had begun. Right here, God willing, was where it would all end. If Abbey came through on her promise, that is.

I took a seat on a bench. We were close to the water and the gnats were swarming, which meant we'd get bitten to holy heck. It also meant we had the riverbank to ourselves.

"How's the ice cream?" she said.

"Good, but I've had better. There are too many chips, which overwhelms the vanilla. If I'd wanted chocolate, I'd have ordered chocolate."

"You're welcome."

If she expected a thank-you, she'd wait a long time.

A light rain started to fall. I pulled my hood up.

"You told me you had answers," I said. "Who are you with? The DEA? The FBI?"

"You have my business card," she said.

"Delmar Investigations, right? How big's this outfit?"

"You're looking at the entire outfit right here."

An ice cream headache stabbed me between the eyes. It was nothing compared to the headache I'd been living with for the past two days.

"Sorry, brain freeze," I said, pinching the bridge of my nose. "So tell me about this justice you promised."

She paced in front of the bench. "We'll get there. But first you have to realize this is all highly confidential. Not to mention there's a lot of money on the line for the insurance company that retained me."

"How much?"

"Enough for them to retain me," she said without a hint of arrogance.

"If you're not supposed to tell me anything you've discovered, why are you doing it?"

She swatted at a swarm of gnats. "I've been asking myself the same question. I could lose business over this. I could lose my license. I didn't know Finn Donnelly. Everything I know about you I learned online. I didn't even vote for you."

"For which race?"

"Any of them," she said. "I wasn't old enough."

"Not even in 2012?"

She shook her head. "Turned eighteen two days after the election."

I didn't have to do any math to know that she was only a few birthdays past drinking age. My first reaction was that she was too young to help me. That's exactly what I'd been, once upon a time: too young. And the people of Delaware not only gave me the time of day, they actually sent me to the U.S. Senate.

"So why are you here, talking to me? With everything on the line."

"I guess because . . . it's the right thing to do. Does that make sense?"

"It makes sense," I said. "It makes all the sense in the world."

40

Abbey Todd hadn't set out to be the Sam Spade of corporate investigations. That was just the way things worked out. She'd always had an insatiable curiosity for the world around her. The world was made of onions, she said. She couldn't stop herself from peeling away the layers.

"I started working crowdsourced cold cases at thirteen," she told me, without stopping to explain what any of that gobbledygook meant. "I caught my first serial killer before I even had my first kiss."

She'd been heavily recruited both by law enforcement agencies and by Silicon Valley, but found that she liked working on her own too much to slog away inside a government or corporate office. I asked if she'd considered college.

She said she hadn't even taken the SAT.

Abbey started her own private-investigation business while still in high school. There wasn't much money in it. "Nobody took me seriously," she said.

"Because you looked like a cheerleader?"

She scrunched her face up. "Because I wore braces."

From then on I decided to keep my mouth shut while she talked.

Abbey was drawn into insurance-fraud claims investigations by a friend on a message board. I assume she meant an online message board, because I was beginning to get the feeling she'd lived most of her life in front of a screen.

Unlike most of her criminal and civil cases, her insurance-fraud investigations promised serious sums of money. Enough that, if she played her cards right, she could be her own boss after graduation.

Five years later, she was one of the top investigators on the East Coast in her particular area of expertise: life-insurance fraud. That's how she came to be involved in Finn Donnelly's case.

"It looked like it was going to be easy," she said. "He died under suspicious circumstances not long after taking out his policy. There were drugs involved. Twenty-four hours, I figure. Twenty-four hours and I'd be home. I was so confident I didn't even give my key to anyone to take care of my cats."

"Are your cats going to be okay?"

"They're very resourceful," was all she said.

"So what changed your mind? When did you realize this wasn't an open-and-shut case?"

"When the president and vice president stumbled into the deceased's motel room."

I felt my face flush.

"There was more, of course. The heroin in Finn's pocket was powder, in a baggie. Ninety-five percent of the heroin in this town is black tar from Baltimore. It's sold in small quantities in —"

"Balloons."

"You've done your homework."

I didn't say anything. Taylor had lied to us, but he'd been smart enough to pepper his story with enough truthful details to make sure it would check out. He wasn't as dumb as he pretended to be.

Abbey said she contacted a friend at the Drug Enforcement Agency to see if he knew how an Amtrak conductor might have encountered this specific kind of heroin. "And that's when I learned Finn Donnelly was already under investigation by the DEA."

If learning about Finn's death was a shock, this was an electrocution. I knew I wasn't going to like what she said next.

"He'd been running drugs for an outlaw biker gang," she said. "They're not competing with the local dealers who traffic from Baltimore to Wilmington. They're operating on a bigger scale, up and down the East Coast."

"The Marauders."

"You're familiar with them?"

"I've heard of them."

Finn knew the Amtrak security protocols inside and out. He knew when the drug dogs came through on sweeps. He knew the undercover Amtrak narcotics detectives. On his daily route, he could move product unmolested across half the eastern seaboard.

"Why didn't the DEA bust him?" I asked.

"It takes time to build a case. My contact didn't give me all the details. Either because he doesn't have them, or because they're so close to making a move that they don't want to risk upsetting the entire house of cards." She stopped pacing. "So that's where we're at now."

"If this is true . . . do you think he stepped in front of that train on purpose?"

"I know what the engineer, Alvin Harrison, told the police. I've read the preliminary findings from the transportation board. Finn Donnelly was lying on the tracks — a 'trespasser,' in their parlance. Either asleep, unconscious, or . . ."

"Dead."

"We'll know a little more when we get those blood test results. But they're not going to tell us the full story. I'd say he knew the DEA was onto him. My best guess is he got high to numb the pain of what he was about to do and then laid down on the tracks. He may not have even been thinking about his life insurance policy at the time. He just wanted out."

"There was a map," I said.

"A map?"

"With my address. The police found it on the train, at his desk. You don't know anything about that?"

She shook her head. "I assumed you were involved in the case because he was your friend."

"He was my friend."

"Then maybe he wanted your help. Maybe he thought you could help him cut a deal with the DEA."

"I once told him that if he ever needed my help, he could look me up. I thought he'd ask me to help move a bookcase or something." I shook my head. "If all you've got is bad news, why'd you ask me to meet you here? It sounds like you've finished your report. You're convinced this was a suicide."

"I didn't promise you good news. I promised you justice. As in the truth."

I thanked her for letting me know what she'd discovered, even if it hadn't been what I'd wanted to hear. As Khaled Hosseini writes, it's better to get hurt by the truth than comforted with a lie. I wanted to believe that she was a liar. She'd passed Steve's background check, but so had Finn. Still, in my heart of hearts, I couldn't deny that all the pieces were falling into place. It wasn't her fault if I didn't like the picture.

We shook hands and she started to walk away.

"Oh," I said, calling out to her from the bench. "One more thing."

She turned her head.

"Thanks for the ice cream," I said.

41

Barack was waiting for me in the Challenger. I slipped behind the wheel.

"Remember the woman from the motel? Abbey Todd?"

"The one who gave you the shiner at the Donnellys' place," Barack said.

"She has a friend in the DEA," I said. "They were shadowing Finn before he died on the tracks. We can stop waiting on those blood test results to see if he was high because it doesn't matter. We can stop worrying about whether that was his blood at the motel. Everything I didn't want to believe about him . . . it was all true."

I brought Barack up to speed on what Abbey had told me. He didn't seem surprised by any of it.

Sirens wailed in the distance. We'd heard so many sirens these past two days, and I hadn't ever noticed. The noises of the city faded into the background when you weren't listening for them.

Barack took some time before speaking. I could tell he was analyzing everything in his mind, trying to make sense of the chaos. Rain pattered on the roof of the car, like spent casings from an automatic weapon.

Finally, he said, "Whatever Finn did, he did it for Darlene. For love."

"Is that what people do for love? Would you do that for me?"

"You're my best friend, Joe. Michelle and our family are part of the Biden clan, through the good times and bad. I already told you that if anyone messes with you, they mess with me. That's what family means. C'mon, Joe, I know I'm not the only one who misses our weekly lunches. You and me, we're like the Three Amigos. Only there's two of us."

If he expected a laugh from that line, he was in for a rude awakening. "Best friends talk to each other," I shot back. "All we've been doing is talking *over* one another. You haven't called or texted me in how long, and then you show up and expect everything to be the same?"

"You never called or texted me either. I thought you wanted to keep your distance."

"Why would you think I wanted to avoid you?"

"Because if you want to have any shot in the next election, you have to step out of my shadow. I thought that was obvious."

"Your shadow's not a bad place to be right now. Your approval rating —"

"Nostalgia for a bygone era. I leave office, and suddenly Obamacare becomes popular? It's flattering, but it says more about the current administration than it does about me. The truth is that I failed, Joe. I had my eight years. There were some wins, but they were few and far between. The slate's being wiped clean. If anything, we're going backward."

"If you failed, then so did I. I was there every step of the way."

Barack didn't say anything.

"But," I added, "I don't think you failed. I've been in this game longer than you. You've got to have patience. It takes more than eight years to build a legacy — and it takes more than a term or two to reshape the world. Change happens incrementally."

"That sounds like something I said."

"If it is, I'll be sure to give you proper credit," I said with a small laugh.

Barack smiled. For a split second, we felt like friends again.

Only for a split second.

"I'm sorry about your friend," he said.

"And I'm sorry for dragging you so deep into this. I feel like an idiot."

"It's been a strange weekend, Joe. I would say it's been fun, but there's nothing fun about people dying."

"It got my heart rate up," I said. "There's that."

More silence.

Finally, Barack said, "Why don't you and Jill come over for brunch next weekend? Michelle would love to see you guys. You could bring the grandkids down. Stay the night. There's plenty of room."

His offer was tempting.

It was also too little too late.

"I appreciate what you've done for me this weekend, Barack — I really do — but it's time for us to go home. And by that I mean for you to head back to the swamp, and for me to head back to the Lake House."

"Joe —"

"I need a little space. It's for my own good, right? Isn't that what you said?"

"Don't be like that."

"Be like what? Upset? I have a right to be upset. Our little adventure this weekend was just fun and games to you. I see it in your eyes. To me it was personal . . . It doesn't matter now. It's over. With any luck, I can sweet-talk Esposito into keeping my name out of the news, or at least reducing me to a footnote. But that would be par for the course, wouldn't it? I've never been anything more than a footnote."

"You weren't a footnote to me. You were my vice president. You were also my friend."

"Friends back each other up."

"What's that supposed to mean?"

"I thought you were going to cover me tonight."

"You told me not to. You said you wanted to go meet your mystery man alone. You're not seriously mad about that, are you?"

"If I'd been in your shoes, I would have *never* let you do something that stupid."

"No offense, but I would never do something that stupid."

"So that's how it is, huh? Just another case of 'Joe being Joe.' "

Barack placed a hand on the dash. "Joe —"

"Don't 'Joe' me this time," I said, starting the car. "Don't ever 'Joe' me again."

Barack's silence spoke volumes. He and I were through — this time, for good. It wasn't Barack's call. It was mine. I drove him back to his Escalade in the Waffle Depot parking lot, and we parted ways without another word.

42

I was halfway home when I remembered our pal T-Swizzle still handcuffed inside the storage unit. The unit was climate-controlled, so there was no chance of him overheating. Still, he would cause me a heck of a lot of trouble if he started screaming his head off and was discovered by some Nosy Nellie. Although I was tired, I phoned Dan and told him to meet me at the storage facility. I said I had a gift for him.

I arrived before Dan. I knelt low and unlocked the padlock. Before I could roll the garage door up, there was a cough from behind me.

It was Dan, half shrouded in darkness. He must have parked somewhere out of sight.

"Jumpin' Jesus on a pogo stick, you scared me there, Dan."

He stepped out of the shadows. "There is no federal investigation. I had a friend check with Service headquarters. You lied to me, Joe."

I rose to my feet. "We didn't have much choice. I just wanted the details kept out of the paper, at least until the funeral."

"But after the funeral, you kept up the lie. What's your excuse for that? You told me this afternoon you wouldn't do anything stupid, and here you are. You say you've got a 'gift' for me. I'm afraid to ask what it is."

"It's a Marauder."

"A —" His mouth dropped open. "You've got one of their hogs in there?"

"I've got one of *them* in there."

"Jesus, Joe. You have some sort of death wish?"

"We're all dead men walking. The road to the Reaper's just longer for some of us."

"You're not just acting like a cop anymore. Now you sound like one too."

I snorted. "Any updates on Alvin?"

"He overdosed. Not sure what you mean."

"Nothing suspicious?"

"They were his pills, legally prescribed. He was trying to end his life." Dan paused. "He was successful. Men usually are, you know. Once they make up their minds, there's no stopping them. He made it easy on us, though — he left a note."

"Notes can be faked."

"They can. An expert will need to review it, but it appears to be in his handwriting. I'm sure you have some sort of wild conspiracy theory, right?"

Alvin was in bad shape at Finn's funeral. In a sense he'd killed his coworker, or at least believed he had. But could he have killed himself? It was possible. Amtrak would have offered him grief counseling, but there is no way to predict how fast and how hard grief can hit you. He could have had the pills on hand. There are more than enough prescription drugs in the average American household's medicine cabinet to do the job.

Dan shoved his hands in his pockets. "For what it's worth, Alvin wrote that he was sorry for what happened. Said there was blood on his hands." He shook his head. "Senseless. All over an accident."

"You're still convinced Finn's death was an accident."

"The transportation board measured the stopping speed, the distances, all that. There was no way to avoid hitting Finn. Alvin blew the whistle. Whether Finn walked onto the tracks on purpose or stumbled because he was high on something . . . It wasn't Alvin's fault."

"How long before we know if there were

drugs in Alvin's system when he hit Finn?"

"We have the results. He was clean."

"I thought it took weeks to get the results back. You said that even with an expedited time frame, we wouldn't know —"

"And we still don't know for sure about Finn. The transportation board has their own labs they go through. None of this explains what Finn Donnelly was doing out there on the tracks, but it does put a bow around one mystery. We can close the case on Alvin Harrison."

I steadied myself with a hand on the door. "I don't know what to believe. Just twenty-four hours ago, if you'd told me that Finn had been involved in drugs — that he'd been smuggling them — I'd have said you were crazy." I paused. "I think I pretty much did say that."

He arched an eyebrow. "Smuggling?"

"According to the DEA."

"You've spoken to them?"

"Not personally, no," I said. "A couple of drug enforcement agents stopped by to speak with Grace Donnelly this afternoon. Maybe 'speak' isn't the right word. They tossed the place like a tornado in a trailer park."

"What were they looking for?"

"If I knew for sure, I'd tell you. There was

a search warrant and everything. I didn't want to believe it, but the more I put together, the more I realize how wrong I might have been about Finn. It's looking like he wasn't just using — he was smuggling."

"For the Marauders? Is that where this is leading?"

I shrugged. "Talk to the DEA."

"They don't always keep us in the loop. Worried about leaks. Damn feds got to stick their snouts in everything, don't they? No offense."

"None taken."

"This thing is turning into a real mess, isn't it? If the DEA tries raiding the Marauders' clubhouse . . . well, I already told you. Biker gangs aren't known for going out quietly. Have you shared what you know about the DEA investigation with the lieutenant?"

"We're not on the best of terms right now."

Dan ran a hand through his thick hair. "Joe, Joe, Joe . . . I don't even know where to begin. You don't know what you're getting yourself into, you really don't. I've been sticking my neck out to help you, but I feel like you just keep getting deeper. I don't want to see you get hurt. So I say this as a friend: stick to the suburbs — it's safer out there."

"Wilmington is my city, too. I know she has her problems —"

"Problems? Delaware is the corporate capital of the world. Over half of all Fortune 500 companies are chartered here. You think a single one of those companies cares about what's really going on in this city? For a place whose motto is 'A Place to Be Somebody,' a whole lot of people in Wilmington sure are treated like nobodies."

I didn't say anything. A light rain started to fall again.

"We have one of the highest rates of homicide per capita in the United States for a city of this size," he continued. "Gang violence and drug trafficking are out of control. The opioid crisis might be new to your neck of the woods, but we've been fighting the drug war inside the city limits for so long that we've forgotten why we even started."

"If the department needs money, I can get you money," I said. "There are federal funds available. I still have friends in Congress. Barack was a community organizer —"

"You're not listening to me," he said. "I'm telling you that it's a lost cause."

"The city?"

"The city. This damn case you keep picking at. Everything. More money would mean more officers on patrol. But it's a superficial fix. There are people who get shot in broad daylight in the middle of a crowded street, and nobody talks to us. Two dozen witnesses. Not one will come forward. The problems run deep in this city."

The problems ran deep in the entire country. I might have been Irish, but I wasn't stupid. I told him I was done playing amateur sleuth. I'd leave the detective work up to the real detectives from now on.

I tossed him the pocket watch.

"What's this?"

"It was Finn's. I found it in the biker's pocket."

"He's a Marauder, you said?"

I nodded. "Goes by T-Swizzle. Real name Taylor Brownsford. You know him?"

"The name's familiar, but I can't place him."

I dangled the key for Dan. "He's handcuffed inside."

"Will you testify in court that you found this on him?" he asked, taking the key.

"If it comes down to it."

Dan opened the watch. "This doesn't prove anything because the chain of custody is broken, but it might be enough to break him down during an interrogation. I take it you've already tried."

"Didn't get anywhere."

"We'll take over now. Maybe we'll get somewhere, maybe not. Bottom line is this is what detectives do every day." He placed a hand on my shoulder. "I appreciate what you've done, Joe. Really, truly appreciate it. So don't take this the wrong way . . . but why don't you make like a tree and get the hell out of here."

He laughed.

I didn't.

I returned to my car in the lot out front. The rain had stopped again. I sat in my car with the windows down, smelling that after-rain smell. Even though I'd pointed Dan in the right direction, I'd abused his trust. Another relationship was on the rocks. I was having some kind of night.

43

I hit the sack without flossing or brushing my teeth. Jill didn't wake when I kissed her goodnight, and that was probably for the best. As I was drifting off to sleep, I remembered I'd forgotten my prescription pills for the second night in a row. If skipping a few days' worth of statins and alpha-blockers was what finally killed me, then I deserved to be weeded out of the gene pool.

When I woke up, I found myself in the middle of the cemetery. I was lying on my back, with the sun beating down on my face. A gentle breeze was rustling the unmowed grass.

Far away, I heard a *thump-thump, thump-thump, thump-thump.* Like a racing heartbeat. The louder it grew, the more distinct it became. It wasn't a heartbeat at all. It was the trotting of hooves. Big, heavy horse hooves.

I sat up just as a white horse emerged

from over a hill. A faceless rider snapped the reins and flew down the slope of the hill, dodging broken tombstones and barren trees. The hooves pounded louder and louder, as if the sound was coming from inside my own head. *Thump-thump, thump-thump, thump-thump . . .*

The closer the horse came, the more indistinct its shape. It was so white that it was glowing. Looking at it was like staring into the sun during an eclipse; I was forced to look away.

Just when it sounded like the horse was about to run me down, the animal came to an abrupt stop. It was so close now, I could feel its warm breath on me. I was vaguely aware that I was dreaming, but every sensation was so vibrant. I desperately wanted it all to be real.

"Need a hand?"

I peeked at the figure on the horse's back through cracks in my fingers. My eyes slowly adjusted to the light emanating from the horse, and the figure came into focus. It was Barack Obama, clad in a white toga.

He pulled me to my feet.

"Thanks," I said. "You wouldn't believe the dream I've had."

"Try me."

"You came to see me one night, and said

my friend had been hit by a train . . . and . . . is that a unicorn?" I asked, squinting at the curled horn sprouting up between the horse's ears.

"I call her Little Beast."

I ran my fingers through the unicorn's silken hair, which left rainbow glitter on my hand. The headache that had plagued me off and on all weekend was gone. There was no pain in my knee, or anywhere else in my body. "Is this heaven?"

"No," Barack said. "It's Iowa."

And then suddenly we weren't in the cemetery anymore. We were on a baseball diamond at the edge of a cornfield. The stalks towered over my head, whispering in the wind.

"I — I don't understand," I stammered.

"Hop on," Barack said. "We don't have much time."

"Where are we going?"

"To set up your campaign headquarters, of course."

"I haven't even decided if I'm running," I said.

What I truly wanted — honest-to-God — was for somebody new to step up in the Democratic Party. Somebody younger. Somebody with fresh ideas. Somebody who had two knees that worked. This was all happening too fast.

"It's now or never, Joe. What's it going to be?"

Before I could give him an answer, my alarm went off.

44

I woke up facedown on top of the bed-spread, still dressed in my clothes from the night before. Daylight filtered into the room through the blinds. I didn't have to look at my clock to know that I'd hit the snooze button more than once. Thankfully, Jill was used to that by now.

I rolled onto my back. Jill's side of the bed was made. She was probably downstairs reading. I could only imagine what she'd thought when she awakened to find some old guy in a hoodie and sagging jean shorts next to her. I prayed she'd forgive me for scaring the bejesus out of her, but I knew it was going to take a lot more than prayer. A trip to the florist might be in order. This time, I'd open my wallet for the roses.

There was a yellow sticky note in the middle of the bathroom mirror:

THERE'S A BAG OF FROZEN PEAS IN

I caught a glimpse of myself in the mirror.
My face bulged in odd places, places I
wasn't even aware I'd been hit. The bruising underneath my eye had ripened into a
good ol' fashioned shiner, the kind you get
from taking a fastball to the face. The only
good news was that it looked worse than it
felt.

My left knee, on the other hand, was a
different story. It looked like an overripe
peach. As I changed into my khakis, sharp
pains shot up my thigh like lightning bolts.
There was no telling when it would give out
next.

I took one look at the stairs and decided
to hold the railing with both hands. I
couldn't smell any coffee. "Jill?" I called out
on my way down.

No answer.

There was a stack of mail waiting for me
on the kitchen table, but no Jill. I shuffled
through it disinterestedly. A couple of
magazines I'd subscribed to because of a
fundraiser my grandkids were mixed up in.
A utility bill, which was always paid auto-
matically online. A letter addressed to me,
with no return address — either fan mail or

hate mail, neither of which I was in a hurry to read.

Jill had left another note for me on the cereal box above the fridge.

AT BRUNCH WITH ALICE. TOOK CHAMP. BOTTOMLESS MIMOSAS, SO BACK BY ??? — LOVE, JILL

That explained that. While eating breakfast, I looked around for something to read, but the newspaper was in the living room. It seemed so far away, now that I'd sat down. It was going to be impossible to hide my injured knee from Jill. Not that I'd even contemplated it.

Okay, maybe I'd thought about it. I wouldn't say I "contemplated" it, though.

I picked up the *New Yorker*. The cartoons always made me guffaw, but the writing wasn't my speed. We had six months' worth of back issues stacked on the back of our toilet. One day the tower was going to tip and break someone's neck while they were doing their business on the john. The subscription was in Jill's name, so she'd be the one getting sued, not me.

The cartoons didn't grab me this time. Not after the weekend I'd had.

I decided to open the fan letter. Jill liked

to tease me about them, until we got a couple of threatening ones. The Secret Service always dealt with those. Since then, I'd just been stacking the letters in my office. I sometimes thought about hiring an assistant to handle the paperwork, but didn't have the income to support the idea just yet. Maybe I needed to do some of those Wall Street speaking gigs that Barack had been making bank on. Trouble was, as soon as you went down that route, you were just spoon-feeding ammunition to your political opponents. It was only trouble if I ran for office again, though . . .

I peeked into the envelope to make sure there wasn't any white powder before removing the letter. You can't be too careful these days. As if you ever could. It looked reasonably anthrax-free, though. I unfolded the letter. It was a regular-sized sheet of typing paper, folded into thirds.

The letter was addressed to me. Both front and back were covered in cursive handwriting. The penmanship was legible, but looked like it had been scrawled out on an uneven surface — in several spots, the pen had poked through the paper. At the bottom of the second page, the letter was signed, *Yours, Finn Donnelly.*

I dropped my spoon onto the table. Of

course. This was why Finn had printed off my address. He didn't have a cell phone. He just searched online and printed the first page he'd found: a map.

I read the letter through once, and then a second time just to be sure I hadn't imagined any of it.

I hadn't.

Breakfast time was over.

Upstairs, I dug out my brown leather bomber jacket from the back of our walk-in closet. I'd already replaced my T-shirt with a navy-blue polo shirt; now I undid the top button. I picked up my Ray-Bans from the nightstand. Slipped them on.

I couldn't have looked more like Joe Biden than if I'd been playing myself in a Joe Biden biopic. Finn Donnelly didn't need Joe Tingler right now; Finn Donnelly needed Joe Biden.

I stopped in my office. The Medal of Freedom was sitting on my desk, where I'd left it Friday night. When Barack had bestowed it upon me, he'd said I was "as good a man as God ever created." Even if the president and I were no longer speaking — even if we never spoke again — just looking at this medal was enough to remind me of all that I'd once been. Of all that I could be again. Of all that I could be right now, today, for Finn. I slipped the medal inside my jacket pocket and headed out.

As the garage door lifted, I started the Challenger. It rumbled to life. Every muscle in my body was vibrating, as if I was in an electric massage chair. A good massage was what I would need after this was all said and done. But first, Wilmington Station. And then Baltimore . . . where Finn's duffel bag was waiting for me.

45

I was waiting like a cat on hot bricks at the counter of the Baltimore Penn Station lost and found. The employee had disappeared into the back room to search for the duffel bag. He was young, portly, and had a bad haircut. Most kids had bad haircuts these days. Too many of them looked like Hitler youth. Heck, too many of them *were* Hitler youth.

The kid seemed decent enough, but he was taking a lot longer in back than I'd expected. Was he on the phone with security? I worried I was being watched, but I didn't dare look around. No reason to act overly suspicious. I was just a guy picking up a duffel bag full of heroin.

I'd taken the first train out of Wilmington, a Northeast Regional. It was the slower cousin of the high-speed Acela, but much faster than driving bumper-to-bumper on I-95. I'd already spent too much time behind the wheel over the weekend.

The regional train was cheaper, though, and that meant more riffraff. Since business class had been full, too, it turned out to be the first time in decades that Amtrak's most famous passenger sat amongst the working stiffs. Instead of feeling out of place, however, I discovered that I felt right at home. I struck up a conversation with the lovely woman seated next to me, and we chatted about our grandkids all the way to Baltimore. It was a welcome distraction from the chaos of the previous week.

But it wasn't enough to distract me from the letter.

Dear Joe,

I hope this letter finds you well.

Things are not going so good on my end. In January, Darlene had a stroke. She is over at Baptist Manor. We do not know if she will recover. All I want to do is bring her home. As you can imagine the costs involved are more than we can afford. This is not to excuse my actions, because there is no excuse.

I met some men one morning at Waffle Depot, who told me, "How would you like to make some extra money." I said, "What do I have to do." They said, "Take

317

this bag with you to DC and give it to somebody." I asked what is in the bag, they said, "Do you want the money or not."

I knew the men were drug dealers. Still I said, "Yes."

The first couple of runs went fine. The money was good. I didn't open the bags, but I had an idea what was in them. We (Amtrak conductors) got a notice to be on the lookout for increased trafficking. Specifically "opioids." Agencies were doing stings on the interstate, and the DEA thought dealers might try alternate routes. I had to laugh at that one, because the DEA was a little late to the party.

Last week, my daughter tells me a girl in her dorm overdosed on heroin. "I thought only junkies overdosed," I said. This girl was a college kid at Georgetown. On the volleyball team. Good grades.

She lived. The next might not.

I never opened the bags, so I can't say for sure what I was transporting. But it wasn't marijuana. The dealers were paying me too much to move a little pot.

There is a black duffel bag in lost and found at the station in Baltimore. I told the man at the counter someone left it in the men's room. I think they believed me. The perks of wearing a uniform!

The drug dealers are in a motorcycle group. "The Murder Town Marauders." I do not know their real names, but the one guy who gave me the bags and the money calls himself "Texas."

I do not know what the men are going to do when they find out I didn't deliver the bag. The men say they are being protected by the police, so I cannot go to them. I do not know if I can trust other government agencies. You are the only one I can trust right now who might be able to help me.

Your friend,
Finn Donnelly

P.S. I am sorry. Give my best to Dr. Biden.

The lost-and-found employee finally returned. He was holding a black duffel bag. Instead of being relieved, my heart sped up. I could feel sweat forming on my brow.

It was real. It was suddenly all too real.

"Is this it?" he asked.

I had no way of knowing. It was black, and it was a duffel bag. It would have to do.

"That looks like it," I said. I tried to smile like I'd just been reunited with a long-lost friend. I suppose it was true, in a way.

The kid heaved it onto the counter with a huff. He reminded me that, in the future, I might want to place a luggage tag on my bags. I said I'd keep it in mind, and reached for the bag.

"Wait," he said, slapping his forehead. "I forgot to have you identify what's in the bag. I'm so sorry, Mr. Vice President."

I kept my grin up, but inwardly was hitting the panic button. "What's in the bag?"

"I know it sounds stupid, that you'd want to take someone else's old gym clothes," he said. "I trust you, go ahead and take it. But you can't be too careful these days, especially after 9/11." He whispered the date like it was a naughty word. "Just so you know, we go through everything that's brought in — not to be nosy, just to be safe. You might want to make sure everything's in there. Sometimes things get misplaced."

The kid didn't look old enough to remember how lax security had been before September 11, but I let it slide. "I'm sure all of my . . . old gym clothes . . . are in there," I said, taking the bag off the counter. It wasn't much heavier than a bag of gym clothes. Could there really be enough drugs in it to be worth killing someone over?

Nobody stopped me as I crossed the concourse. Nobody swarmed in with guns drawn and told me to drop the bag and get on the ground. Still, I lowered my head and quickened my pace until I reached the men's room.

Inside a locked stall, I set the bag on the back of the toilet. There was piss all over the seat. I'd never understand how some men couldn't aim their pistols. Half of 'em probably had handguns at home, too — a terrifying prospect.

I unzipped the duffel bag quickly, like I was tearing off a Band-Aid. I knew there was no reason to draw things out. It wasn't going to change what was inside.

I breathed deep and looked.

Sneakers.

A couple of T-shirts.

A pair of shorts.

A Monster energy drink.

That was it.

I rifled through the bag, feeling for a false bottom or hidden compartments. Nothing. Finn had given me one job, and in the end I'd failed him. Taylor and his biker buddies had been searching for the bag all week — in Darlene's room at Baptist Manor, at the Donnellys' home in Riverside. Had they beat me here?

I stuffed everything back in the bag. I could return to the lost-and-found counter later, when somebody else was working. See if there was another black duffel bag. *Damn you, Finn,* I thought. I knew why he hadn't left his name and address inside the bag, but he could have done *something.* Of course, it was futile to get upset with him. He'd been working with what he had. He hadn't planned this out. He'd been acting impulsively. I could hear Jill's voice in my head: *Now who does that remind you of, Joe?*

Wait.

I pulled the energy drink out again. Finn and I might have both been impulsive, but we both had something else in common: we didn't drink alcohol . . . and we didn't drink caffeine. The likelihood of Finn buying one of these highfalutin beverages was zero to zilch.

I popped the tab. Though the drink was supposed to be carbonated, there was no release of air. The can weighed about the same as it would if it were filled with liquid, but there wasn't any liquid inside. Instead, there was a plastic bag, packed with bright-white powder and taped up tight. Good night, nurse.

46

I boarded the Acela and took my seat. I'd bought a one-way return ticket on the faster train because I needed to get back to Wilmington as quickly as possible, and there was no faster train in the United States than the Acela. I was back in first class, where there would be less of a chance of talking about my grandkids. People don't pay first-class prices to talk about their families. It wasn't that I'd exhausted the topic — far from it. But it was impossible to think about anything other than the duffel bag in the overhead compartment.

I'd debated calling someone from inside the station, but I couldn't think of a single person eager to help me. Lieutenant Esposito was in charge of the investigation . . . or she had been, until she'd told me the books were basically closed. What I'd handed Dan last night should have been enough to reopen the case, although there was a chance he'd shuffled it over to the narcotics division. The DEA was involved. What their angle was is anyone's guess.

All of this was complicated by the fact that the Marauders alleged they had help from inside the Wilmington PD. I sure hoped this was a bluff. As much as I personally disliked Esposito, she was a good cop. The thought of her or anyone in the department being corrupt was difficult to stomach. Some of my biggest and most loyal supporters work in law enforcement — and I believe they have some of the toughest jobs in this country. But I also believe they're not infallible. None of us are. Not me, not Barack.

Well, maybe Barack.

He would know exactly what to do. Exactly who to contact. As much as it infuriated me sometimes, Barack could always be counted on to have the right answer.

I looked out the window as the train beside us pulled out in the opposite direction. I felt the medal in my pocket. Had I really spoken to Barack Obama for the last time in my life? It didn't seem possible, yet there wasn't any other way to interpret how we'd parted ways. Neither of us had said "goodbye," but it had been a goodbye all the same.

"Is this seat taken?" a man asked, hovering in the aisle beside me.

Without looking up, I motioned that the seat across the table was free.

"Thanks," the man said, sliding into the padded chair.

It was Dan Capriotti.

His appearance on the train was so unexpected, I was having trouble forming thoughts, let alone words.

"Lift your shirt," he said.

"Excuse me?"

He moved his jacket to the side to show the butt of his pistol. "You heard me. Lift your shirt."

The first-class cabin was filling quickly. I waited for the attendant to pass us, and then I leaned in close to Dan. "I'm not armed," I whispered.

"Don't make this any more difficult than it has to be, Joe."

I sighed, and looked around. When I was certain there weren't any prying eyes, I flashed Dan my naked gut for half a second. "Happy?"

"Now your backside," he snapped.

I turned around in my seat and showed off my lower back. "I think there's been some misunderstanding. The bag isn't mine. I was —"

He put a finger to his lips as another passenger scooted past. There were dark circles under Dan's eyes, like he hadn't slept well last night. Or at all. Had the department had me under surveillance? Regardless, he'd caught me red-handed with the duffel bag.

"There's a letter," I said in a hushed tone. "It explains everything."

He glanced around. There were no other police around, unless they were plainclothes like Dan.

"Let's see it," he said wearily.

I dug it out of my pocket. "It's from Finn."

He put on a pair of reading glasses and scanned the letter, front and back. The engineer blew the whistle, and the train slowly pulled out of the station. There were several open seats in first class, including one across the aisle from us. I didn't know if the relative privacy decreased or increased my anxiety.

"He mailed this to you?" Dan asked.

"The envelope's at home. It was post-marked in Maryland. The date was smudged, but it showed up either Friday or Saturday. I didn't see it until this morning, or else I'd have told you about it sooner."

He returned his glasses to inside his jacket. "You could have saved yourself the round trip and called and told me this morning."

"I could have," I conceded. "Lucky for you, you happened to be in Baltimore this morning."

"It wasn't luck. I followed you here."

"Because you suspected me of something."

"Because I knew you weren't finished playing cops and robbers."

The first-class attendant interrupted us with a smile, and dropped a couple menus on our table. It was another new hire. I didn't recognize her, and I didn't introduce myself. She moved on to the next row.

The train was winding out of town at thirty-five, forty miles per hour. The Acela wouldn't hit its maximum speed of a hundred and fifty until later on, and only for a couple of short stretches of track. There were too many twists, too many turns. I'd always wanted to take a high-speed train out west, where there was enough room to really fly.

"You know why they call Delaware the Diamond State?" Dan asked.

"Thomas Jefferson," I said. "He called the state a 'jewel,' because of its prime location on the eastern seaboard."

"It's also a prime location for drug trafficking. Delaware's on a direct route between New York City and DC, with Philly

327

and Baltimore along the way. I-95 was practically paved with illegal drugs, until the DEA started cracking down."

I knew all of this. We were in the midst of a public health crisis that had already proven more lethal than the crack cocaine epidemic of the eighties.

"The Marauders worked out a pretty decent plan," I said. "Finn had the inside track, so to speak. But the bad guys didn't count on one thing."

"What's that?"

"Finn Donnelly had a conscience."

"You believe all this?" Dan said, waving the letter.

"What other explanation is there?"

"Maybe he didn't feel he was getting paid what he deserved. Maybe he wanted a bigger piece of the pie."

"And then he decided to tell me about it?" I said. "No. That doesn't make any sense. Not unless you think Finn and I were in cahoots."

"Were you?"

"How long have we known each other, Dan? I can't believe you'd even ask that."

"You're telling me that when you read this letter, you didn't wonder if *I* was the one protecting the Marauders? Not even for a second?"

"It may have crossed my mind, but —"

"Relax," he said. "I'm just messing with you. Had to ask, though."

My blood pressure was returning to normal. Or what passed for normal these days. "So what happens now?"

"The way I see it, I turn this paper over to my boss, who's been working with the DEA. Your friend's name gets dragged through the mud. Your name gets dragged through the mud. Everybody loses. But that's life, right?"

He paused to gauge my reaction. I didn't have one.

"Or there's a second option," he continued, his voice low. "We forget about this letter. Your friend can rest quietly. No one ever learns about his trafficking scheme. And, most importantly, you walk away clean."

"The bag," I said. "What about the bag?"

Dan shrugged. "I'll turn it in anonymously, like one of those babies left on church doorsteps."

"Don't you need it to convict Taylor Brownsford?"

The attendant stopped for our lunch orders, but neither of us were hungry. Dan watched her walk away and then turned back to me. "Taylor's dead."

"What happened?"

"I had to re-cuff his hands behind his back, you know. His hands were free for half a second, and he went for my gun. There was a struggle. The gun went off." Dan paused. "There was no way he was going to turn state's witness and rat his brothers out. If an outlaw biker flips, he's as good as dead."

I took off my sunglasses and rubbed between my eyes. My headache from yesterday was coming back.

"Everything all right, Joe?"

"I'd rather we went with the first option, that's all," I said, replacing my glasses. "I know there will be fallout from the letter, but I can handle it. Whatever happens, happens. What's important is getting the truth out there. I couldn't live with myself if I had to keep the letter from his daughter. She deserves to know what happened."

"If that's your only objection, we can let her know."

"There's this old joke. Two Irishmen are talking. One has a bag of donuts. He tells the other, 'If you can guess how many donuts are in my bag, you can have them both.'"

I waited for Dan to laugh, but apparently he'd heard that one before.

I continued, "What I'm trying to say is,

the Irish aren't known for keeping secrets. We like to talk, and I can't guarantee the truth wouldn't just slip out of me at some point. So let's get everything logged as evidence. I'll go on the record. Whatever you need me to do."

Dan stashed the letter in his jacket. "You're right. I hope I didn't offend you."

"Offend me?"

"I know you're all about doing the right thing. I'm just trying to look out for you, that's all."

"I appreciate it. Don't get me wrong, I really do appreciate it. It's tempting to just forget about this letter. It would make my life easier. Lord knows, it would make your life easier too, I'd bet."

He shrugged. "Paperwork's part of the job."

"Still, this thing is going to blow up. Whoever's covering for the Marauders down at the station isn't going to be happy. There might be a target on your back."

"You handle yourself. I handle myself." He glanced around the cabin, then leaned across the table. "Say, did you open the bag? Is it all there?"

"There's something there. Whether it's all of it or not, I don't know. Looked like a pound or two, sealed up."

"It's good you didn't touch it. Fentanyl is dangerous stuff. Touch it without rubber gloves, and it can kill you." He snapped his fingers. "Just like that."

"Fentanyl?"

"A synthetic opioid. Dealers cut heroin with it to increase the potency. Fentanyl is fifty times more powerful than heroin. That's why you can fit over a million dollars' worth into a Monster can."

Fentanyl. Of course. Regular heroin was passé. Kids today wanted heroin as extreme as their energy drinks.

Energy drinks . . .

I hadn't told Dan about the energy drink. There was a slim chance he'd gotten the detail from Taylor, but Dan had said Taylor wasn't going to sing. Dan might have known traffickers used vacuum-sealed packages hidden in cans . . . but there was only one way Dan could have known the brand. My left leg was bouncing under the table like a Jack Russell terrier. The first-class attendant was a few rows away, pushing a cart.

"Everything okay, Joe?" Dan asked.

The room was spinning around me. "Stomach's just a little upset. If you'll excuse me."

"Don't let me stop you," he said, gesturing to the aisle. "I'm getting a drink. You

332

want a Sprite or something?"

"Thanks, but I'll manage," I said, heading for the restroom at the end of the car. I didn't look over my shoulder, but I knew that Dan was watching my every move. The train was just about halfway to our destination, humming along at over a hundred miles per hour on the open track. In approximately twenty minutes, we would pull into Wilmington Station. Once the doors opened, Dan would step off . . . and I knew that I'd never see that duffel bag or letter again.

47

"Pick up, pick up . . ."

The line rang and rang. After five rings, Barack answered.

"Thank God!" I shouted, doing a poor job of staying quiet inside the first-class lavatory.

"— but I'm not in right now, so if you'll leave a message after the beep . . ."

I listened to the beep, slack-jawed. By the time Barack discovered I'd called and then tried to ring me back, it would be too late.

I slumped back on the toilet seat. The fact that Dan had come after me by himself — and then suggested we just "forget" the letter — had raised my suspicions. The fact that he knew about the Monster can all but confirmed them. I didn't know if Dan was the dirty cop protecting the Marauders. I just knew that something wasn't adding up.

I wanted somebody with some authority to meet us at Wilmington Station to ensure that Dan didn't go back on his word. I tried dialing Esposito but she didn't answer, either. And I didn't have the direct numbers to the DEA agents who'd hit the Donnellys' home. There were any number of law enforcement agencies I could call. Getting them to believe my identity was a laughable prospect at best. There was a saying in the Biden family: If you have to ask for help, it's already too late . . .

Wait. The train was scheduled to arrive at Wilmington Station in twenty minutes. But what if it was delayed? Regular riders knew that delays were part and parcel of traveling on Amtrak. The frequent holdups were usually attributable to the freight companies who owned the tracks and gave priority to their own trains. If I could manufacture a delay, I could buy some time for Barack or Esposito to get back to me.

Heading straight to the conductor onboard would raise Dan's suspicions. Luckily, I didn't need to get to the conductor directly. I flipped excitedly through my contacts until I found the number I was looking for. The Wilmington Station manager. Grant.

There was a loud knock on the door.

"Somebody's in here," I shouted.

When I returned to my phone, the screen

was dead. I tried powering it back on. No luck. I hadn't plugged it in last night, and hadn't charged it in the car on the way to the station. Jill had stuck one of those mobile chargers in my Christmas stocking last year, but for all I knew it was still in the stocking, somewhere in our basement.

I'd figure out something, though. I always did.

When I returned to my seat, Dan was missing. *Probably in one of the other restrooms,* I thought. *Either that or he decided to hit the café car.*

Five minutes passed, however, and he hadn't returned. I glanced around once more for him, and pulled the duffel bag down from the overhead bin. I tried to look as casual as possible as I rifled through it, but there was no disguising my panic:

The energy drink was gone.

48

My most incriminating evidence was gone. I should have stopped to copy the letter before heading out of the house. I always knew my lack of forethought would land me in a pickle. I never imagined the pickle would be this big.

The first-class car was the last passenger car on the train. That left five other cars where Dan could be waiting: four business-class cars, and the café car sandwiched in between. All of which I had precious few minutes to search. If Dan debarked in Wilmington before I could stop him, it would be his word against mine. My word carried a lot of weight . . . but so did Dan's. He was a decorated officer. To accuse him of wrongdoing without hard proof wouldn't earn me any favors.

I charged into the next car, full of business-class passengers. A few faces looked up, but most people were in their own little worlds, pecking at their cell phones. I moved quickly down the center aisle, checking each seat.

The restroom at the end of the car was unlocked. I checked inside just to be sure Dan wasn't there — no dice. My luck was no better in the next car either.

Then came the café car. At a glance I could tell Dan wasn't there because there were only a handful of seats for passengers. I passed through as fast as I could without bending my legs. "Mallwalking," Jill called it.

"Virgin daiquiri, Mr. Biden?" asked the café car attendant. He had a thin, wispy mustache.

I could have asked him to contact the conductor for me. Any of the first-class attendants could have put me in touch with the conductor as well. Unfortunately, Dan was armed. I couldn't risk involving any of these good people in my confrontation. Dan had likely killed Taylor Brownsford to protect his secret. He might kill again.

My only hope was that I could talk him into doing the right thing. If I could appeal to him, as his friend . . .

"Just getting some exercise," I said with a nod. I scanned every face in the next car, but there was still no Dan. Had I passed him already? There was zero possibility he'd jumped off the train — that was suicide even at twenty miles an hour, let alone a hundred and twenty. Had he forced himself into the power car at the head of the train?

Impossible, I thought. He wouldn't risk drawing that kind of attention. Dan might have been a criminal, but he wasn't crazy. He was planning to get away with this. To walk off with the mother lode. His only obstacle was . . . me.

I stepped into the vestibule between the last two cars. As soon as the door behind me closed, I was blindsided with a bear-hug tackle from the left. My lungs went flat like a couple of whoopee cushions. I didn't recognize my assailant until he had me pinned against the exit door. It was the speed-demon biker — with the southern accent, who I realized was in all likelihood the one Finn called "Texas."

Dan stepped through the automatic doors.

"I know what you're thinking right now, Joe. You're thinking, *Why, Dan, why?*"

"Something like that," I said, gasping for air under the weight of the biker.

Dan refused to look me in the eye. "I'm retiring next year, and it terrifies me. The state pension fund is depleted. I've got no savings. I've been shot and stabbed more times than I can count, and I can count pretty well for a blue-collar guy. What kind of thanks do I get? A Christmas card every year from Joe Biden, champion of law enforcement. Not signed. Not even a paper card. An *e-card*."

"I can take you off the mailing list," I said.

"Look at you! You're a decade older than me. You were the freaking vice president of the United States. What do you have to show for it? A house in the suburbs, that you still owe money on. A vacation home on a bed of rocks that can only charitably be called a beach. A couple of cars that you haven't paid off. You've got *nothing*."

"I have a family. I have a legacy."

"I had a legacy once, too. But a legacy doesn't pay the bills. A legacy doesn't put food on the table. A legacy will get you a room in Baptist Manor someday, and not much more. That's why I started taxing these bastards."

"The Marauders?"

"All the criminals. You want to do business in my town, you need to pay for the privilege. Finn decided to go into business for himself, and that's where his troubles started."

I was seething inside, but had stopped pushing back against Texas. He was too big.

Too strong. My only hope was to conserve my energy.

Dan went on: "As soon as I found out he had a sick wife, I knew he was a liability. And when the duffel bag went missing . . . well, he forced my hand. I can't skim money that isn't there."

He wrenched the phone from my pocket. As soon as he saw it wouldn't power on, he smiled. He knew there was little chance I'd called somebody for help. If I had, I wouldn't have come looking for him.

"You killed Finn," I said.

He stuffed the phone back in my pocket, where it nestled next to my Medal of Freedom. "Taylor roughed your friend up in his motel room. He was in bad shape when I arrived. He was bleeding like a burst pipe all over the floor. He still wouldn't talk, so I hit him one time. One time! And his head caved in like a rotted pumpkin. It's scary how fragile our bodies become as we age, isn't it?"

"So you laid him on the tracks and staged it to look like an overdose. Pretty sloppy work," I said. The longer I kept him talking, the greater the chance that somebody would cross through the vestibule between cars.

"No one was ever going to take a second look, not in that part of town. And then the

341

next conductor found that printout with your address in his travel orders . . . and things started to get complicated. Until I read the letter today, I thought you had a hand in this mess. I honestly wasn't sure where the bag ended up."

"Drugs are one cookie jar I've never stuck my hand in. You should know that. You and I were friends."

"Friends?" he shot back. "I worked security for your rallies a few times when I was off duty. You weren't a friend. You were a job."

He couldn't have known what I'd been going through with Barack, but his words stung nonetheless. Maybe adults weren't meant to have friends. We could have acquaintances, and we could have coworkers. We could have bosses and employees. But friends?

Friends were for children. It was time for me to grow up.

Dan unlocked the side panel that operated the exit doors. At first I thought he was hoping to be the first one off the train. Then I realized he didn't need to make a quick getaway. Not if Texas tossed me out of the moving train first.

"He's going to keep the drugs for himself," I told the biker, trying to sow a seed of discontent. "That's been his plan all along."

Texas grinned. "The fentanyl? We never found it."

Of course. How could I have been so blind? "You're both working together to screw over the club."

Dan pressed his hand on the latch. If he opened the door right now, all three of us would be sucked out. "What can I say? If you see your shot, you have to take it. The bag was lost. The Marauders don't need to know it was found. It's the perfect crime."

"He killed Taylor," I told Texas.

The biker looked surprised, but not shocked. "Taylor was a moron," said. "He was never going to earn his colors."

"Taylor nearly torpedoed this entire operation by picking up the watch that fell out of Finn's pocket," Dan said. "An idiot like that doesn't deserve to live. He sealed his own death warrant the day he was born. You, on the other hand . . ." He smiled at me. "You're too smart for your own damn good, Joe."

Through the windows of the exit door, I could see that we were on the outskirts of Wilmington. Soon the train would be slowing down. I just had to keep stalling. I had about as much chance as a Democrat in Alabama to stop Dan from making his getaway. If I was lucky, though, I could at least escape without winding up splattered along the side of the tracks.

Dan nodded to Texas.

My time had run out.

So had his.

I head-butted the biker in the nose with my forehead. There was a sickening crunch as bone struck cartilage. Blood erupted from his nose, and he staggered backward. I'd never done anything like that in my life. One more hit and I could take him down.

Before I could charge him, something hard as steel pressed into my right temple. Dan's gun.

"You won't get away with this," I said. "There will be an inquiry. There will be —"

"I don't think so. Every year, five or six passengers open these doors while the train's in motion. Usually they're old and confused. Just like you. I'm sure people will come forward and testify that you'd been acting strange this past week. Delusional. Talking about conspiracy theories."

Dan pressed a button inside the control panel. The exit door opened with a *woosh*. Wind whistled into the train, popping my ears. "Goodbye, Joe."

Before I could even come up with some witty last words, Dan clubbed me in the temple with the butt of his pistol. Stars flashed before my eyes. I was in so much pain that all I wanted to do was lie down and go to sleep. *You got knocked down,* I heard my father's voice say in my head. *Now it's time to get up. Get up, Joe. Get up.*

I staggered on my feet, but Dan had the advantage by a country mile. He grabbed the back of my shirt and hurled me like a shot put through the open door. My legs went out from underneath me, and the world turned upside down.

49

I'd heard that in our final moments, we see our entire lives flash before our eyes. But I had more urgent things to worry about. Tumbling out, I'd managed to catch the door frame with my left hand. Physics pinned my body against the side of the train. I'd been spared, if only momentarily. My Ray-Bans were laying shattered on the rocks a hundred yards back, a preview of what would happen if I let go. If I was lucky. If I wasn't lucky, I'd get sucked underneath the train, where the wheels would have their way with me.

My fingers were slipping from the door frame one by one. My pinky was the first to go, then my ring finger. I tried to swing a leg back up inside the train, but the high-velocity forces working against me were too strong. I needed more "core strength." That was what Jill would have said. A year or two's worth of daily sit-ups and crunches would tighten my abs right up.

Unfortunately, I didn't have a year or two.

My middle finger slipped free. I was down to my final moments.

Review or not, I'd lived a good life. I closed my eyes and pinched my last two fingers into the frame as hard as I could, hoping for another few seconds so I could make peace with my maker.

If you're listening, Saint Benedict, help me out, buddy. Protect my body and my soul . . . but mostly my body.

My heart skipped a beat as my index finger gave way.

Then a hand grabbed my wrist. My eyes snapped open. It was Texas. My first thought was that he was trying to pry me loose, but he reached out his other hand for my forearm. He was pulling me toward him. With one great burst of energy, he yanked me into the train and we both fell to the floor.

Dan's gun was tucked into the front of the biker's jeans, digging into my hipbone.

Dan was slumped in the corner, eyes closed.

"The name's Jeremy," Texas shouted over the hiss of the tracks and the wind. His southern drawl was far less pronounced, on account of his busted nose. "I'm with the

Drug Enforcement Agency."

"So you *were* following us yesterday."

He shook his head. "I had no idea that was you driving that Escalade. Not until you showed up at the clubhouse."

"Good thing I didn't back into you. That would have really put a dent in your operation. And your bike."

He grunted in the affirmative.

I lifted myself off him. "Waited long enough to save my ass just now, didn't you?"

"To be fair, you gave me quite the stinger," Jeremy said, pinching his nose.

"You have the drugs?"

"They're in Capriotti's jacket."

The train was drawing closer and closer to the station. We were going slower than usual, though, and decelerating at a rapid pace. "Did you ask the engineer to stop the train?" I asked Jeremy.

He got to his feet. "I couldn't risk contacting anyone."

"Maybe the open door triggered an alarm. Or maybe . . ." I braced myself against the wall. I searched the horizon. Not sure what I expected to see. A fleet of cop cars? A helicopter packed with Navy SEALs? The forty-fourth president on the back of a unicorn?

Instead, what I saw was a blur of leather

and denim as Jeremy tumbled out of the train. His body smashed into the rocks along the tracks and was out of view within seconds. The Acela couldn't have been going more than thirty or forty, but even that was thirty or forty miles per hour too fast when it comes to falling out of a locomotive.

I turned around. Dan was on his feet, feeling the back of his head. He looked at the fresh blood on his fingers. "He got me good." Dan grinned. "I got him better."

The train came to a smooth stop in the middle of the warehouse district, stomach-churningly close to where Dan and Taylor had staged Finn's "accident." The conductor came over the intercom and asked everyone to remain in their seats. Dan and I wouldn't be interrupted, unless an Amtrak employee decided to move between cars.

Outside, beneath the low hum of the overhead electrical wires that powered the train, I could hear a cacophony of sirens growing in the distance. Dan could, too. His eyes flicked from me to the open door. I was standing between him and freedom. Papa Biden told me never to back someone into a corner, where the only way out is through you.

Papa Biden had never met a stone-cold

killer like Dan Capriotti.

The keys were still hanging out of the control panel to my right. If I hit the correct button, the door behind me would close. Dan would be trapped. Trouble was, there were half a dozen buttons. Hit the wrong one, and the other exit door behind Dan might open instead, letting him waltz his way to freedom.

"How'd you know I was lying?" he asked. Neither of us were in any kind of shape to duke it out. He was still bleeding badly from the blow Texas had given him. He appeared woozy, like he was concussed. The hit I'd taken to the temple wasn't as bad. Still, if he slipped past me, there was no way I could catch him in a footrace. Not with my bad knee.

"You first," I said. "What's my tell?"

"Easy. You're a politician. You're all phony. I can tell when you're lying because you move your lips."

"If that's how you see me, then you were right. We were never friends."

Dan grinned. I couldn't believe this was the same guy I'd met at Earl's just a few days earlier. All the time I'd known him, he'd been wearing a mask. One of us was phony, and it wasn't me.

"You want to hit me," Dan said, goading

me on. "I'm not armed. I'm already bleeding. A couple of hits is all it would take. I'd
drop easy, just like Finn Donnelly."

"I'm not like you — I'm not a killer. Texas.
Finn. Alvin —"

He waved a finger at me. "Whoa. Alvin
Harrison overdosed. That was all him. I
found him after he'd already stopped
breathing. I was in the apartment when you
showed up, pressed up against the wall in
the hallway. If you'd only looked to your
right, you would have seen me. I don't know
if you got lucky or I did. It doesn't matter
now."

"I'd say your luck has run out." The sirens
were getting louder by the second. "You
wanted to know how I knew you were lying.
I didn't know for sure, not really, until I
came back from the restroom and found
the drugs were missing."

"So if I'd just stayed put . . ."

"You might have gotten away with it. But
here we are."

I heard a familiar *thump-thump, thump-
thump, thump-thump.* Like a racing heartbeat. No, it *was* my heartbeat. But there
was something else, too . . . not a sound,
but a feeling. A violent rumble shaking the
ground. It was as if a great chasm were

351

about to open beneath us and swallow us whole.

"If you turn me in, hundreds of criminals are going to go free," Dan said. "Everyone I've ever arrested — they'll all walk. I've arrested some bad, bad men. You think the streets are dangerous now, wait 'til you see this town in six months. It'll be on fire. Do you really want to be responsible for that?" He shook his head slowly. "Step aside, Joe."

Dan smiled. He was right, and he knew it. Convictions would be overturned if they depended on his testimony. Not every one of his arrests, but enough.

Not enough to make me rethink turning him in, however.

I slapped the big red button on the wall.

The exit door behind Dan hissed open. He spun around.

I hit the button again, but the door was stuck.

Dan wasted no time. He slipped through the door and jumped off the train. His boots landed hard on the rocks, but he didn't lose his balance. The rumble was growing louder.

Dan jogged a couple steps, then paused on the other set of tracks. At first I thought maybe he'd twisted an ankle or jammed a knee when he leapt out. But no. He turned around to face me. His lips twisted into a wry smile. He put his index and middle fingers up to his eyebrow and bid me adieu with a good ol' fashioned two-finger salute. I was contemplating whether to return the gesture or shoot him a one-fingered salutation when he was hit by a screeching train.

50

The first vehicle to arrive on the scene wasn't a police car or an ambulance.

It was an Escalade.

The Little Beast plowed through the six-foot chain-link fence and skidded to a stop inches from the open door of the train, where I was sitting. The interior sliding doors on either side of the vestibule were locked. I'd peeked through one of the windows, hoping to converse with the conductor or the café attendant. Employees and passengers were bent over in their seats, heads between their knees, hands covering the backs of their necks. Waiting for the all-clear from law enforcement.

Steve hopped out of the driver's side door. He left the SUV idling. "Is Dan —"

"Neutralized," I said, nodding over my shoulder. "Hit by another train." The Acela that hit Dan had finally come to a rest farther down the tracks. I didn't know where it threw his body, and I didn't care. The cadaver dogs would be around soon enough to start the search for what was left of him.

"Help is on the way," Steve said, examining the bulge on my temple. He looked like he needed help more than I did. He had a shoulder sling on his left arm and was still wearing his hospital bracelet.

"Barack got my message," I said. A slight breeze blew through the vestibule.

Steve moved a finger back and forth in front of my face. I followed it with my eyes. "You didn't leave a message, so the president didn't think anything of it, really. In the meantime, though, I contacted the DEA to straighten some things out. They told us they were investigating Detective Capriotti. That, of course, raised some red flags, and when we couldn't reach you, well . . ."

"How'd you find me?"

"Traced your phone, of course."

"That takes a court order, doesn't it? You can't do it in real time."

"If you're suggesting President Obama has some sort of backdoor into the officially dismantled NSA surveillance program —"

"Say no more," I said. They'd had the train stopped. That was what mattered. If it hadn't been for them, Dan could have slipped away when the conductor opened the cabin doors at Wilmington Station.

"There's a man," I said. "Jeremy. A Drug Enforcement agent, undercover. He was the biker we chased yesterday. Dan threw him off the train a couple of hundred yards back."

"There's a medical helicopter on the way," Steve said. "We'll have them look for him."

Barack stepped out of the SUV. He was wearing the Phillies cap again.

"What did we miss?" he asked. "Did you and Dan fight it out on the top of the train?"

I climbed down onto the rocks and pointed to the electrical cables running over the tracks. "Touch one of those, and you'll be fried to the tune of twenty-five thousand volts."

"Guess they don't call you Amtrak Joe for nothing."

"I know some things," I admitted.

A trio of cop cars pulled into the gravel parking lot on the other side of the fence, lights flashing. They killed their sirens. A police helicopter circled overhead.

"They're not going to give us a hard time, are they?" I asked.

"Lieutenant Esposito's in charge," Steve said. "So maybe."

Barack ran his hands over the Escalade's

bumper. The Little Beast had sustained minor damage in the weekend's festivities. There was a scratch or two on the hood. A minor dent on the front side panel if you looked at it in the right light. Other than that, it could have been fresh off the lot. "We'll run through a car wash on the way home," Barack announced to no one in particular.

Steve answered his phone. He waved up to the helicopter, letting someone — Esposito? — on the other end of the line know that they could call off the SWAT team.

There was a loud clank behind me. I turned in time to see a bloodied, mangled figure entering the train vestibule through the far door that was stuck open. There was nothing human about the creature except for the whites of its eyes.

It was Dan.

He'd been torn to shreds.

Somehow, despite it all, he'd found a way to gather his broken limbs into something resembling a human form. His breathing was shallow, ragged. In his right hand he held a snub-nosed pistol, which he must have hidden in a holster.

I realized he could have pulled it out and shot me during our standoff, but he hadn't. Perhaps he'd had second thoughts about killing me. Perhaps he'd simply known it was futile. Now, however, he was past rational thought. He was fueled by rage. A thirst for revenge.

"Gun!" I yelled. I launched myself shoulder-first into Barack, knocking him to the ground and out of harm's way. Steve dropped his phone and pulled out his own piece.

The smell of gunpowder was in the air. Shots had been fired. I hadn't even heard them. All I could hear was the ringing in my ears. I was lying on top of Barack and rolled off onto the rocks. Steve was racing for us, gripping his smoking SIG Sauer with his one good hand. The shootout was over.

Dan was finally dead.

Barack and Steve helped me up into a sitting position. Barack showed no signs of injury. It took a lot more than an old man to knock the wind out of him.

I grabbed my aching love handle, and my index finger went through a tiny hole in my bomber jacket. A bullet hole. I'd been hit.

Barack threw open my jacket and patted me down. There was no blood, no entry or exit wound on the pink skin of my abdomen. "It went through your jacket but missed your body," he said, his voice muffled. My hearing was slowly coming back.

"You're lucky to be alive."

"It wasn't luck," I said.

I reached into my pocket and pulled out the bullet. Its nose was bent at an angle. I tossed it into the sand. There was a small dent almost dead-center in the Medal of Freedom, with cracks in the enamel overlay radiating around it. The dent would need to be pounded out, and the paint would need touching up. I knew my auto-body guy would fix it for a pittance, especially compared to what a jeweler might charge. All in all, the medal wasn't in bad shape.

And, all things considered, neither was I.

51

Steve and I gave statements to the Wilmington PD. Steve's hands were trembling; he'd never shot someone before. My hands weren't the steadiest, either — I'd never been shot before. Neither of us mentioned the president playing games on his Black-Berry.

Dan wouldn't be mentioning him, either. The fact that Dan had died instead of entering the Delaware penal system was probably for the best. The Marauders would have surely put a hit out on him once they found out what he'd done to Taylor.

Esposito approached me after I'd finished giving my statement. "I should apologize for being so hard on you," she said.

"You should, but . . ."

"But I don't believe in apologies."

I shook her hand. "I appreciate the gesture nonetheless."

She promised a full internal investigation

into Detective Capriotti's illicit activities. I didn't blame her or her department. I believed that the Wilmington police force did the best they could with the tools they were given. Police officers were, by and large, good people. A single bad egg, however, was all it took to spoil the bunch. At least as far as public perception is concerned. It would be up to Esposito to clean up the mess.

A pair of DEA officers — one man, one woman — introduced themselves to me. I recognized their names from the search warrant for the Donnellys' home. "Do you have a moment to chat?" the female agent said.

An EMT was wrapping a blood pressure cuff around my upper arm. "As long as you don't say anything to spike my numbers," I said.

They explained to me that the Marauders' trafficking encompassed the entire eastern seaboard. The scheme involving Finn Donnelly had been just one piece of a larger pie they were tracking. I apologized for royally screwing their investigation, but they told me not to sweat it. When they realized Dan Capriotti was crooked, the entire DEA operation had been thrown into disarray. The DEA couldn't trust Esposito or anyone else in the Wilmington PD. They didn't know how far the conspiracy to "tax" the Marauders' local chapter went, or if Finn Donnelly had truly gone into business for himself. For a while, everyone who crossed their radar had been suspect.

"Including me," I said.

The agents looked at each other, but didn't deny the charge. "We had an undercover operative and an informant to protect," the female agent said. "We couldn't trust anyone."

"Jeremy was the undercover operative. Who was the informant?"

"Alvin Harrison," she said. He was dead now and the operation had fizzled out, so there was no risk in revealing his name. "He'd turned in a tip that Finn was smuggling something."

"So rather than confront Finn directly . . ."

The male agent cleared his throat. "There was a reward involved. A substantial reward."

It couldn't have been easy for Alvin to turn in one of his railroad brothers. I wanted to believe Alvin had been motivated by more than money. A sense of justice, perhaps. I assumed that Alvin had his reasons for doing what he did, just as Finn had his reasons for doing what he did.

Whatever the reasoning behind Alvin's actions, I now understood the pit of despair he'd fallen into after the accident. Even though Finn was already dead when Alvin's train hit him, Alvin *had* killed him, in a way. And he'd known it. The weight had been too much to bear.

Even though the good guys ultimately prevailed, the bad guys had landed some hard punches. Dan's betrayal stung. We were entering a new age, one where there were no absolutes like right and wrong. The worst part was that it felt like everyone else had already been living there for a long time. I was finally just catching on.

52

We retired to the Lake House for the evening, and Jill cooked us a big Sunday dinner. She had a million questions, but she was willing to wait and let me rest before hearing the full story. I promised not to leave anything out. Not this time. Not ever again.

After dinner, Barack and I took seats on opposite sides of the couch in the living room. Champ was chasing fireflies in the yard. So was Steve. They'd shared a package of hot dogs at dinner, and now they were the best of friends.

"You want to do this again?" I asked Barack.

"Have dinner? Sure, why not?"

"I meant the whole private investigator thing. You can get a license for cheap in Delaware. Cheaper than a crab-fishing license."

"Joe, don't take this the wrong way, but

we would make terrible private investigators. Plus, we've got a lot on our plates already. You've got your university work and your foundations. I've got some books to write."

"I was kidding."

"It's hard to tell sometimes, Joe."

I sighed. "It's not like I'd have the time, anyway. I've been thinking about running."

"Really."

"I'm no spring chicken, but I'm not dead yet. It's like my mother used to say, 'You're not dead until you see the face of God at the Pearly Gates.' "

"You'd be the oldest guy to ever run for president."

"President?" I said with a laugh. "I'm talking about *running*. Like maybe a 5K. As soon as I bounce back from this bum knee."

Barack shook his head. Jill was doing the dishes in the kitchen. She only did the dishes when she was ticked off at me — otherwise, that particular task fell under my purview.

"Besides the knee, I'm in better shape than any other old guy you know — you have to admit that," I said. "And that's just from being a Biden. Imagine what kind of shape I'd be in if I actually started working out."

"If you actually want to run — for office, that is . . ."

"You'll be the first to know."

I wasn't just saying it to say it. I meant it. Barack was an honorary Biden. Through good times and bad. Through the ups and the downs. This was definitely one of those down times, but, God willing, it wouldn't last forever. Nothing does. Not even grief. The first year after you've lost someone is the most painful, but the second year is excruciating in its own way. The grief fades, and it's only on birthdays, and anniversaries, and holidays that you realize you've become accustomed to their absence. That you don't think about them every day.

I picked up a deck of cards on the coffee table and shuffled them. "Rummy?"

Barack nodded.

For a long while, neither of us said another word. We just played cards. Jill started the dishwasher and went upstairs to call the grandkids. It was something we did together, at the same time every Sunday night. Not this week, though.

Barack drew from the discard pile. "Do you know why I came to see you last week?"

"To tell me about Finn."

He nodded. "I could have called, though."

"You could have."

"But I didn't. Michelle was the one who told me to drive up here on Wednesday. I'm usually as cool as cucumber lotion, but I asked Steve to pick me up a pack of smokes on the way." He paused. "That was the first cigarette I'd had in seven years."

"I don't know why you were so nervous. It's just me — Uncle Joe."

"I thought you'd be mad."

"I was."

"You were?" he asked, genuinely surprised.

"Did you think I was happy as a clam, sitting at home watching you go kite-surfing and Formula One racing and who knows what else with guys half my age?"

"I never went Formula One — no, wait, I did. But I don't see why you were mad. You've never liked extreme sports."

"I wasn't mad," I said, discarding a ten of clubs. "I was jealous of your never-ending parade of celebrity playmates. As soon as we parted ways, you started holding open auditions for a new best friend."

He took a Nicorette from his pocket. It was his third package this weekend. "I was trying to keep my distance. I told you this."

"How was I supposed to know at the time? We're brothers, not twins. We don't have a psychic connection."

"I don't think that's how twins really work."

"That's not what Jenna Bush Hager told me," I said. "Bipartisanship. Try it sometime and you might learn something new."

Barack played a meld. The six, seven, and eight of hearts. He discarded his final card.

Game. Set. Match.

"Are we keeping track of score?" I asked, tossing my cards faceup onto the table.

"You're only asking because I won, aren't you?"

I grinned. Barack was the most competitive person I'd ever known. It drove him up a wall when somebody suggested playing a game "just for fun." If there wasn't a clear winner and loser, he tended to lose interest. He lived for elections. He withered in office.

I handed him the deck. "You shuffle this time."

"The most important people in my life have always been women," Barack said, dealing the cards. "My grandmother. My mother. Michelle. My daughters. Not saying I haven't had male friends, because I have guys I play ball with. Guys I have beers with. But with you, it's different. Once we figured each other out, it was like our friendship was on autopilot. It was so easy,

368

for so long, that once we left office, I didn't know what to do. I didn't know how to just text another guy without inviting him over to shoot hoops. I didn't know how to call you just to talk, even though that's what I wanted to do. I didn't know, and I'm sorry, Joe."

I looked at the cards he'd dealt me. It was a crap hand.

"I'm sorry, too," I said.

"You didn't do anything."

"Jealousy is an ugly sin. You're allowed to have other friends." I drew a new card. "As long as I'm your best friend."

"Aren't we too old to have best friends?"

Maybe he was right. Maybe I was being silly.

"I'm too old to be jumping out of airplanes," I told him. "I just think it'd be nice to go golfing sometime."

"You said something just a minute ago," Barack remarked. "You called us brothers again."

"I didn't mean anything by it," I said.

Barack wasn't having any of it. "Don't be bashful, Joe. As far as I'm concerned, we never stopped being brothers," he said, holding out a fist. I punched him with too much force, but it was the best fist bump we'd ever had.

"Watch the knuckles there, Joe," he said, shaking out his hand.

"Say, I've got another lightbulb that needs to be changed, in the upstairs bathroom. I'm in no shape to stand on a chair right now, and —"

"You're putting me to work?" he asked.

"You're taller. You've got longer arms."

"I'll do it," he said, rising from the couch.

"Thanks," I said. "Bulb's on the counter."

Barack mounted the stairs. A few seconds later, he called out to me. "Hey, Joe?"

"Yeah?" I shouted.

"Why does your dart board have Bradley Cooper's picture on it?"

"It's not important," I said. "Not anymore."

53

Three months later, I boarded the express train at Wilmington Station with a round-trip ticket to DC. It reminded me of my days in the Senate, except the train was leaving at ten thirty instead of before dawn.

I'd awakened early to do my morning run with Jill. I couldn't keep pace with her, but I was getting closer. My knee still hobbled me a bit. An MRI over the summer revealed an ACL tear. If I was a professional athlete or under the age of forty, they would have reconstructed my knee. For someone my age, the best they could do was prescribe a regiment of ice, forced rest, and twice-weekly rehabilitation appointments. "That's it?" I'd asked. The doc said there was one more thing. She wrote me a script for extra-strength ibuprofen to lessen the inflammation. I'd asked how long I should take it, and my doc laughed. Like most drugs people my age were on, I was to take it until, well, the end.

The end, with any luck, would be a long time coming.

The first-class car was less than half full. I took a seat in the back, across from an empty chair. After last call, the train rolled out. The seat across from me was still empty. I was going to have the table to myself, at least until Baltimore.

I spread out the morning newspaper. Earlier in the week, grand jury indictments had come down for several members of the Marauders, and the $1.4 million fentanyl bust was front-page news again. It had dominated the *News Journal* headlines over the summer, but barely cracked national news. The White House's daily self-inflicted crisis du jour left little room for stories not originating from Twitter tantrums. Somehow, though, the *News Journal* had found the resources for an in-depth, five-part story, which was culminating its front-page run with today's paper.

The paper's reporting team cast Finn as a hero for blowing the whistle on the smuggling operation. I didn't think that's how he would have viewed himself, even though he'd surely known he was committing suicide by turning on the Marauders. The insurance company was going to have a real

372

bitch of a time fighting the life insurance payout now. Especially since Abbey Todd quit on them and Finn's blood tests came back clean.

The undercover DEA agent had recovered from his injuries and was now back in the field, under a different assumed name. A spokesperson for the agency told reporters that they'd received assistance taking down Dan Capriotti from an off-duty Secret Service agent, who happened to be traveling on the train. The unnamed agent had since been promoted to the Secret Service's tactical Counter-Assault Team.

There was no mention of either Joe Biden or Barack Obama.

The train rumbled by the Wilmington and Brandywine Cemetery. I set down the paper to watch the parade of gravestones. Only a couple of weeks had passed since I'd set foot in the cemetery. The trees were bare now, but when I was there last the cemetery had been a sea of red and yellow. The leaf peepers flocking to Massachusetts and New Hampshire had no idea what they were missing.

I hadn't been at the cemetery to enjoy the leaves.

I'd been there for another funeral.

I wasn't alone. Jill had come with me,

against my wishes. "You don't need to keep putting on that brave face for me," she'd said. "I know you're brave. Sometimes, however, we just need someone to hold our hand."

She was right. Like always.

I was wearing a new black suit, which had mysteriously shown up in the back of our walk-in closet a few weeks ago. The tag on the inside of the jacket bore Fred O'Flanaghan's name. The same tailor I'd been visiting for more than thirty years. Jill hadn't asked what had happened to my last suit, and I hadn't offered any details.

Before trying on the new slacks, I'd worried I was going to have to return for an adjustment. To my surprise, I was able to both zip and button them. It wasn't the most comfortable fit, but it was a welcome surprise — the time I'd been putting in working out was paying off. Besides the knee injury, I was healthier than ever.

The same couldn't be said for Darlene Donnelly, God rest her soul.

After what happened over the summer, her already precarious health had taken a nosedive. Even though she'd been unresponsive, it seemed she knew Finn had passed, that his visits had been the only thing keeping her tethered to this planet.

When she went into intensive care, Jill and I offered what we could to make her comfortable. To our surprise, Grace — who had forgiven me — told us that an anonymous donor had already taken care of her mother's medical bills. The donor had also started a trust fund for Grace and wiped out her student loans. I had an idea who the mysterious benefactor was, but didn't say anything. Grace had no idea that Barack had helped me track down her father's killer. If someday he wanted her to know the full extent of his involvement, he would. The story was his to tell.

"We should go say goodbye," Jill said, tugging at my sleeve. Darlene's service had ended. Most of the crowd had already paid their respects, but we were still seated, waiting — for what, I didn't know. I was the first one to leave at parties, but the last one to leave at funerals. Saying goodbye to the living was hard enough; saying goodbye to the dead was an impossible task.

"Why not hold funerals when people are still alive?" I said. "What's the sense of getting all your friends and family together, and not being around to enjoy it? It's rotten, I tell you."

"We do have funerals for the living," Jill said. "They're called birthday parties."

As we approached the casket, my hands shook. Jill squeezed my fingers. Every death reminded me of the losses I'd suffered in my own life. For once, though, I didn't turn away from the deceased. I took a moment to look upon Darlene's face. She didn't look at peace; she looked dead. I knew, however, that she was with her beloved now. Her husband's pocket watch, recovered from evidence, was on a chain around her neck. She and Finn were together again, without the pain that had separated them near the end of their earthly lives.

To the left of the hole the groundskeepers had dug for her casket sat a small polished marker. FINN DONNELLY. Beneath the dates of his birth and death, it listed him as CONDUCTOR, FATHER, FRIEND TO ALL.

Despite the excitement over the summer, the world seemed to finally be settling back into its natural rhythms. I'd finished the first draft of a new memoir about hope and hardship, scheduled for publication in the fall. There were still two Wilmingtons — the haves and the have-nots. There were still two Americas. It wasn't my burden to fix the broken system, but that wouldn't stop me from trying. I would do what I could. There are certain things worth getting mad about. Injustice is one of them. The greatest sins on this earth are committed by people of standing and means who abuse their power.

Those are my father's words.

They're also mine.

"Didn't see you sneak on. Heading all the way to DC?"

I turned from the window. The conductor — a young woman I didn't recognize — was examining my ticket. Her eyes were as green as shamrocks.

"Erin. Erin Brady."

"Irish?" I asked, shaking her hand.

"A wee bit," she said, affecting the worst Irish accent I'd ever heard.

"My name's Joe."

"I thought it was you," she said with a grin. "I've been working this line six months now and was beginning to feel like the only one without an Amtrak Joe story. Would you mind if we took a picture?"

Of course I didn't mind.

We posed for a selfie, our arms wrapped around each other. I still remember the days when you needed someone else to take a selfie of you. The days when you had to wait a week to know if your pictures turned out.

"I'm sure you hear this all the time, but we miss you," Erin said.

"I'm still around. I don't ride Amtrak as

much as I used to, but I guess I have fewer places to go."

"No, I mean, the *country* misses you."

I slid back into my seat. "Absence makes the heart grow fonder."

People hadn't forgotten me — that much I knew. Book tour events for later in the year were already selling out. Some political prognosticators suspected I was testing the waters for another presidential run. They must have forgotten who the real Joe Biden was. I'd always flown by the seat of my britches. I wasn't going to start planning ahead now.

The country clearly needed a change in direction; there was no question about that. But did the country need Joe Biden more than my family did? I wasn't sure I knew the answer.

Barack once told me that, at the end of the day, every one of us is just part of a long-running story. All we can do is try to get our paragraph right. Whether I would make another run at the highest office in the land was still up in the air. I learned long ago to never say never. Fate has a strange way of intervening. All I knew for sure was that I wasn't done writing my paragraph yet.

On her way out, Erin tripped over my bag

of golf clubs, which had been sticking out into the aisle by a hair. She had great balance — you have to if you want to ride trains for a living — and she caught herself before taking a spill.

"Sorry about that," I said, pulling the bag closer. "Hitting the links today."

"It's a good day to be outside. Business or pleasure?"

I smiled. "Meeting a friend."

I didn't have to say the friend's name. Anyone with half a brain could tell by the twinkle in my eye who I was on my way to see. And as long as we didn't talk business, it would be pleasure. All pleasure.

ACKNOWLEDGMENTS
(REPRISE)

They say that nobody reads the acknowledgments page. But you — you're not nobody. Chances are, you're somebody close to me, hoping to see your name in print. Did you make the cut, Grandma? Read on . . .

Thank you to my editor, Jason Rekulak. This book went through many iterations, and Jason was there to hold my hand every step of the way. A recent study by researchers at the University of Colorado at Boulder and the University of Haifa suggests that hand-holding may have positive health benefits, including reducing pain. This has been my experience as well. Revisions weren't entirely painless — they never are — but having an editor as skilled as Jason at the helm made the writing enjoyable and rewarding.

I am indebted to the rest of the Quirk Books team, especially Brett Cohen, Nicole De Jackmo, Moneka Hewlett, Rebecca Gyllenhaal, Jane Morley, Ivy Weir, Kelsey Hoffman, cover designer Doogie Horner, and, of course, Mr. Pringles. Their enthusiasm and support for *Hope Never Dies* has never wavered.

Jeremy Enecio provided the kick-ass cover illustration. Check out his work at jeremy enecio.com.

Thank you to my agent, Brandi Bowles at UTA. She recognized the brilliance of my pitch immediately, responding with an email reading, "OMG."

My wife punched up many of the best jokes in the book. I was going to thank her here, but she requested I donate her thanks to our sweet, sad cat, Honeytoast. So, thank you, Honeytoast.

I owe a special thanks, of course, to Joe Biden, who has overcome numerous tragedies and hardships to become one of the United States' most celebrated public servants. He's more than a meme — he's a man of action. A man of action who loves his ice cream almost as much as he loves his country.

ABOUT THE AUTHOR

Andrew Shaffer is the *New York Times* best-selling author of more than a dozen books. He lives with his wife, the novelist Tiffany Reisz, in Lexington, Kentucky, where he teaches at the nonprofit Carnegie Center for Literacy and Learning. *Hope Never Dies* is his debut mystery.

The employees of Thorndike Press hope you have enjoyed this Large Print book. All our Thorndike, Wheeler, and Kennebec Large Print titles are designed for easy reading, and all our books are made to last. Other Thorndike Press Large Print books are available at your library, through selected bookstores, or directly from us.

For information about titles, please call:
  (800) 223-1244

or visit our website at:
  gale.com/thorndike

To share your comments, please write:
  Publisher
  Thorndike Press
  10 Water St., Suite 310
  Waterville, ME 04901